CONTENTS

BETRAYAL

ORLA
KELLY
PUBLISHING

By

Susan Newman

Dedicated to my beautiful granddaughter,
Martina Newman Alvarez
And her late grandfather, Ted Newman

CHAPTER 1

Tuesday 30th April 1969

She cut a forlorn figure through the mist.

The Atlantic-borne rain had eased but the hunched form seemed oblivious. Her attention was focussed on the open grave, the mound of earth to the side in readiness to cover the coffin of her young daughter.

The mourners remained at a distance, almost fearful of intruding. The monotonous voice of the priest as he intoned a decade of the rosary merely added to the oppressive atmosphere.

Her husband stood awkwardly by her side. Occasionally he raised a gnarled hand to his eyes, surreptitiously, as if unsure, probably wondering if it was alright for a grown man to cry in such a public place.

Once or twice he had reached out to touch her hand, seeking comfort, offering comfort, but she had swatted aside his gesture. Her grief was iron-fenced around her.

The mourners tutted as they left the graveyard, some overcome with pity, yet all glad in a way that it wasn't their turn today.

And though they left in groups, each was aware of the fear which seemed to keep step with them, the danger which had suddenly and inexplicably invaded their space.

Sixteen years old and tossed in a drain on the Belgooly road, her bicycle lying beside her, her schoolbag partially submerged in mud. A few copies peeked through the open flap, half used. Fully used.

The middle-aged couple were alone now, staring abysmally into the gaping hole in the ground. The long empty years stretched out before them. Death had robbed them, had torn apart their plans, the promise of all their tomorrows.

CHAPTER 2

Friday May 2nd

Superintendent Alderton exhaled a deep sigh of satisfaction as he surveyed his lair. There was nothing superfluous here, no photos, no certificates and no knick-knacks. His wife had made several attempts to persuade him to inject a bit of personality into the space. Books, apparently, exuded a certain aura and would do wonders to improve his 'general air of vulgarity and ignorance'. When that suggestion was swatted aside she had mooted a few pastoral landscapes, to show his 'human side', a comment which seemed to be the source of much hilarity though Alderton had failed to see the funny side of that particular input. Maybe she was a secret drinker, he mused idly. She had then ceded any hope of success when she suggested displaying a few strategically placed photos of him and herself in order to convey a sense of normality.

Alderton had immediately hidden all evidence of their union and co-habitation up in the attic. Perhaps, worryingly, she hadn't missed them but, much to his relief, the saga of interior design had petered out.

This was *his* space. His desk dominated the room, its size rivalled only by his enormous chair. In front of the desk was a single chair, the most uncomfortable one he could locate and it was there, he fancied, that his subordinates squirmed while he 'set them straight' and issued his very succinct instructions.

He was a man who had little time for pleasantries or niceties preferring instead to go for the jugular. Of course he enjoyed the good things in life but he kept that side hidden. A man was entitled to his pastimes, without fear of interference or prosecution.

He was feeling particularly energised this morning. A phone call, a very important phone call from the Commissioner all the way from Dublin, had initially almost paralysed him with fear. But he relaxed when he realised that the import of the call concerned some murder or other in Kinsale. Alderton almost stood to attention as he was informed of the details, all the while scribbling a few incoherent notes. And, even though it hadn't been explicitly expressed, or even hinted at if he was honest, it was most gratifying that Alderton had been chosen as the most capable of resolving the mystery surrounding the event.

The mention of Detective Inspector Morecamb and his sterling work rate and success record had somewhat deflated Alderton. By the end of the conversation, he had sunk into the aforementioned chair while he digested the Commissioner's insistence that he should convey his best wishes to Morecamb and went on to remind Alderton that he should do all in his power to be of assistance to Morecamb, albeit from a safe distance.

So his initial sense of bonhomie was rapidly dissipating and he was now pacing the floor while he waited for 'God's gift' to the Garda force to put in an appearance. It was now one hour and thirty six minutes since he had ordered Sergeant Moloney to contact Morecamb and tell him to present himself at the station, urgently. But, of course, he knew that any mention of 'urgency' was Morecamb's trigger to drag his heels and let his boss stew.

*****

Alderton was right. When Morecamb received the garbled alert from Moloney, who was never very coherent after one of the Superintendent's communiques, he decided to run a bath, followed by a leisurely breakfast and topped off by a brisk walk. When he felt that an unsuitable amount of time had lapsed he took himself off to the station, the long way round, but was still in a peevish frame of mind when he reached his destination. He was, after all, officially still on holidays but Alderton didn't dignify any such entitlements with any degree of compliance.

It was thus, in a spirit of mutual disrespect that the two men squared up to one another on Friday morning.

Morecamb tried to remain calm as he endured Alderton's endless preamble and self-aggrandisement rhetoric. Presumably he would soon get to the point. So he filtered out the rant and focussed on the shaft of sunlight fingering its tentacles through a gap in the blind. Dust motes danced chaotically, as if drunk on the sheer exuberance of the daylight and Morecamb mused pathetically that they seemed to have it all.

"Are you listening, Morecamb?"

Morecamb assured him that he was hanging on his every word and now his attention settled on a bluebottle, wheeling wonderfully close to his boss's shiny, bald head and made a silent promise that if he completed the landing successfully he would never again annihilate a member of that species.

"Poor lassie. Only fifteen years of age. Or maybe sixteen."

Morecamb snapped out of his reverie on the flight pattern of the bluebottle and realised that, in the midst of his boss's spiel, he might possibly have missed some salient nugget of information.

"So, can you do a quick re-cap of all that, sir, in case I missed anything?" asked Morecamb, knowing that his boss liked nothing better than to hear the sound of his own voice and would happily comply.

"No. Now, get out. Oh, and just for your information, I did try to dissuade the Commissioner from appointing you the Senior Investigating Officer but he was insistent. He seemed to think that you had acquitted yourself well in that earlier murder in Ballyroe____"

"Triple murder actually," Morecamb reminded him.

"Naturally I didn't point out to the Commissioner that the body count increased exponentially with every day you spent there. Or that you and your men left an entire village traumatised in your wake. I stand by my men, you see, whatever their shortcomings."

"And what's the victim's name? I like to know____"

"O' Donovan," Alderton replied, squinting at a notepad in front of him. "And that's all I know. She was discovered near Kinsale, a place dear to the Commissioner's heart. He has a sailing boat down there. Look, you'll get all that information when you go down there. I told them you'd be down there… " he consulted his watch… "Two hours ago!" he finished on a shout.

"And who's in charge down there?" asked Morecamb.

"Detective Spillane. But they're short-staffed. A few of them are scheduled to go on their holidays__"

"Might I remind you that I'm also meant to be on holiday? Two weeks, starting yesterday to be precise."

"Oh, don't be so selfish, Morecamb. That's bloody typical of you. Just go. And I suppose you'll be taking the usual suspects with you?"

"Well, that's my call, sir."

"Well, you can't have Finin. I need him here. So I want you to take McClean instead. That boy is on his way to the top so I want him to get some experience. And you can take one other body. Hopefully that Murphy fellow though he's a complete waste of space. But I don't want him cluttering up the station here. He always makes the place look untidy."

He was still rambling on when Morecamb shut the door behind him.

Spillane?

Why did that name ring a bell? He was still mulling it over as he headed to the glorified canteen where he spotted Sergeants Kilroy and Finin. He went over and joined them and informed them that they were heading to Kinsale.

"Why Kinsale, sir?" asked Kilroy.

Morecamb explained the sailing habits of a certain Commissioner and also the fact that they were short-staffed down there as some stations actually honoured the holiday arrangements of their members.

"Where's Murphy?" he now asked, looking around for his long-suffering sergeant who, he knew, regarded work as his only refuge from the turmoil of his domestic arrangements.

"He said he might be a bit late this morning as he had to bring the missus to the outpatients' clinic," Finin volunteered.

"Nothing trivial, I hope," muttered Morecamb as he went over to fetch himself a cup of tea.

Just as he re-joined his men at the table Murphy burst through the doors, apologising and hurriedly tried to straighten his tunic. Morecamb stopped him in mid-stream explaining that Kilroy had already informed him.

"We're going to Kinsale today, Sergeant," Finin explained.

"Bit of an exaggeration there, Finin. You're not going." He went on to scare the life out of Finin by informing him that Alderton seemed to find him indispensable and he would be staying put. Finin looked ready to cry.

Murphy started to count on his fingers and announced that there would be just the four of them travelling.

"I can't go," Kilroy supplied. "I'm off on a course. Something to do with the rights of criminals and supports and that for the families."

Morecamb knew that the course concerned the rights of victims and their families but Kilroy was never one to concern himself with details and Morecamb couldn't be bothered correcting him. He'd find out soon enough and then he'd know the difference between victims and criminals when the course directors realised Kilroy's limited knowledge and cavalier attitude.

Murphy's fingers appeared again but before he could deliver his findings Morecamb delivered the coup-de-gras and told him that he could add McClean to the total. Murphy emitted a loud groan followed by a string of profanities and announced that he wasn't going.

In truth Morecamb shared the same reservations about McClean but decided not to encourage and prolong Murphy's expletive-laden diatribe.

McClean was a university graduate. First Class Honours, Alderton had announced proudly, the previous week, as if he had spawned the wonder-boy himself. Added to that nugget of information Alderton had said that he was to be treated with the utmost respect, Murphy was to be kept away from him for fear of contamination and Morecamb could do worse than absorb some of the superior intelligence and undoubted refinement of this fine upstanding specimen of humanity. Or words to that effect.

So naturally, from the outset, McClean was regarded with suspicion. 'Alderton's snitch' was one of the more kindly judgements and most steered a wide berth when he was in the vicinity. Murphy had pronounced that he had a screw loose.

"Finin, will you see if you can locate McClean and send him in here. And, Murphy, your inclusion is non-negotiable. You're going and that's that. Would you prefer to be in Finin's shoes? Mmmm? Because that can be arranged. McClean may not be flavour of the month but it's hardly his fault that Alderton thinks that the sun shines out of his nether regions. Well, not his fault entirely. So, we all work together. Best way to get results."

*****

Forty minutes later and they were still only on the outskirts of the city. Murphy wanted to know if there were only two gears in the car, first and second, but McClean pompously informed him that as a member of the Garda Siochana he wasn't in the habit of breaking the law and had no intention of exceeding the speed regulations which were in place for the safety of the good citizens of Cork.

"You'd best find fourth gear pretty sharpish, McClean, or you can get out and wait for the next bus to Kinsale," Morecamb bellowed.

McClean relented and went into fourth but still maintained a snail's pace.

A pall of gloom descended and nobody spoke until Murphy suddenly breached the silence.

"Met the wife around here," he said morosely.

Morecamb looked around for a dwelling or anything that might have provided shelter for the virago that had hitched herself to Murphy.

"She was driving a few head of cattle just along here," Murphy elaborated. "Her father had a small bit of land and every so often, when the cattle looked as if they were about to fall down with the hunger he would send them into the neighbour's farm, in the dead of night, to graze. It would be a few days before they were discovered and then all hell would break loose. But of course there was always the farm on the other side then and the same thing would happen. Always in the dead of night. Helped them a few times myself when I started courting Maisie. The guards were called several times but Maisie's old man threatened them with a shotgun."

At the end of Murphy's narrative McClean picked up speed, considerably, and the rest of the hair-pin bends were conquered at an alarming rate. Only when the town of Kinsale appeared on the horizon did the driver ease his foot off the accelerator and eventually they cruised to a stop outside the barracks.

They all took a moment to admire the scenery as they got out of the car. It was truly spectacular. They were only a short walk from the marina where they could see boats and a few yachts bobbing at their moorings on the silver water. In the distance solid, double-fronted houses nestled into the cliffs which flanked the harbour.

It was a town of hills and the houses seemed to be set in layers, each rising above the one beneath, residents taking full advantage of the sweeping views and elevations. The three spires of the local Catholic Church loomed over the picturesque town and a religious person might feel comforted and secure under its towering shadow.

Reluctantly, Morecamb and his men turned their back on the view and contemplated the barracks. The outside was painted in a dark blue colour, in its entirety. No surface had been spared; door, window sills, chimney, door step. Obviously a rogue batch of paint, dismissed by everybody with a scintilla of taste. The whole effect was quite hideous.

The contrast between the brightness of the day and the darkness within was quite staggering. Furthermore, the place seemed deserted. The only evidence of habitation was a sergeant's jacket slung across the back of a chair.

"What are you lot doing here?"

A burly individual had come through one of the internal doors and they could hear a toilet flush behind him.

Morecamb did the introductions, refusing to shake the man's hand when he announced that his name was Sergeant McGrath.

"Put on your jacket, there's a good man," said Morecamb. "Are you the only one here?"

"God, no, there's a lorry load of us a few doors up the street. Giving the lads a bit of a send-off on their holidays. Not the best timing, I know, but their holidays are booked so nothing we can do about that."

"And a few doors up are … what?" asked Morecamb, interrupting the trivia.

"It's the local hostelry. Detective Spillane likes us all to have our lunch in there. Says it helps the investigative juices. Great man with words is our boss. I'll take you up," he finished as he buttoned up his tunic.

The salubrious hostelry went by the name of, 'The Hoor and Hounds'. It was dark and dingy inside and Morecamb vowed it would be the last time he would set foot in the place.

A long, crooked counter took pride of place, liberally dotted with cigarette burns. A young barmaid stood sentry in front of shelves of un-labelled bottles of uncertain provenance, and Morecamb was sure that a cursory sniff would point to the existence of a poteen-still somewhere nearby, no doubt masquerading as a war monument.

McGrath led them over to a table laden with plates of half- finished food.

"And who are ye?" asked an insolent looking individual.

"Where's Detective Spillane?" asked Morecamb, ignoring him.

"He's at a meeting," said McGrath, jumping in quickly. "In Cork".

Morecamb noticed the others glance at each other on hearing this bit of news and ordered them all back to the station. There were some dark mutterings as the chairs were scraped back and they headed out the door like a bunch of recalcitrant schoolboys.

"Sit down," Morecamb instructed them when they were all assembled.

There were six in all, including McGrath.

"Names please!"

"Garda Hancock, sir." *Clueless, if his vacant stare was anything to go by.*

"I'm Garda Williams." *Late forties, Morecamb reckoned and rapidly going to seed.*

"Garda Rooney at your service!" This from the lippy individual. *Late twenties. A pup. Fancied himself a bit of an Elvis; hair slicked back, pointy-toed shoes which were certainly not standard issue and was that a gold medallion around his neck?*

"I'm Garda Harrington," said a man who looked as if he wasn't long out of nappies. *Early twenties, if even that, with a permanent grin on his face like a child at a circus.*

"And I'm Sergeant Foley," came the final response. *Might be the only sane one of the lot of them.*

"Right. I'm Detective Inspector Morecamb. We're from the Serious Crime Unit in Cork and we're here investigating the death of the sixteen year old girl. So, who's going to fill us in on the progress so far? Let's start with you, Rooney, shall we?"

"Just back from the old holliers, guv. So I'm not exactly up to speed."

"Get your feet off the table and straighten yourself up. Sergeant Foley, what can you tell us?"

"Well, the girl's name is Mary O'Donovan, fifteen years old, going on sixteen and doing the Inter Cert at the Convent of Mercy here in the town. She was obviously on her way home from school when some bastard murdered her."

"Was there any weapon found?"

"Great big lump of a rock."

"Any suspects in the frame?" he asked.

"Nothing concrete, sir," said McGrath. "Really we're only just beginning to get our heads around what happened. Detective Spillane asked us to make a list of potential suspects but we hardly know where to start. See, we get a lot of visitors down this way, especially in summer. So, it could be anybody."

"And who gave the go-ahead for her funeral?"

"That would be Detective Spillane," chimed in McGrath.

"Indecent haste, I would have thought," said Morecamb.

"Well, in fairness, he was thinking of the poor parents. They were distraught so Detective Spillane felt that once all the proper procedures were adhered to, the pathologist should release the body. Then, there was no reason why we couldn't just work with the material we have."

"And how has that been working out so far?" Morecamb cast a baleful glance around the room. "Using the local pub as a major incident room and swilling back a few pints hardly constitutes serious policing."

"Well, we conducted a few interviews while we were there as well," Harrington said in wounded tones.

"Shut up, Harrington," hissed Rooney.

"And where are the records of these so-called interviews?" snarled Morecamb.

"Oh, we didn't take notes," countered the irrepressible Harrington. "There was no need. Nobody had any worthwhile information."

"Where are the photos of the victim and the crime scene?"

"In here, Inspector," said Foley as he ushered them into a room towards the back of the station. And there, in gory detail, pinned to the wall, was a single photograph taken in situ, depicting the desecration of a young life. Her long, brown hair was matted with dried blood and mud, there was a gaping hole at the base of her skull and her mouth was open, as if in mid-scream. *Had she registered her fate before the life was beaten out of her?* Her satchel seemed to be a parody of what might have been, what should have been. As Morecamb leaned in to study the bicycle he noticed that the back wheel had a flat tyre. Maybe a puncture, forcing her off the bike to walk the last part of her journey.

"And where are the rest of the photos? Are they in a drawer some-where?" asked Morecamb, looking around.

"Ah, no, there's just the one," answered McGrath. "Detective Spillane felt that one was enough. As he said, a picture paints a thousand words. Great man with the words_____"

Morecamb turned his back on him and ordered Foley to drive himself and Murphy to the crime scene. The others eyed each other warily, sud-denly sobered up and contemplated life under this new regime none too enthusiastically. Only Hancock and Williams were unperturbed while the others cursed their fate and wondered if they could somehow devise some half-baked excuse for absenting themselves from duty, temporarily.

*****

CHAPTER 3

"We're taking the road that Mary usually cycled. It's kind of the back road to Belgooly," said Foley as they left the town behind.

"Beautiful scenery," remarked Morecamb, "especially on a day like this."

The ditches sported as many blossoms and colours as any garden. Sod's Law, he mused. There were people up and down the country who toiled away on their patch of ground, keen gardeners, and they could never recreate what nature produced at will. Magnificent fuchsia with their delicate heads tossing in the breeze, rhododendron flourishing with glorious colour and a magical profusion of heathers. Yeats's line, 'and noon a purple glow' came to mind. Morecamb was quite pleased with himself. Lines learned in a room full of testosterone and unbridled rage from a distraught teacher had had some benefits, he supposed.

"Bloody countryside!" exclaimed Murphy.

"You're not a fan then?" smiled Foley.

"Nope! Too quiet. Not a soul for miles around. Except dead ones of course," he added darkly. "Most murders take place in the countryside, did you know that? Wonder is it boredom? Remember all the murders earlier in the year, boss? I honestly think that the countryside encourages people to go out and kill all around them."

Foley looked in danger of losing control of the car. Morecamb just ignored his sergeant's musings. He had heard it all before and knew there was no point in trying to reason with him. Those earlier murder investigations seemed to have tainted Murphy's perception of the countryside and, Morecamb suspected, the rural background of his wife simply cemented his thwarted view of country living. And probably all forms of living.

After a few minutes silence Foley pulled into a gap.

"We'll walk from here," he said. "It's just up there."

Their footsteps echoed eerily on the deserted road. Not much traffic around here, Morecamb noted. Then he saw the drain running along the side of the road and soon they were at the locus. Police tape ringed the area. No blossoms around here. The whole area was shrouded in shadow; large oak trees canopying the narrow road. It was quite secluded, equidistant from two sharp bends.

The drain had obviously dried up considerably over the past few days, leaving a thick residue of mud. Mary's satchel and bicycle had been removed and would be undergoing forensic examination at the lab in Cork. But you could still see the outline where the body had lain.

The three men stood around, taking in every detail. The area had been combed for any traces in the immediate aftermath of the crime but there was still hope that something, anything at all, might be lying around to help unlock the mystery.

Morecamb broke the silence. "Where would the murderer have parked his car? It would have been too dangerous to simply stop his car here."

"I imagine where we parked ours," said Foley. "Then he simply walked up to her, took her by surprise and killed her".

"So, do you think it was opportunistic or was it planned?"

Foley looked like a man who had been asked to explain the theory of Quantum physics and stared vacantly at Morecamb. Eventually he offered the opinion that it was an 'either or situation', translated thus, "if it was planned we have to ask why. And if it wasn't planned we also have to ask why."

"What possible reason could anybody have for killing a sixteen year old schoolgirl," Morecamb muttered, not bothering to dwell on Foley's chaotic assessment. "Are there any houses around? Any near enough that they might have seen or heard something?" he asked, looking around.

"No, sir, not in the immediate vicinity. About a half mile up the road is the nearest house." Morecamb's interest piqued. "But the house is deserted. Nobody's lived there for years. Place is falling down. The next house is about two miles further up."

Morecamb wondered bleakly why Foley had bothered to supply that useless piece of information about the first house. He alternated between wanting to tell Foley that the word 'dwelling' usually meant that there was somebody living there or giving him a good thump.

"Let's go back to the station. The first thing we need to do is to establish if this was random or did somebody follow Mary once she left the convent or possibly lie in wait for her. But surely somebody would have noticed a car if it was parked up, with the driver just sitting there. C'mon, let's head back."

*****

"I think we should take the lead here," said Rooney belligerently, when Morecamb arrived back and started to divvy up the tasks. "After all_____"

"You haven't got any experience in Serious Crime," Morecamb snapped. "End of discussion. McClean, I want you to work with Garda Hancock and Garda Williams_____"

"Actually, sir, as of now Garda Williams and myself are on our holidays," said Hancock, hesitantly. He was never so glad to be making his escape. There was something deeply unsettling about this new fellah and while not given to philosophical musings Hancock was reminded of a rabid Alsatian which one of the neighbours had owned and which had to be eventually put down. The family pet, they called it until it turned savage on its owner, who was lucky to escape with his limbs intact. The story had left a lasting impact on Hancock.

"Right. That's good," said Morecamb, enigmatically. "So, clear off, the two of you. Now, Harrington, isn't it? You going anywhere soon?"

15

"No, sir."

"McClean, you work alongside Sergeant McGrath, Sergeant Murphy and Garda Rooney. Collate all the information you've gathered so far and put it up on the board over there. Take down those betting slips. Harrington, do you drive?"

Harrington assured him that he did. He was Detective Sweeney's designated driver and, thanks to the detective's foresight, he had insisted that Harrington should take the advanced garda driving course for emergency occasions and he was now an expert. He had the State's permission to exceed all speed limits without any danger of imprisonment. And detective Sweeney loved speed. "'The faster the better' is his motto."

*****

"Where would you like to go, sir?" asked Harrington, revving the engine and threatening to take off before Morecamb and Murphy had engaged their seat belts.

"I want you to take us to the victim's parents. I presume you know where they live?"

Harrington assured him that he did and within seconds they were almost airborne. Morecamb began to miss McClean's more cautious attitude to driving.

"It's about a mile up here," Harrington announced after a surprisingly short few minutes.

"So they're farmers then," said Morecamb.

"Yes, sir, a small dairy herd and a few pigs and that."

"Must be hard to make a living," Morecamb mused.

"Well, the wife cleans houses and that for a few of the wealthy farmers' wives. She also takes in washing, I think. Bloody hard worker, she is. And the husband slaves away on the farm. Here we are," announced Harrington, who then informed them that he might have to slow down a little as the condition of the boreen leading to the farmhouse was full of craters and could be highly dangerous if taken at speed.

16

"On second thoughts maybe I won't bother," he announced and they were treated to the worst excesses of Harrington's elite driving skills. When they slewed to a stop Murphy refused to get out of the car, citing chest pains and a pounding headache for his inability to put one foot in front of the other.

Harrington, completely unaware of the trauma he had inflicted on his hapless passengers, bounded out of the car and proceeded to slosh through the puddles like a big child. Morecamb followed at a more sedate pace, keeping his distance from Harrington in case he was overcome by his emotions and launched a savage attack on him.

Whilst the house wasn't lavish in any way it was still a solid-looking dwelling and bespoke care and attention. It had obviously been painted in the not too distant past and some pots by the front door were a blaze of summer bedding.

Morecamb told his driver to stand back and knocked on the door, gently at first and then a little more loudly when there was no response. Surely their approach must have been noticed. But then, this was a house in mourning and he couldn't even begin to imagine the pain of burying a sixteen year old child.

"Herself is round the back," said a voice. "Are ye selling something?"

Morecamb turned to face his interlocutor. He was a man of indeterminate age, anywhere between fifty and seventy, a haggard, weather-beaten face and a cap pushed back off his forehead. His hands hung limply by his side and they waited silently as he seemed to feel his way towards them.

"Mary's father," whispered Harrington.

Morecamb went forward to meet him and offer his hand.

"Mr O'Donovan, my name is Detective Inspector Morecamb and this is Garda Harrington. May I offer you my deepest condolences?"

The man slowly took the proffered hand. He seemed almost shy.

"Terrible," he muttered and Morecamb could hear the catch in his voice. "I'll take you round to Moll."

They followed his shuffle towards the back of the house where a straight-backed woman, possibly late forties, was dressed from head to toe in uniform black. She was busily throwing feed to a bunch of cackling, hungry hens. When she realised they had company she lifted her head and as Morecamb moved forward her eyes raked his face. There was no warmth there, just a barely concealed anger. Slowly she put down the bucket of meal.

"Mrs O' Donovan, my deepest sympathies on your loss."

She took his hand and inclined her head. Morecamb was surprised by the strength of her grip which spoke of years of hard, manual labour.

"Would you like to come inside, officers?" she asked stiffly. "I'll make some tea."

They followed her inside to the kitchen. It was dark after the sunlit farmyard and it took Morecamb a minute or two to adapt to the sudden change. When he did he was surprised by the chaotic nature of the kitchen. He didn't know what he'd been expecting but certainly not this. Clothes were strewn around the place, newspapers littered most surfaces and the sink was almost hidden by unwashed crockery.

"Excuse the mess," she said in a tired voice. "I just don't seem able… you know… "

"Quite understandable, Mrs O'Donovan. Take no notice of that. I'm leading the investigation into Mary's death and I wanted to meet you before initiating the inquiry."

"Sit yourself down then," said Mr O'Donovan. "Just move the papers to one side. We don't usually buy the papers at all but with all the reports and stories and that on poor Mary, well… herself is keen to keep them. Isn't that right, Moll?" he finished as he turned toward his wife for confirmation.

His wife ignored the remark and came towards them, a pot of steaming tea in her hand which she abruptly laid on the table. Then she produced three cups and saucers and started to pour.

"Do you want a cup, Tom?" she asked as an afterthought.

"I will. I'm parched. Haven't had one since I went out this morning."

"Well, I did call," Moll said a little defensively but there was no anger in her words.

She gave him her own tea and then went to fetch another cup and saucer for herself from the dresser.

As soon as she was seated Morecamb turned to both of them.

"Can you tell me a little about Mary," he asked gently.

"Well, she was just like any other girl her age," said Moll. "Worked hard at school, helped out here at home and… well, that's it really."

"Aye, she was good around the farm, like," added Tom. "She was right fond of the animals. And she was mad about the chickens. When she was little she'd spend hours just sitting with the chicks, when they were newly hatched."

"Head in the clouds a lot of the time," put in his wife.

"And she never ate chicken for her dinner," continued Tom, "not when she realised that they were the fluffy things that she used to play with. She said she'd rather go hungry."

"Well, it was all a bit silly, really," countered his wife. "I thought we should make her eat it but Tom said to let it be. He spoiled her a bit."

Tom made no reply but Moll continued. "I said to him, what will happen when she realises that the calves are one and the same beef that I boil for the dinner? And sure enough… " Suddenly she broke off, perhaps wishing she could have it all back again. Morecamb could sympathise, knowing the pitched battles that went on in households up and down the country, between parents and their teenagers.

"So, she could be a little stubborn at times?" he asked, but with a smile, to let them know that he wasn't being critical of Mary in any way.

"Oh, no," Moll put in quickly, "she always did as she was told."

"What about friends?"

"She has a very good friend, Leila Flynn, who lives in the town," Tom volunteered. "They became friendly in Primary school and thick as thieves ever since."

"So did Mary go to Primary school in the town then?"

"Yes," said Moll. "A relative of his," nodding in Tom's direction, "lives about a mile up the road. Bridie Sugrue's her name and she has three sons around the same age as Mary so she used to give Mary a lift."

"Do you have a car, Tom?" asked Morecamb.

"I do now," he answered, "but I didn't when Mary was small."

"We're not exactly rolling in money here," said Moll, "but things are a little better now. I bring in a bit of money otherwise I think we'd starve." This was said quietly but Morecamb thought he detected a little bitterness in the tone.

"Don't get me wrong, Inspector," she added as if realising she may have sounded a little harsh. "Tom does his best but we've nowhere near as much land as most people around here."

Tom kept his eyes fixed firmly on his cup of tea.

"So where does your cousin live, Tom?" Morecamb asked, hoping to draw Tom back into the conversation.

"Over in Currach, not too far up the road," he said, once more glancing at his wife.

"She won't be much use," said Moll. "Full of gossip and stories. Of course we're not good enough for her. Sends her sons to Christians in Cork. The school in Kinsale isn't good enough for her. Drives them up and down every day herself. Madness."

Moll seemed to be on the verge of tears, no doubt thinking that some people had all the luck whilst she and Tom were doomed to hard graft all their days. And now their only daughter was lying six foot under.

"Well, her husband, Dennis, went to school there himself," said Tom gently, hoping no doubt to inject a bit of balance.

"And Mary's friend, Leila. She lives in the town, does she?" Morecamb asked.

"Yes, in Ardbrack," said Tom. "Will you write down the address, Moll?" asked Tom. "I'm not much of a man for the writing and all that," he added, almost apologetically. "Yes, Leila is a nice wee girl."

"So Mary cycled to and from secondary school every day," Morecamb continued. "What time does school finish in the evenings?"

He knew he should have asked the cretins back in the station that question before he left. That was a stupid oversight on his part.

"At four o' clock," said Moll.

"And she would have got home at what time?"

"It would take her about forty minutes," said her mother.

"God, I could do it in half that time," exclaimed Harrington.

All eyes swivelled towards him. Morecamb had almost forgotten that he was in the room and now wished he wasn't. Should have ordered him to finish feeding the hens.

"Bit of a trek," said Morecamb, turning back to them.

"We all had to do it, Inspector," bridled Moll. "And we couldn't drive her. Tom was busy on the farm and I can't drive."

"Of course," said Morecamb soothingly. "So, at what time did you realise that maybe something had happened?"

"About half past five," answered Moll. "I went over to the haggard to Tom and told him Mary wasn't back. Then he got into the car and drove towards town hoping that he'd see her."

"I passed the spot where she was lying in the drain and I never even saw her," he gulped and then the tears came, huge heaving sobs which seemed to cut a swathe through his entire body.

"He called into the Garda station," Moll took up the story. "That was after he had called to a few houses and the school. Nobody had seen her. Then, for some reason, he drove around some of the other roads around the town, though God knows why. She'd never have taken those roads, I said."

"And what did the guards say?"

"Well, Foley isn't it, Tom? He said they'd organise a search. We stayed up all night, and then a knock came to the door about two in the morning. Gave us a fair fright and then Tom said to me, 'tis all over, Moll.' And when we went to the door there were two policemen standing there."

There was silence when she finished, punctuated intermittently by Tom's hiccups.

"Would you have some recent photos of Mary, by any chance?" asked Morecamb. "I'd like to take them with me. I'll return them of course as soon as I can. And I'll take her friend's name and address too, please."

*****

Shortly afterwards Morecamb and Harrington took their leave. Morecamb pulled Harrington aside before he got behind the wheel and told him he'd break his two arms if he went above third gear. As soon as he was belted up Morecamb filled Murphy in on events and then all three men lapsed into silence. Except Harrington who seemed to be humming a little ditty under his breath. Maybe it's nerves, thought Morecamb, willing to give him the benefit of the doubt.

The Angelus bell was ringing as they went into the station and McClean seemed to be holding the fort on his own.

"The others not back then?" asked Morecamb as he removed his cap.

"Been and gone," said McClean as he considered his escape routes.

"What do you mean?" roared Morecamb, as McClean headed towards the nearest door. "Come back here and explain yourself."

McClean sat back down, silently conceding defeat. "They were back around five," he said, "and when there was no sign of you they said they might as well head off. Foley said they'd be back around ten in the morning."

"Did he indeed. Does Foley have a phone in his house?" asked Morecamb, turning to Harrington.

"I'm not sure but if you want to talk to him your best bet is to ring The Spaniard pub. He usually drops in there for a few pints on his way home. Himself and Garda Rooney. Oh God, please don't tell him I told you that," pleaded Harrington.

Murphy was ordered to ring the Spaniard and tell them to be at the station at eight o' clock in the morning. And there was still no sign of the elusive Detective Sweeney. Morecamb was starting to wonder if he existed at all, maybe a figment of Alderton's imagination. When Murphy re-joined them he declared his 'mission a success' and he could guarantee that all hands would be on deck 'as per your orders, boss' in the morning.

In a way Morecamb was glad they had left early. He didn't know if he could stomach them right now. So they said goodnight to Harrington and made their way out to the car.

*****

On the journey back to Cork McClean, none too pleased with his sub-ordinate role, as he saw it, in Kinsale, took his ire out on the car and whilst falling slightly short of Harrington's cavalier road habits nonetheless his adherence to fourth gear had Murphy clutching his chest again and Morecamb gripping the 'fuck it' strap over the passenger window.

In an effort to distract him Morecamb filled him in on their visit to Mary O' Donovan's parents but when that failed to elicit any response Morecamb told him he would book him for dangerous driving and get him banned from getting behind the wheel of a car for the rest of his miserable career.

*****

It was almost seven o' clock when they reached base in Union Quay. Naturally there was no sign of Alderton but Finin was obviously under instructions to wait until they arrived.

"Are you on over-time, Finin?" asked Murphy as they trudged to-wards him.

"I wish. I've been here since seven this morning and the Super told me not to budge until ye got back. Told me to ask if ye had solved the crime. I'm to ring him with the answer."

"Tell him that there's no sign of Spillane and his men are a bunch of cowboys, "said Morecamb.

"Do you know who Spillane is?" asked Finin after a pause. "He's the Super's brother-in-law."

"Good God," moaned Morecamb.

"Bloody hell," spluttered Murphy. "Isn't he …?"

"Complete loose cannon," supplied Morecamb. "Drink. He actually makes Alderton look adequate."

"So, what will I tell the Super?" Finin persisted. "I have to tell him something. I want to go home. I'm dead on my feet."

"Tell him… tell him that I need to see him in the morning. For a private chat. That'll do."

*****

When Morecamb opened his own front door he breathed a deep sigh of relief. He could smell cooking coming from the kitchen. Oh thank God, he whispered.

"God, you're very late," scolded his aunt. "I've been reheating this stew since five o' clock. I thought you were on annual leave. That's what you said last week."

"Long story, Dot," said Morecamb as he went over to the sink to wash his hands.

"So, you're back at work already or were you with some woman?" she asked, peering at him closely. Dot was on a personal mission, trying to find a suitable replacement for the totally unsuitable woman he had been married to and who had left him after a few short years.

"No such luck. I was called back into work, wasn't I? There's been a murder in Kinsale."

"Nice place," said Dot as she put his food on the table. "And plenty of loose women down there, especially at this time of year. I've fed Willow, by the way. A neighbour's nephew met a grand girl there last year. They nearly got married. Until her husband turned up out of the blue."

Morecamb decided to change tack. "What did you feed Willow?"

"Oh, just the usual. She has an abnormal appetite you know."

"Well, we'll have to cut back on her feed. I had her at the vet the other evening and he gave me an earful about her weight."

"Sure what do vets know?"

"A lot, I hope," answered Morecamb, "considering the extortionate rates they charge. She has to go on a diet. It's either that or exercise. And you know how successful that has been in the past. So, we'll start with the diet and take it from there. Just give her water tomorrow."

"Certainly not. She'd have me eaten before I got to the front door. You can take charge of her diet yourself. Tell you what. I'll bring her a big bone tomorrow from the butcher's and she can chew on that until you get home. I'll drop it over in the morning and leave something cold for your supper. I have Bingo tomorrow night so I won't see you."

About an hour later, after Dot had left to go to her own house, Morecamb grabbed himself a beer, went into the front room and sank into an armchair. He didn't bother to turn on a light, preferring instead the faint glow from the street lamps. He thought about the case, about poor Mary. And his mind kept returning to Tom and the misery and heartache etched in every line of his face. Suddenly he didn't even feel like drinking anymore and gave the rest of his beer to Willow. Wonder what the vet would make of that diet, he mused, as he trudged his way upstairs to bed.

CHAPTER 4

Saturday May 3ʳᵈ

"What do you mean; there was no sign of him?" Alderton bellowed.

It was seven a.m. and Morecamb was seated in his boss's office. Alderton had the temerity to feign surprise at the absence of his brother-in-law the previous day.

"Of course he was there. You obviously didn't look hard enough."

Morecamb stared at him open-mouthed.

"Sir, this isn't a household pet that has gone AWOL. This is a fully grown adult who has decided to take himself off to God knows where. Meanwhile, his men are taking advantage of the situation and it's only a matter of time before we have a mutiny on our hands."

"Poppycock," spluttered Alderton. "You're always one for drama."

Morecamb decided to explain slowly. "Sergeant Foley said he was at a meeting in Cork ____"

"There you go, then."

"But nobody believes that. McGrath even looked embarrassed saying it."

"Right. Well, leave it with me. Once again your boss to the rescue. I'll get in touch with Joseph... Detective Spillane. You just take yourself off to Kinsale and get on with things. I thought you'd have it all wrapped up yesterday."

Morecamb felt like screaming as he banged out of Alderton's office. Alderton just pushed all the wrong buttons, whether deliberately or not. It was a miracle he had survived unscathed for so long.

As he made his way to the canteen he met Finin coming against him.

"Sir, I was wondering if I could have a word."

"Okay, come into my office but make it quick. I want to get on the road as soon as I can. Take a seat."

"Thanks, sir. I was wondering if… "

Five minutes later a distraught Finin couldn't even summon the energy to close the door behind him. He had tried everything; terminally ill relatives, threats to the safety of Superintendent Alderton, blackmail and finally an arson attack on Union Quay. But Morecamb wouldn't budge. Finin would have to stay with the unpredictable, and in Finin's opinion, the clinically insane Alderton. Morecamb refused point blank to revisit Alderton's office and plead on Finin's behalf.

"Look, maybe tomorrow," Morecamb said in an attempt to stem the growing panic in Finin's face. "That's the best I can do for now."

*****

Shortly afterwards, when they were trapped in the car, with McClean at the wheel, Morecamb announced that there would be no talk on the way down, no reminiscences about the past and if McClean, who had reverted to his torturous slow pace of the previous morning, didn't find fourth gear pretty sharpish he would find himself hitching a lift to Kinsale.

Morecamb felt a little calmer when they reached the barracks in Kinsale. And, if McGrath and his crew had obeyed orders and presented themselves in good working order, he had high hopes that his blood pressure wouldn't be a source of alarm for some unsuspecting local G.P.

"Good morning, sir. All present and correct, as you instructed."

McGrath seemed in ebullient form, obviously not contagious judging by the scowls on the faces of the other officers.

"Detective Spillane just rang," McGrath continued, "and said the meeting in Cork ran over last night but he said to tell you that he'll be in first thing this morning."

Morecamb didn't believe a word of it and asked for a review of the previous day's actions. The results were pitiful. Some of them had called on the houses near the scene of the crime but a lot of them were empty.

"Like the *Mary Celeste* empty or were they hiding?" asked Morecamb.

"Hard to say," said McGrath.

When Morecamb pushed him and asked how many houses they had visited he was given a choice of two numbers. McGrath said two and Rooney said four. But, Foley added hastily, they had also called on some of the houses near the convent and that was a lot more fruitful as a lot of the residents were there. No, they had no useful information, he was sorry to say but they were more than willing to assist the Gardaí and offered to call to their relations and ask them if they had any sighting of the victim prior to death. One of them had asked if they could have a garda car at their disposal to speed things up. McGrath said he'd make enquiries.

Murphy excused himself and headed to the toilets. Harrington contemplated offering his services as a designated driver but in a rare moment of insight decided against it at the last minute. He had also noticed a vein protruding from Morecamb's forehead and while he stared at it the moment had passed.

Morecamb drew a deep breath but before he had time to unleash the mother and father of all screaming lectures he was interrupted by the appearance of a man with a spectacular girth, a complexion to rival the fuchsia bushes he had seen yesterday and an almost comical look of confusion on his face. Then he seemed to get his bearings.

"You must be Alderton's lad," he addressed Morecamb as he weaved unsteadily towards Morecamb. "How do you do... it?" he continued. "Had an earful from him this morning. Not the kind of thing you want to hear first thing. He told me I was missing, you know... lost! I think he might be a heavy drinker. Morecamb, isn't it?" he finished as he offered his left hand.

Morecamb took it and studied the man in front of him. At least he was impeccably dressed, but Morecamb's eye was immediately drawn to the intricate array of burst blood vessels in his eyes and the red-veined nose was no less unattractive.

"Good to meet you, I was the person who reported you missing, I'm afraid."

"Yes, well, I wasn't feeling too well yesterday. The wife wanted me to go to the doctor and do you know, I just hadn't the energy. A virus, I reckon. So she insisted on making a few hot toddies for me. Not my favourite tipple but they seemed to do the trick. By the way there are two reporters outside looking for information. Get us a cup of tea, will you, Harrington. I need to sit down. I'll be in my office."

And he was gone.

Morecamb turned to Murphy and ordered him to go out and threaten the journalists. He then turned to the others intending to continue where he had left off but, once again, Spillane reappeared, in some distress.

"Just had Alderton on the phone. Seems there was a disturbance down at the Marina last night. Some boats were damaged. Said to tell you to deal with it, Morecamb. My God, twice in the one day." And his office door clicked shut behind him.

Morecamb told Rooney to go down to the Marina to see what was going on and to have a report on his desk by lunchtime.

Rooney grumbled his way to the door and Morecamb was glad to see the back of him. But part of him sympathised with him. This was a complete waste of resources and an unnecessary distraction. So what if some hooligans had thrashed half the yachts in the bay, the Commissioner's included. The murder of a schoolgirl was far more important though he doubted if Alderton could tell the difference.

"Foley, I want yourself and Harrington to visit a woman called Bridie Sugrue. She's a cousin of Tom's and she used to give lifts to Mary to Primary school. See if she can add anything to our enquiries. Sergeant Murphy and myself are off to the convent where Mary went to school. I believe it's not far."

Out of courtesy he decided to inform Sweeney of their plans but when he knocked gently on his door and went in there was no sign of him. How was that possible?

Retreating he explained his dilemma to the others.

"Oh, there's a back door, sir," McGrath explained. "It's over at the very corner. Hard to spot behind the coat stand."

*****

In spite of Murphy's protestations Morecamb announced that they would walk to the convent. He assured Murphy that the exercise would be good for them. He decided not to mention that there were over sixty steps to be negotiated.

"For you maybe, boss, but I always feel desperately unwell after walking. And I'm still recovering from yesterday."

Morecamb ignored him and moved off at a brisk pace until he came to the steps. Half way up he stopped and began to regret his decision. But when he looked out over the bay his resolve returned. His companion experienced no such epiphany as he clung to the railing with his head bowed.

"God, look at that magnificent view, Murphy!"

Down below they could see the sparkling water of the harbour with boats of all shapes and sizes swaying together by the quayside. Masts soared gracefully towards the sky. Across the bay they had a bird's eye view of those magnificent, elevated houses, their occupants looking down on the fruits of their inheritances and, no doubt, on the lesser mortals who toiled away on their fishing vessels.

Morecamb guessed that the so-called merchant classes had homes up there, those rarefied species of big business. Some of the houses probably served as bolt-holes for the weekend where the occupants indulged their own brand of hedonism, a fan-club of mutual admiration. Chief among them, no doubt, was their illustrious Commissioner.

"Would you like to live up there, Murphy?"

"Up where? In the bloody convent?"

Eventually they found themselves at the solid, mahogany doors of the convent. A prominent plaque proclaimed, 'St. Joseph's Convent of Mercy', its brass lettering testimony to years of scrubbing and polishing. Murphy pulled on a bell to the side of the door and it was opened almost immediately by a scowling individual dressed in the traditional garb of the Mercy order. The wooden rosary beads at her waist could be classed as a lethal weapon if she chose to wield it in anger.

"Yes?"

"Hello, Sister. We're from the Serious Crime Division in Cork and we're investigating the death of one of your students, Mary O' Donovan," said Morecamb as he offered his warrant card.

"And you?" she asked, addressing Murphy.

"The same, Ma'am."

"Follow me."

And with a swish of her habit she sashayed down the highly-polished floor, walls adorned with a vast array of saints staring superciliously down at them, and she stopped at another mahogany door at the end of the corridor.

"In here," she said. "I'll fetch Mother Superior for you."

They were ushered into a magnificent parlour, with two large, bay windows offering a spectacular view of the harbour. Large portraits of dead clerics, mostly bishops judging by the inscription on the brass plates, seemed to follow their every move. An upright piano stood in the corner, with a sheet of music displayed on its stand. Luxurious armchairs were strategically placed in front of an open, unlit fire, with a beautiful marble surround.

"They take a vow of poverty, don't they, boss?" said Murphy as he glanced up at the ornate cornicing.

A light tap on the door and an imposing woman came into the room.

"Inspector, I'm Mother Josephina," she smiled. "It's nice to meet you."

Then she turned to Murphy and extended her hand in greeting. Thankfully Murphy had the good grace to stand up as he took her hand.

"Please sit down," she said, as she indicated a sofa. "Now, how may I help you?"

She was much younger than Morecamb had anticipated, not much older than himself. Her warm smile endeared her to the hardened officers and her direct gaze seemed to invite confidences but also commanded respect. A good friend and a formidable adversary, Morecamb reckoned.

"We're here about Mary O' Donavan's tragic death, Mother," Morecamb began. "We've already called to her parents and spoken with them."

"How are they, Officer? Of course I met them at Mary's funeral and I called to see them the day after. But I didn't stay long. Father Leonard was with them and I think a cousin of theirs was there as well. So I told Tom I'd call back again later on."

"Yes, they seem devastated, Mother. We're trying to build up a picture of Mary. We've gathered from our enquiries so far that she was a quiet girl. Is that your assessment too?"

"Well, yes, Officer. Obviously I no longer teach but I've been speaking with the other Sisters. Some of them taught her. And yes, she was quiet and diligent. As far as I know she intended leaving school after her Inter Cert. She talked about wanting to do a commercial course."

"And would her parents have wanted that?"

"Well, I can't say for certain but I imagine they wouldn't have objected. She had just turned sixteen in March and I suppose the extra money coming in would be appreciated."

"Yes," said Morecamb, "I gather the father and mother work hard and it's not a large farm."

"Well, it's not so much that it's a small farm but Tom got it when his father died. I believe the father, though it isn't right to speak ill of the dead, had a drink problem so the place was a bit run-down when Tom eventually got it."

"And is Moll a local woman?"

"She's from outside Garretstown, about ten miles away. She probably had it hard when they married because they lived with his father until he died. I imagine it was difficult."

"And what age would Mary have been when her grandfather died?"

"About six or seven, I'd say."

"It can't have been easy for her either," put in Murphy.

"I'd say not. But Tom doted on her. Moll is more practical, tougher maybe but as I say she didn't have it easy either."

"I believe Mary was quite friendly with a girl called Leila," said Morecamb.

"Yes, Leila Flynn. They're in the same class or were in the same class I should say. Leila is a different kettle of fish," Josephina laughed. "Nice girl but as mad as a March hare. Apparently she wants to leave school in June as well. She wants to do fashion design." This was said with raised eyebrows. "Don't ask."

"And is that likely?" asked Morecamb, intrigued by this woman's quirky insights.

"Have you met Leila's parents, Officer?" Again the quizzical smile.

"Not yet," he admitted.

"I think they have loftier ambitions for Leila."

"Would it be possible to speak to Leila, Mother, do you think?"

"Well . . . yes, I'll summon her. The exam classes come in on Saturdays to do study. At least that's the theory. It seems to keep the parents happy, at least they know where their teenagers are for a few hours. But another adult will have to sit in with Leila. Protocol, you understand. I'll fetch her now."

With that she bade them goodbye and assured them of her full co-operation in their attempts to catch Mary's murderer.

"A fine cut of a woman," opined Murphy as the door closed softly behind her. "She's wasted in here, you know. When I think of all the bloody women who think they're cut out to be wives . . ."

A deep sigh was followed by a moment of intense melancholia. Morecamb almost felt sorry for his sergeant.

They were interrupted by a sharp rap on the door and in marched a very self-assured, gum-chewing young girl. She was accompanied by the waspish-looking nun who had opened the door to them.

"I'm Sister Assumpta and this is Leila," she announced. "Sit down over there, Leila. And pull down your skirt, for God's sake."

Leila threw a murderous glare in the direction of her chaperone. She plonked herself into a chair and defiantly hitched her skirt a little higher.

She was quite a pretty girl, under the scowl and could have passed for a woman of twenty. The make-up was discreet, a nod to conformity but also rebellion. The latter would emerge victorious in that battle, Morecamb reckoned.

"I believe you wish to speak to Leila, Officers," said Sister Assumpta, in clipped tones. The subliminal message was, 'get on with it.'

"Yes, of course," said Morecamb, turning to Leila. "We believe you were best friends with Mary O'Donovan so I want to start by saying how sorry we are."

Leila continued to stare at the two officers, unblinking.

"So, could you describe Mary for us?"

"Well . . . about five feet tall, long brown hair, small eyes but I showed her how she could make them look____"

"Shush, Leila," interjected Assumpta. "The officers know what Mary looked like, dear. I'm sure they mean what she was like in terms of personality.

"Is that what you meant?" asked Leila, her piercing eyes boring into Morecamb. "It's just you didn't say."

"Well, yes," said Morecamb, foolishly feeling a little intimidated.

"She was lovely. Quiet. But we were working on that," said Leila.

"Did she have lots of friends?"

"Why is *he* here?" she asked, nodding in Murphy's direction. Morecamb could feel his sergeant squirming a little and noticed how his gaze remained fixed on the fireplace. "He hasn't said a word. Is he dumb?"

"Leila!" barked Sr. Assumpta. "Have manners."

"I was just asking," she pouted.

"I'll do the asking," said Morecamb deciding there was little point in adopting the soft approach. "What about other friends?"

"Well, we used to hang around with some of the other girls. But they're real swots. Mary and me had planned to leave school this summer after our Inter Cert and make lots of money. Of course I'll still do that."

"We're trying to prepare ourselves for the void, Officers," said Sister Assumpta in acerbic tones.

Maybe you're not so bad after all, Morecamb mused. Personally he felt that he would want to hack off his head if he spent every day wrestling with the likes of Leila Flynn.

"And what about boyfriends?" pursued Morecamb.

"Who? Me or Mary? Well, seriously, I'm hardly going to discuss our love lives in front of Sister Assumpta," she said scornfully.

Sister Assumpta blushed a deep crimson and Morecamb felt sorry for her.

"It's a fairly straightforward question, Leila," said Morecamb. "Was Mary seeing anybody?"

"No."

Morecamb didn't believe her but he knew there was little point in pursuing that line of questioning at the moment.

"Well, were you aware of anybody who might want to harm Mary?"

"Nobody. I mean who would want to do that? She was just an ordinary girl who went to school and never hurt anybody in her life."

The bravado seemed to have vanished, Morecamb noticed, and she seemed close to tears.

"We'll leave it at that," he said, kindly. "Thank you for seeing us. And thank you, Sister Assumpta, for your time."

Leila remained sitting where she was and Sister Assumpta escorted them to the door. No words were spoken but Morecamb could sense sadness in the nun as she bolted the door behind them.

Murphy pronounced that he was the victim of a second horrendous experience in as many days. On this occasion it was the existence of teenage girls who make it their life's mission to inflict as much mayhem as possible and destroy all in their path. Murphy felt as if he had been castrated and went on to ask if that was the reason that Morecamb had his dog at the vet the previous week.

When Morecamb pointed out that his dog was female Murphy became even more animated and suggested euthanasia.

Morecamb knew he wasn't going to be able to discuss the case with any clarity at the moment. Murphy was practically jogging away from the convent until they got to the steps. But at least it was all downhill now and Murphy led the way, in fact.

To help calm him down Morecamb suggested that they stop at a restaurant on the way back to have some lunch.

"About time," grumbled Murphy. "I was hoping they might have given us a bite to eat at the convent. I'm sure I could smell food."

"Presumably for the students, Murphy. Would you like to share lunch with the lovely Leila and her buddies in the refectory? Well?"

A scowl was the only response he got. They went into the first restaurant that they saw and when their food arrived Murphy's mood soared several octaves and he didn't lift his head until his plate was clean.

"Now I feel human again, boss," he announced as he patted his ample stomach. "You're very quiet. Something up?"

"Well, I didn't want to upset your digestion while you were eating but I was thinking about Leila Flynn____"

"Can you wait until I've had my dessert, boss?"

"No, you've eaten enough. Now, Leila Flynn. What did you think of her evidence?"

"I was afraid of her to be honest. Do you think she might be the murderer? Or what about one of the nuns?"

Morecamb was dumb-struck and immediately left the table to pay the bill.

When they returned to the station Harrington and Foley were back and, judging by Spillane's open door, he was still missing.

"How did you get on in Sugrue's, Sergeant?"

Well, began Foley, apparently it depended on how you looked at things. She was a very nice woman, gave them the tea and sandwiches. She introduced them to two sons, grand lads, who are studying for their Inter cert and she didn't want them upset in any way with talk about murder and such which is quite understandable really. Anyway, the upshot of it all is that she will only talk to the person in charge, somebody from outside the jurisdiction.

"She said she was afraid that Sergeant Foley would blab when he had too much drink taken," Harrington added.

Foley turned crimson and assured Morecamb that Mrs Sugrue has a strange sense of humour and mustn't be taken seriously. You had to know her and even though this was their first meeting he could tell straight away that she was joking.

"I'll tell him about the phone call," said Harrington in a high state of excitement. "There was also a call from an old man who claimed that he saw a young girl answering Mary's description in a car with some man. Mr. Egleston is the caller's name."

Morecamb felt a frisson of excitement. This could be a lead.

"Mind you," continued Harrington, "he said he was coming home from the pub, a little the worse for wear according to himself, and he had to drive the car into the ditch to avoid a collision. A neighbour of his had to tow the car out of the drain with a tractor."

Shit!

Morecamb wanted to beat somebody.

"Right, well we won't hold our breath on that one," said Morecamb. "Still, no harm in calling on him. Where does he live?"

"About two miles down the road from where the O'Donovan's live, according to himself. But then he added 'as the crow flies'. So, who knows."

"I see there's still no sign of your detective," said Morecamb to Foley. "Think I'll just make a phone call. I'll use Spillane's parlour."

Morecamb closed the door behind himself and dialled the station in Union Quay.

"Moloney, Morecamb here. Will you put me through to the Great Man?"

A few minutes later Alderton peevishly answered his phone.

"Morecamb here, sir. I was wondering_____"

37

"Solved it, have you? Or are you ringing to whine and annoy?"

"I'll do my best, sir. Your brother-in-law put in the briefest of appearances at ten thirty this morning before vanishing again."

"Well, he's obviously out trying to solve the case."

"Do you think so, sir? Do you *really* think so? I don't think he's in any fit state to even be out in public representing the force. So here's what I'm going to do. I'm off down now to the Marina and I'm hoping to meet the Commissioner there. Apparently he likes to swoop in at this time of year. Just so that I can update him on the case, you understand, and the unorthodox resources at our disposal." Morecamb could hear an incoherent spluttering at the other end of the phone. "Do you want me to pass on your regards to said Commissioner? Yes?"

With that he slapped down the phone. When he came back into the day room McClean informed him that a Mrs McCarthy, who works up in the convent, had also rung. She wanted to speak to one of them so he had told her to call to the station on Monday morning.

Good, at least that was something, Morecamb thought and then he told the men he was off down to the marina, ostensibly to see what Alderton had been spouting about earlier concerning the vandalism but, really, he just wanted to clear his head and enjoy the soothing calmness of the harbour. Suddenly he spotted Rooney in the corner.

"What are *you* doing here?" he asked him.

"It's lunch-time. We *are* entitled to eat you know."

"Only if you deserve it. Where's your report?"

"Well, I'm not finished down there yet, am I? Not much point in writing half a report. What if something kicks off in the afternoon?"

"Get your lunch and then get your arse back down there. And don't attempt to sneak off like you did yesterday before I give permission. Understood?"

Morecamb didn't wait for a reply. He beckoned to Murphy and once outside informed him that they were going to take a stroll. Murphy had the good sense not to complain and seemed happy enough to take in their surroundings as they walked along, in silence. Morecamb didn't feel like breaking the silence anyway as he nursed bleak thoughts about Alderton.

His mood lifted suddenly when they reached the quayside. There was something infinitely peaceful in the gentle lapping water against the boats as they stood in line, some patiently waiting for their owners. Others were occupied and a number of people were dining out on their decks.

"How the other half lives, eh, boss?"

"Let's pretend that they're jealous of our relative youth, Murphy. Most of them look ready to pop their clogs. Would you swop your life for what's left of theirs?"

"Yes," grunted Murphy.

They continued walking along until Murphy grabbed hold of Morecamb's arm.

Good God! Spillane!

"This looks interesting," said Morecamb.

The Detective was weaving his way towards them, his hand raised in greeting.

"I was looking for you," slurred Spillane. "Then I met Jim . . . you know . . .Jim Dunworth . . . no, Dunphy. Do you know him? Decent man. Went for a pint . . . haven't seen him in . . . anyway, salt of the earth and all that . . . said to say hello, so I couldn't refuse. Do you know him at all . . ."

"Come on," said Morecamb, "we'll walk back to the barracks with you."

"No, no, no . . ." he objected. "I hate the bloody barracks . . . do you know Alderton?" he asked, trying to focus on their faces.

"Yes," said Murphy. "He's our boss."

"Terrible bloody man. Always interfering. Is he here now?" he asked, hiccupping. "Going to call him out. Long overdue."

"He's back in Cork, Detective," said Morecamb as they nudged Spillane in the direction of the barracks.

"Married to my sister, you know. Terrible bloody woman too. Aldert . . . you know . . . himself tried to be a member of the sailing club here . . . barred. Only time they all agreed on something. Awful man."

"Right, here we are, Detective. Careful of the step now."

As soon as they got in Morecamb called Foley to one side and told him to take Spillane home. When the door closed behind them Morecamb turned to the rest of the team and brought them up to date on their findings at the convent. Then he turned to Murphy and informed him that they were going to see Mrs Sugrue.

"Harrington, you drive. Presumably you know the way." Harrington took off like a hare. "McClean, you stay here and update the crime board. Here," he said, removing Mary's photos from his pocket, "put these up on the Crime Board. We need to remind ourselves that Mary was once a living, breathing human being. She's not just a statistic."

Morecamb's earlier admonishment of Harrington's driving habits seemed completely forgotten and he took off like a bat out of hell. Morecamb resolved that it would be the last time that he would be a passenger in his car. Speed limits were completely ignored and he seemed to regard yield signs as purely decorative.

When they arrived at their destination a very ashen-faced Murphy stumbled out of the car. McClean was ordered to stay put.

Morecamb and Murphy walked a little unsteadily towards the front door which was opened before they had a chance to raise a hand to knock. A young man, probably late teens, was just on his way out and did a double-take when he almost collided with the two men.

"Who are you?" he demanded, with all the charm of a male version of Leila.

"I'm Inspector Morecamb and this is Sergeant Murphy. And you are?"

"Trevor. Why?" Then he took a few paces back and bellowed over his shoulder, "MAM!" And turning back towards the officers he muttered something about catching a bus and slouched off down the drive with his duffle bag dangling from his shoulder.

"How may I help you?"

Both men turned back towards the voice. She was in her mid-forties, well turned-out, as Murphy would say, dressed in a sensible tweed, twin-set and what looked like a string of pearls around her neck.

"Inspector Morecamb and Sergeant Murphy, ma'am," said Morecamb, raising his warrant card.

They were ushered into the parlour and Mrs Sugrue excused herself while she instructed 'my maid', Peggy, to make some refreshments.

The room was an explosion of pinks and purples, every surface was gleaming, silver-framed photos dotted here and there and a large white rug in the centre. It was in stark contrast to poor Moll's house but a poor relation of the parlour down at the convent. Returning she exhorted them to make themselves comfortable but the room's appearance didn't lend itself to any such liberties.

Both men perched on the edge of the sofa and started to dread the arrival of the so-called refreshments. Would they have to balance everything on their knees? Murphy was warily eyeing the white rug while Morecamb felt like a specimen under a magnifying glass.

"Ah, here we are," said the hostess as Peggy carefully wheeled in a trolley and handed a cup of tea and a plate of biscuits to each of the men. There followed a few anxious moments while Peggy was ordered to fetch a side table, reposition it three times, to be careful of 'my best china,' and to rearrange the rug which she had almost tripped over, sending the entire set of china into the fireplace.

Morecamb and Murphy would have helped poor Peggy but a glare from Mrs Sugrue stymied any such overture. There was also the issue of what to do with the tea in any such manoeuvre. Sensibly, Peggy beat a hasty retreat.

"Now, Mrs Sugrue_____"

"Bridie, please, Inspector. No formalities here."

"Right, Bridie, some officers called here earlier. They got the impression that you would prefer to speak to myself."

"Oh, they were in no doubt. I told them I would only address the man in charge. Now, what would you like to know?"

"I believe you're related to Mary O' Donovan's parents."

"I'm related to Tom, that's all. We're second cousins. Once removed. Nice man. Shame about his wife."

"I've met Moll," Morecamb pointed out, "and I found her very amenable. You also knew Mary, I believe?"

"Well, yes, I took pity on poor Mary so I used to give her a lift to and from Primary school. But then we sent our sons to a fee-paying secondary school in Cork."

"So would you have seen much of Mary in recent times?"

"Hardly, Inspector," she answered primly. "Moll and I are hardly bosom pals."

"Did you have a falling-out?"

"Well, we're from very different backgrounds, shall we say. And of course Moll's father put a gun to poor Tom's head to make him marry her when she got in the family way. Tom could have done so much better for himself, I can tell you. Quite a shock to the family when he brought *her* home."

"So, what kind of woman was his father expecting? When he was sober, that is," asked Morecamb with raised eyebrows. "See, our understanding is that Moll has been a huge asset in that relationship," continued Morecamb. "Practically keeps your cousin's farm afloat, so to speak. Now, is there anything useful you'd like to tell us?"

Bridie glared at the two officers, her lips drawn in a straight line.

"What about your sons, Mrs Sugrue?" asked Murphy. "They must have come across Mary at some stage. Perhaps in town?"

"Certainly not."

"Are they never down the town, chasing girls and that?" continued Murphy. "They're probably a bit young for the pubs but lots of young ones take to the back streets and parks and get plastered on bottles of cheap ale."

Mrs Sugrue had become decidedly pale as Murphy plundered on. Morecamb sat back and started to enjoy the scene.

"We just bumped into a strapping lad of yours at the door. Trevor, isn't it? He looks like someone who'd enjoy a bit of mischief. I'm not saying he's one of the druggies or that…..or is he?"

Mrs Sugrue drew herself up to her full height.

"Trevor will be studying Law in UCC in September, as soon as he gets his Leaving Cert results. Have you ever heard of a barrister dabbling in drugs?"

"Actually I would have thought, given their dealings with the criminal elements_____"

"Mrs Sugrue," interrupted Morecamb, sensing an imminent ejection, "please sit down. What ages are your other sons?"

"Fourteen. They're twins. And no, they don't cavort around the town either."

"We'd like to have a word with them, nevertheless. Are they here?"

"They're studying but I'll get them if you insist."

She flounced out of the room and they heard her at the bottom of the stairs calling up to her sons. After a few minutes they could hear the thump of her footsteps on the stairs followed by a heated argument. Eventually she shepherded two sullen-looking boys into the parlour.

"Marcus, Damien, these men wish to speak to you."

"About what?" mumbled the boy called Marcus.

"Oh, just a few questions about Mary O'Donovan," said Morecamb calmly, noticing a quick glance pass between both boys before looking at their mother. "Sit yourselves down, lads."

"We prefer standing," said Damien, obviously the leader of the two.

"Suit yourselves. Now, when was the last time you saw Mary O'Donovan?"

"Ages ago," said Damien.

"Could you narrow that down?" asked Morecamb, all the while holding his gaze.

"About three weeks ago," said Marcus obviously more eager to co-operate.

"Not that long ago then. Did you speak to her?"

"Of course," said Damien. "We're cousins."

"Well, hardly that," snapped his mother. "Only indirectly. Once removed."

"Just said hello," said Damien answering Morecamb's question. "You know, the usual."

"You'll have to elaborate on 'the usual'", Morecamb put in. "We may have a different interpretation of that. After all, your understanding of 'ages ago' and mine are somewhat at variance."

"We asked her what she was doing outside the chipper."

"Was that unusual for her?"

"Well, it's on the edge of town, hardly on her way home," smirked Damien.

"It's just she seemed to be waiting for someone," Marcus added. "A bit dressed-up like."

"And was it a school day?"

"Yes."

"But she wasn't wearing her uniform?"

"No." This in unison.

"And if it was a school day what were you doing in town?" asked Morecamb. "I thought you were ferried to school and back."

"Mum's car was in the garage so we had to get the bus." Marcus again.

"And did Mary say what she was doing there?"

"She said she was waiting for a friend. She blushed like a beet root." Again the smirk from Damien.

"Do you think she was waiting for a boyfriend?"

"How should we know?" snapped Damien.

"As I explained, Officers, my sons didn't exactly mix socially with Mary. Even if she was waiting for some boy or other they're hardly likely to know who he was."

"So, do you know who it might have been?" Morecamb asked the question anyway. They both glanced at Mama and then shook their head.

"And what is the name of the chipper?"

"Lorenzo's," said Damien, "and that's all we know. Can we go now?"

Morecamb nodded and without a backward glance they left the room and thundered up the stairs.

"You've upset them," Mrs Sugrue declared even though there was scant evidence for such an accusation.

"What time do you expect Trevor to be back?" asked Morecamb, ignoring her. "We'll need to speak to him too."

"Is all this absolutely necessary, Officer? I've already explained_____"

"Yes, it is. We need to eliminate as many people as we can from our enquiries."

"I hope you're not seriously suggesting that my Trevor is a suspect?" she squealed. "I've never heard anything so ridiculous in all my life."

"So, what time would be convenient to talk to him? We can do it here or down at the station."

"He'll be here on Tuesday afternoon," she fumed. "They get a half day on Tuesdays for study purposes. But of course if you insist on harassing him he'll just have to forego that essential activity, won't he?"

"Precisely. Tell him to expect us sometime in the afternoon. We'll bid you good-day."

Their exit was a lot frostier than their welcome and Morecamb felt their next interview would probably be conducted in the kitchen, if not in one of the outhouses.

"Do you think it's something in the water, boss?" asked Murphy as they headed back into town. "We've met some terrible people since we arrived here. No offence, Harrington."

"None taken," came the response, as he drove over a pigeon, scattering feathers in all directions. "Oops!"

*****

45

Morecamb called a brief meeting for updates as soon as they got back. He hadn't felt so tired in a long time. He should really corner Alderton when he got back to Cork but he hadn't the energy. It would have to wait until Monday, so he decided to call it a day. He reminded Foley and Harrington that they were meeting Mrs McCarthy on Monday morning and that it was standard practice to take notes.

Next up was Rooney who proudly presented his report from the Marina, all the details scribbled down on a piece of paper torn from a sum's copy. When he noticed Morecamb's less than enthusiastic response he boldly added that there was nothing to report. Obviously, somebody was 'taking the piss.'

Finally, and perhaps foolishly, Morecamb asked who was manning the station over the weekend. He was met with blank stares all round and then McGrath informed him that the whole thing was on an ad hoc basis, an arrangement which had always worked very well and, 'as the old saying goes, if it's not broken why fix it?'

Harrington and Rooney marvelled at McGrath's quick thinking, momentarily, until Morecamb found his voice and let loose a volley of ear-splitting expletives accompanied by a rearrangement of the station's furniture.

Foley resolved that he wouldn't be around on Monday.

"Rooney, take the first shift from eight a.m. until two tomorrow. Harrington will relieve you. Foley, check in at regular intervals and see if there's any progress. Notify the barracks in Union Quay immediately if there's any information."

"That's fine, sir," answered Foley. "But I'll only be able to make myself available until twelve because as of midnight on Sunday, I'm on holidays." Foley felt quite chuffed with himself after that statement because initially he had been dreading having to tell Morecamb but now a sense of panic had set in and, furthermore, he reckoned that the case might be solved by the time he got back and he wouldn't be around for any fall-out. And even if it wasn't he would take sick leave until he was certain that Morecamb was out of the way.

"Really? You'll do no such thing, Foley. And if you go near an airport or a ferry terminal I'll have you arrested. You can go on your holidays when this case is solved and not before. Do I make myself clear? Right, we're off."

He left a stunned silence behind him and wearily trudged out to the car. His men followed at a safe distance.

CHAPTER 5

Monday 5ᵗʰ May

After a poor night's sleep Morecamb didn't arrive at the station until eight o' clock on Monday morning. Sunday had been spent recovering from a massive hangover and a gargantuan attempt to recall the details of Saturday night when he had charmed a young woman to spend the night with him. He vaguely remembered them exchanging names as she left his house in the small hours and praying that she hadn't stolen anything before she had tottered off in her high heels.

He wondered if the whole experience constituted a blackout and if he should ease up on the drink. And then he thought of Alderton and decided, not yet.

His late arrival was grist to the mill for Alderton. He could now go on the attack and, sure enough, he was waiting at his office door, obviously spoiling for a fight.

"In here, you. Shut the door. Because I'm a reasonable man I'm prepared to overlook the tardiness of your arrival. But I might well bring it up the next time you cast aspersions on a family member."

"Look, sir, we need to set some ground rules here," said Morecamb, trying to ignore the ringing in his ears. "I want Spillane to take annual leave while I'm working this case and I want_____"

"Want, want," muttered Alderton.

Morecamb raised his hand for silence and continued, "I want complete control while I'm down there. At the moment it's a free-for-all. Nobody's in charge, least of all your brother-in-law. They're all just pissing around_____"

"Language please."

"_____whenever and wherever they please. The locals seem to regard them as a joke so unless I get complete autonomy I'm going to the Commissioner with my complaints."

"Always drama with you, Morecamb," roared Alderton.

"And it now transpires that some of them have decided that they're in need of a holiday so they have simply taken off. So, I suggest that Finin_____"

"Finin has been seconded to the station in Rosscarbery. They're short-staffed. I was going to send your friend, Murphy, but I'm not a vindictive man. So, you'll have to make do with what you have. Obviously they couldn't wait to get out of the place when you arrived. See, that's the thing about a bad reputation_____"

"The newspapers are now sniffing around," continued Morecamb ignoring him, "and it's only a matter of time before they go up the chain of command and park themselves at your door. Before moving onto the Commissioner. And I wouldn't want to be in your shoes, sir, when the fan starts scattering_____"

"Alright, alright, you've made your point. On and on . . . what newspapers?"

"Locals. Nationals. All straining at the leash, teeth bared. You get the picture."

"Yes, yes. As I say, always the drama queen. What do you want me to do about it?"

"Sanction Spillane's leave and notify him before I set foot in the station in Kinsale. Then get onto Sergeant McGrath and inform him that I am now in sole charge of the investigation. So from now on they doff their cap to me."

"Like you do to me?" sneered Alderton.

"Along those lines, yes, but with more feeling. I'm calling on the lab now to get an update and I'll come by here on the way to Kinsale to check that everything is in order."

"Will you indeed?" snapped Alderton but Morecamb knew he would do the necessary. The power of the media was a wonderful thing not to mention the fear of the Commissioner.

*****

Alderton sank back into his chair as soon as Morecamb had left. What now? He wasn't a man usually given to introspection, preferring instead to stick to the glaringly obvious. But he now realised that perhaps he had been a little hasty in promoting his brother-in-law to the position of detective. But the wife had been insistent and Alderton had succumbed after he had been caught, *in flagrant,* with some woman who had practically thrown herself at him.

Such was the price one had to pay for such exalted positions as he now occupied. An occupational hazard, really. The fact that the woman was tanked up on a vat of wine was simply by the by.

But something would have to be done about Joe. He knew he would have to be cunning and subtle in how he approached the dilemma. Somehow he would have to persuade him that taking early retirement would be ideal for him and allow him ample opportunity to pursue his various hobbies. But then he remembered that Joe had only one hobby, an addiction if you like, and a retirement package would go nowhere near financing that particular past-time.

Mmm…he would need to be very clever. Maybe he'd enlist McClean's help. What good was a college education if you couldn't solve a fairly simple, straightforward conundrum.

*****

Morecamb and Murphy rolled up outside the forensic laboratory twenty minutes later. Their contact was Malcolm Heffernan, a man who could easily measure six feet were it not for the permanent stoop. Hours spent peering at exhibits, no doubt.

"Morning, Heffernan," boomed Murphy who laboured under the impression that if Heffernan got an almighty fright he would jump and straighten up. 'A bit like having a squint,' Murphy had explained. 'If you come up behind someone with a squint and suddenly roar in their ear the squint will straighten out.'

"Morning lads," smiled Heffernan. "Got something for me?"

"We were hoping you had something for us, Malcolm," said Morecamb. "You have exhibits from the murder scene in Kinsale, I believe?"

"Oh yes, come on in."

They were led through a cavernous warehouse with shelving and presses lining both sides as far as the eye could see. To say that everything was haphazard was an understatement but Heffernan seemed to have an innate knowledge of the location of each item.

"Here we are," he announced pointing to a press halfway down. When he opened the door a bike almost toppled out on them.

"Very little, really," he said as he grabbed the bike. "The only prints on this belonged to the victim. As you can see the back tyre is punctured. Big bugger of a thorn. We also seem to have the weapon – a great big lump of a rock. You see the dark patches there? Blood spatters. But of course no fingerprints. Impossible to get prints from a stone. Just blood," he joked.

"Yes," said Morecamb, "very little to go on really."

"Well, I presume you'll be talking to Pettigrew, the pathologist, too. He'll be at lectures now though, sowing the seeds of doubt and confusion in young minds."

Heffernan's opinion of Pettigrew almost reflected his own.

"Yes. Might keep that pleasure until tomorrow. Don't want to have all the fun today. Right, we'll be off, Malcolm. I suppose it would be stretching things a bit to suggest that every effort was made by the lot in Kinsale to preserve the exhibits properly and avoid all risk of contamination before depositing them with you?"

"Yes, it would, so I won't upset you by telling you that the bike was retrieved from the boot of the garda car, squeezed in beside a bag of coal and the rock was rolling around on the back seat."

When they got back to Union Quay Morecamb headed straight for Alderton's office but Moloney, the desk sergeant, stopped him in his tracks. He was told to pass on a message from the Super to the effect that Morecamb wasn't to go anywhere near his door and, at great inconvenience to himself, and with huge misgivings, he had informed Kinsale that Morecamb was indeed now in charge.

Moloney had then glanced over his shoulder and gleefully told Morecamb that his last sighting of Alderton was through the station's rear exit door, lugging a bag of golf clubs. "A new hobby, sir," smiled his informant.

Morecamb decided that he didn't like Moloney very much. The fat slob just sat behind his desk all day, probably dreaming up ways to impart bad news and revelling in the pall of depression which beset the recipients of his twisted sense of humour.

Bastard, muttered Morecamb as the thrum of his headache intensified and threatened to blow his head to smithereens.

Nothing for it but to head off to Kinsale.

*****

Foley's palpitations hadn't subsided until he'd heard the pilot announce that they were cruising at 42,000 feet.

McGrath had been bribed and Foley was well out of pocket but he had no regrets. Two weeks with Fiona in the Canaries was worth it. Morecamb was to be informed that Foley had been suddenly and inexplicably taken seriously ill in the middle of the night and was now undergoing tests in an unspecified hospital. Couldn't have Morecamb ringing the so-called hospital, enquiring about him and discovering the lie.

Of course McGrath was a hopeless liar. Maybe he should have engaged the services of Rooney. He was a bloody natural.

He suddenly remembered some snide comments that Rooney had once made about his Fiona, even suggesting that he'd had his wicked way with her. As if she would! He reached across to hold her hand but she slapped him away. She was still seething about the midnight flit and the three hour drive to Dublin airport. She hadn't even had time to apply her make-up, which was a bit of a revelation for Foley. He almost felt as if he was sitting beside a stranger really and not a very pretty one at that.

CHAPTER 6

For once McClean behaved behind the wheel and they got to Kinsale without rancour. When they entered the station Morecamb immediately saw that their number seemed seriously depleted. Mercifully, Spillane was absent but Foley was nowhere to be seen either.

"Where's Foley?" he demanded looking around with a thunderous glare.

"Well, see, here's the thing ….." stammered McGrath. All eyes swivelled towards him and he could feel himself squirming. "Sick….hospital, and that," he added vaguely. "He left a message….yes, with my wife and that…….." He could feel his bladder beginning to give way.

"You never mentioned that," said Rooney. "Is it serious? We'll have to visit him. He could be dying. Wow, another death. What are the chances of that?"

"He's not dying," McGrath put in. Christ, maybe he'd been too convincing. "I think it's maybe a very heavy 'flu. And vomiting. And that."

There was an ominous silence as his voice petered out. Hurriedly he excused himself and headed for the gents but Morecamb ordered him back. He demanded to know which hospital had cleared their decks and admitted the stricken patient and when McGrath stammered, 'Ardkeen' Harrington helpfully pointed out that Ardkeen is a hospital in Waterford.

"All the hospitals in Cork are full," McGrath pointed out. "I think some of them are undergoing renovations."

Phew, he thought, that was close!

Morecamb spent the next five minutes staring at McGrath and then asked him who was doing the painting and decorating at the hospitals.

"Come on, any name will do," he shouted. " Pick the first name that comes to mind. Pluck it out of your_____"

"Boss, maybe we should press on," Murphy intervened, suddenly feeling sorry for the sergeant who seemed like a decent sort.

Morecamb dragged his mad gaze away from McGrath and informed everybody that Sweeney was on sabbatical...... "Thrown out, Harrington, for gross incompetence"....and they were fortunate to have himself at the helm now.

He ignored the stunned looks around the room and ploughed on. There would be a new regime now. It was called, 'Professional' and its cornerstone was organisation, with a side helping of dedication, sacrifice and abject grovelling to himself.

'Violet! That was the woman's name from Saturday night! He felt quite chuffed that he had remembered it. He could continue with his drinking, knowing that he would get his memory back eventually at some stage, and sometimes in the strangest places and most unexpected moments.

"Any questions?"

Several hands shot up in the air but Morecamb ignored them. He felt like slapping Murphy who seemed to have raised both hands.

"Now, Harrington, so it was just yourself interviewing Mrs McCarthy this morning. How did that go?"

Yes, and it was extremely unfair that he had to do it on his own as he felt, for safety reasons, there should be at least two personnel in attendance. And what would happen if Mrs McCarthy took a shine to him and later made accusations of sexual harassment when he spurned her. Because make no mistake, he most certainly would.....

Murphy practically cleared the nearest chair, guided Harrington outside and quietly asked him for a very brief summary of the outcome of his chat with the McCarthy woman.

When he heard the full, sad story he decided he would have to edit Harrington's rather frightening account of the obviously chaotic meeting between the two combatants. Mrs McCarthy had never said that it could have been the local rector, dressed in a school uniform, who was waiting for Mary O' Donovan. Harrington had accused her of changing her mind, several times, and telling lies. She then said that the suspect looked a lot like Harrington himself and it was only when Rooney, who had been looking on with amusement, suggested that Harrington should give a description of Trevor that she finally conceded that it sounded a lot like the 'hobo who was loitering with intent'.

Murphy advised the 'narrator' that it might be best if he remained outside for about half an hour, until he got the signal to come back in. Then, cautiously, he re-entered himself and judiciously conveyed the bare necessity.

"It was definitely Trevor Sugrue, boss, so it's obvious that Mary had a boyfriend. Her mother doesn't know everything.

"You were out there a long time with Harrington, Sergeant Murphy," Rooney opined, with a big grin on his face.

Murphy ignored him.

Meanwhile, Morecamb pondered how much of Harrington's account he could trust. It was quite possible that he was recreating an episode from some television programme he had watched the previous night.

He decided that they would have to go back to talk to Leila Flynn again. Maybe she could shed some light on it. She must surely know more than she claimed at that meeting in the convent.

"McGrath, ring the convent and let them know I need to speak to Leila Flynn again. Garda McClean, you will have the honour of talking to the lovely Leila. She might be more willing to speak to somebody youngish."

"Like yourself, sir?" smirked Rooney. "Maybe I should go with you. I have a way with the young ladies."

"Rooney, were *you* ever questioned regarding the murder and you a ladies' man?" asked Murphy, still smarting from Rooney's earlier comment.

Rooney's mouth flapped open but no sound came.

"Leila isn't in school today, boss," said McGrath coming back into the room. "Apparently she's poorly."

Nothing for it but to ambush her at home. Meanwhile, McGrath and Harrington were to check out that Mr Egleston again. See if he was more forthcoming today. Then they would reconvene at lunchtime.

*****

Shortly afterwards they were negotiating the narrow avenue which led to the Flynn's front door. A very new Austin Martin was parked to the side of an imposing, two-storey, ivy-clad house. Morecamb spotted a tennis court off to the side of the dwelling.

Not short of a few bob obviously, mused Morecamb as he lifted his hand to the knocker. The door was opened by a middle-aged woman who squinted against the sunlight at them.

"Yes?"

"Mrs Flynn?"

"Good Lord, no," she laughed. "I'm Nora. I just work here. Hold on and I'll get somebody."

They stepped into the hall and took in their surroundings. McClean seemed awe-struck. A most magnificent sweeping stair-case took centre stage, flanked on one side by an antique grandfather clock while on the other side a stag's head glared menacingly at the two officers. Piano music could be heard coming from the room which Nora had entered moments before.

"I wonder what Mr Flynn does for a living, sir?" whispered McClean. "Something in the city, maybe. Probably a shipping magnate. Wonder if my father knows him."

"Well, he certainly isn't working for the Department of Justice," said Morecamb.

Their discussion was cut short by the re-emergence of Nora.

"You can go in now," she said.

Morecamb's entire downstairs area would have fitted into the room they entered. It took both men a few minutes to get their bearings and to locate the pianist who had continued to play as if oblivious to their presence. Slowly the final notes faded and a ridiculous looking man rose to greet them. He was dressed in what Morecamb presumed were 'plus-fours' with a bright yellow cravat around his bulging neck.

"Don't you just love Bach?" he asked as he advanced towards them. "Food for the soul. Ahhh. Transports me to another place every time, where there is no beginning and no end."

Drugs, thought Morecamb.

"So, to what do I owe this pleasure?" he asked as he extended his hand.

His nasal tones immediately grated on Morecamb's nerves.

"You must excuse my attire," he continued, not waiting for an answer to his question. "Just managed to get a round of nine holes in and haven't changed yet. But I always don the old cravat when I play the piano. It seems only right to do so when one is paying homage to the great composers. Don't you agree?"

"Yes," said Morecamb, "very interesting. I'm Detective Inspector Morecamb and this is Sergeant McClean. We're from the Serious Crime Division in Cork."

"Oh, really?" he announced advancing towards them. " Will you join me in an aperitif?"

"No, thanks. We're on duty. Actually we were hoping to speak to your daughter."

"Oh?"

"Yes. We spoke to her at the Convent on Saturday. She was friends with the murdered schoolgirl, Mary O'Donovan."

"Who?"

Both officers exchanged glances.

"Of course," he said, snapping his fingers. "My dear wife was talking about that at the dinner table."

"Did you know Mary O'Donovan at all, Mr Flynn?"

"I've no idea. Does her old man play golf?"

"I wouldn't think so," said Morecamb.

"Sail?"

"No."

"Dear, oh dear."

The news that Mary's father didn't indulge in those pastimes seemed to upset Flynn more than her death. And he wasn't quite sure if his daughter was at school or not. Nora was summoned and on being told that Leila was feeling sick and had stayed out of school, Flynn revealed that his daughter was very delicate, 'like fine bone china' and always needed to be treated very sensitively. Morecamb translated that as a holy terror, liable to violent tantrums and her father no doubt lived in a constant state of fear. Maybe he'd introduce him to Murphy.

While they waited for the inevitable tornado Flynn told them that he had two sons in Clongowes, all the while glancing nervously at the door. His dear wife had also wanted to send Leila to boarding school but he had argued that he would miss her too much. It all seemed so long ago now and at the time he was on a lot of medication, for gout. But of course he was on triple dose of tablets now for his ulcer and blood pressure and did they think it might be too late now to change his mind and send her to boarding school after all. Money was no object and he wouldn't be averse to a school in England. He was babbling now and Morecamb almost felt sorry for him. He might be a twat but nobody deserved Leila.

"Two boys," he repeated. "Yes, indeed, in Clongowes. My old Alma Mater, actually."

"And what line of business are you in, Mr Flynn?" Morecamb asked, trying to calm him down.

"Oh, a bit of this and a bit of that," came the vague reply with a lofty wave of his arm. "Import and Export, that sort of thing . . . Oh, God!" The door was flung open and Leila flounced in.

"You again!" was her greeting to Morecamb. "I'm feeling sick and I've already told you all I know."

"You'll have to excuse me, officers. Got to change and that...."

"Mr Flynn," interrupted Morecamb, "I'm afraid that I have to insist that you stay while we're talking to your daughter. It's standard procedure. I'm sure you understand."

"Really? Oh right. I'll just return to Johann Sebastian and tinkle the ivories quietly. Won't disturb you. Poor darling. She's delicate as I say." And with a frightened glance at his daughter he hastily made his way over to the piano.

Leila rolled her eyes heaven-ward and then glared Morecamb and McClean.

"I'm sorry to hear you're feeling unwell, Leila," began Morecamb.

"Oh, just the usual female ailment," she smirked. "Still, it would be worse if I wasn't afflicted . . ."

McClean seemed to be sinking deeper into his chair.

"I want to follow up on our conversation from last Saturday," said Morecamb, refusing to get side-tracked. "When I asked you if Mary O'Donovan had a boyfriend I detected a slight hesitancy in your answer."

"Did you?" she asked with her chin raised.

"Yes. Well?"

"She might have had," she responded with the same arrogance they had witnessed previously.

"Do you know who he was?"

"Maybe. But I don't think it's anybody's business."

The music started to creep up a notch as Leila's voice started to rise.

"This is very important, Leila. It is quite possible that Mary knew her assailant."

"Well, it wasn't her boyfriend because she had broken up with him. And I know he wouldn't have done it."

"But how can you know that?"

"Because I was seeing him before he took up with Mary. I was finished with him and it was I who suggested that he ask Mary out. She needed the experience and while he wasn't the greatest . . . you know . . .I thought he might be good for starters."

Mr Flynn seemed to have switched to jazz.

"Mary didn't seem that keen," continued Leila, "but I said she should persist. 'You must persevere at all things,' as Sister Benedict tells us in Maths. Anyway, she only met him a few times and then he ditched her. He said she was frigid but I told him he couldn't expect every girl to roll over for him. 'Rome wasn't built in a day', I told him. The nuns are always saying that as well."

Good God, had the nuns any idea of how their various mottos were being adapted?

"So, to the best of your knowledge Mary wasn't seeing any boy around the time she was killed?"

"I didn't say that. But she definitely wasn't seeing Trevor. But there might have been someone else . . ."

Suddenly she stopped as she realised what she had just said.

"Is that Trevor Sugrue?" asked Morecamb quietly.

"You tricked me," Leila shouted as she jumped out of the chair. "Father," she shrieked, "throw them out." And she stormed out of the room.

But Bach's 'executioner' ignored her and continued to mangle the great man's oeuvre as the two officers let themselves out the front door. Morecamb felt they had narrowly escaped with their lives. But he also felt that McClean had been treated to a valuable life lesson.

*****

Even though Morecamb had sworn that he would never again set foot in the 'Hoor and Hounds', it was a case of 'needs must'. It was lunch-time and there was no point in traipsing around the town looking for an alternative. McGrath and Harrington had already arrived back so Morecamb informed everyone that they would have a meeting after lunch. There were cheers all round when Morecamb announced that they were going to 'The Hoor and Hounds' for lunch.

Morecamb went up to the bar to put in their order, the set lunch for everybody and a round of soft drinks. The latter caused some raised eyebrows when it arrived but nobody was foolish enough to comment.

"Do you want us to fill you in on our visit to Egleston, sir?" called Harrington from the other end of the table while they waited for their food.

"No, this isn't the time or the place. We'll discuss all that when we're back inside." *Had the clown no savvy at all.*

"I fancy a bit of fish", said McClean when the waitress arrived with the food.

"You'll eat what you get," said Morecamb.

"But this is the fish capital of Ireland, if not the world."

"Be that as it may . . ."

"Actually, that would be Torremolinos," said Rooney knowledgeably. "Best fish and chips I ever had. You can't beat it after a few pints of their local brew. God almighty, it would blow your head. A bit like the women. Wow, wow, wow . . . serious stuff."

"Shut up, Rooney," said Morecamb. "We're trying to eat here."

The rest of the meal was eaten in silence and there seemed to be a collective sigh of relief when they all headed back into the station.

Morecamb immediately called them to order.

"Let's have a review of this morning's actions then. Sergeant McGrath, you're up first."

"Well, that's what young Harrington was trying to tell you in the pub, sir. He wasn't there."

"Who wasn't where?"

"Egleston. He was at the Mart. The wife said he'd be back in the afternoon. So we headed off to the Mart but there was no sign of him there either. Place was bloody cold, even for this time of year. According to one of the farmers there Egleston's cattle were in the ring early so he took off to the pub to celebrate. Got a good price apparently. Do you know," said McGrath turning to the others in the room, "what a heifer will fetch in today's market?"

"We're not interested," said Morecamb. "And it's not relevant."

"Twenty shillings a kilo," Harrington contributed in tones of near awe. "My auld fellah_____"

"Thank you, Harrington," snapped Morecamb. "So that's it? Shall we call it a wasted morning? Yes?" he asked turning back to McGrath.

"We tried looking in a few of the pubs around the Mart," Harrington felt obliged to add, no doubt in solidarity with his sergeant. "The Sergeant was frozen so I bought him a hot toddy. You didn't thaw out until you got the second, sure you didn't, Sergeant?" The last word was followed by a yelp as somebody's boot connected with Harrington's shin.

Morecamb filed that bit of information to the back of his mind. But he wouldn't forget it.

He went on to tell them about his own visit to Flynn's and Leila's accidental revelation that Trevor Sugrue and Mary O' Donovan were acquainted with each other. But, the most important bit of news was the revelation that lately she seemed to be in a new relationship, based on the information which they got from the Sugrue twins.

"Will one or two of you call on that chipper......what's it called.....?"

"Lorenzo's," supplied Harrington. "Best fish 'n' chips in the whole_____"

"Right, whatever. Show them a photo of Mary and ask them if they noticed her hanging around. Harrington, you can take Murphy and myself to the Egleston place."

Harrington was beaming behind the wheel when Morecamb and Murphy joined him in the car a few moments later.

"Where to, sir?" asked the incorrigible driver.

"To Mr. Egleston's, lad," put in Murphy, much to Morecamb's relief. "You know, the place you went to this morning with Sergeant McGrath."

Shortly afterwards, too shortly for Morecamb's liking, they pulled up outside a rather sad looking house. It was a two-storey, grey, pebble-dashed affair and the front door had long since relinquished any paint that might have been applied in the dim and distant past. When Morecamb glanced up he saw that several slates had begun a downward spiral. A strong wind and the whole thing would lift.

Still, the place was filled with bird song and when Morecamb gazed skyward he saw some birds flitting to and fro, busily ferrying twigs and saplings and depositing their stash, with the most graceful movements, on trees which seemed at one with the sky. His musings were interrupted by the sudden appearance of a belligerent looking woman standing at the door glaring at them, her hands folded over an ample bosom.

"I hope you've come to arrest him. He's an absolute menace on the roads," she called as they approached.

"Mrs Egleston, isn't it?" asked Morecamb calmly.

"And who else were you expecting? And who's the eejit revving the car?"

"I'm Detective Inspector Morecamb, Mrs Egleston and this is Sergeant Murphy," said Morecamb as he turned to signal to Harrington to take his foot off the accelerator.

"He was here this morning, wasn't he, with that other fellah. I told them he was at the Mart but they didn't seem too interested. Go on in and do your duty. In there to the right. Call me if you need help."

The room into which they were ordered was multi-functional and a sight to behold. Only the table and the Range indicated that it was a kitchen. The entire contents of a shed seemed to be stacked in one corner of the room while a tattered sofa almost certainly doubled as a bed. A few blankets and a pillow were thrown on it. No prizes for guessing who slept there.

"Mr Egleston?" asked Morecamb as he approached the rather morose, hunched figure at the table.

"That's me," he responded in a deceptively strong voice. "Who's asking?"

Morecamb once more went through the formalities.

"Would ye like a drop of tea? The kettle's still warm."

"That would be grand," said Morecamb, "if it's no trouble?"

"No trouble at all." Gingerly he went to a cupboard and eventually found two cups and proceeded to make the tea. "Help yourselves to the milk and sugar. Would you like a slice of bread?"

"No, no, the tea is fine. I believe the Mart was good this morning, Mr Egleston," said Morecamb as he tested the tea.

"Call me Jimmy. Yes, 'twas. Sold five cattle. Bit short of fodder at the moment. A dry Spring, you see. Still, that's farming. Can't control the weather. Do you farm at all yourselves?"

"No, Jimmy, we're policemen."

"Ah, right, you said that. I was talking to some of your lot already, I think. Was it Thursday?"

"Yes," said Morecamb. "We wanted to follow up on that. You mentioned that you had to go into the ditch to avoid_____"

"Jaysus! That's right! Bastard came round the bend like a hoor and nearly made bits of me. I went right into the drain and had to be towed out by Billy Twomey. Got a fair fright, I can tell you."

"Do you remember the date at all?" asked Morecamb.

"Not a clue . . . wait a minute . . . it was a Mart day. Forgot that. That's right. I was selling a few sheep that day. Hardly worth feeding them. No money at all in sheep", he continued, fixing his gaze on the two officers, "fierce stupid animals. Ever try getting them through a gate? Bloody nightmare…….."

Morecamb raised his hand to stop the invective.

"Jimmy, you told my men that there was a female in the passenger seat of that car that ran you off the road."

"I'd say he must have been doing forty miles an hour coming off that bend. Imagine the speed he was doing going into it. I'm surprised he_____"

"And his passenger, Jimmy? Any idea of age? Any clear description?"

Jimmy furrowed his brow in deep concentration.

"Well, I couldn't swear to anything of course but I'd say she was youngish."

"How young?"

"Twenty five, maybe? Thirty? No. I'd say she was nearer the twenty mark. Hard to tell these days, isn't it? But she had long hair. Brown, I'd say. When the driver braked I just caught a glimpse of her hair falling over her face. So it was definitely long."

"Did you know Mary O'Donovan, Jimmy?"

"I know the parents. Grand people. Can't say I know the wee lass who was murdered. Terrible business. Have ye caught him yet?"

"Not yet, Jimmy. Now, what about this driver?"

"Well, I didn't get a good look at him at all. I was too busy trying to stay alive. Just automatically headed for the ditch. More tea?"

"No thanks, Jimmy. And what about the make of car?"

"Bigger than mine anyway. Not sure of the make. Big, dirty thing. Course on these roads . . "

"Do you think he could be a farmer?"

"Could be, yes. I'd say so judging by the car. Is it important?"

"Could be, Jimmy. Would you mind coming to the station with us? I want to show you a photo of the victim. See if she resembles the passenger in that car. And I also need a statement from you. Would that be okay? One of my men will run you back again."

"No bother."

He followed them out into the hall.

"Eileen," he shouted up the stairs, "I'm off now to the station with the guards."

Suddenly they heard the thump of footsteps and a very pale Mrs Egleston appeared at the top of the stairs.

"My God, what have you done now? You've no right to come in here and arrest my husband," she shouted at Morecamb.

"We're not arresting him, Mrs Egleston. He's simply helping us with our enquiries."

"And who's going to milk the cows? Tell me that."

"He'll be back before long," answered Morecamb.

66

"Will he indeed?" she harrumphed.

And the belligerent stance was back in place as they left her at her front door, scrambled into the already moving car and headed out onto the road.

On the way back their 'witness' insisted that they stop where 'that mad-man tried to do for me.' But as soon as they slowed, a large tractor, towing an unwieldly harrow, came bearing down on them. Harrington, probably for the first time in his life, mused Morecamb, put the car into reverse and hugged the ditch. A wave of the hand from the driver and he disappeared in a plume of toxic fumes.

"That's Billy Twomey, actually," offered Egleston. "He's the fellah that pulled me out of the ditch. Grand man. Owns a big farm a few miles up the road."

After much revving and stalling, including a suggestion from Harrington that they all get out and push, a request which was studiously ignored, he eventually got the car out onto the road and hurtled on towards the garda station.

It was now late afternoon. Murphy brought Egleston into Sweeney's office and Morecamb snatched a photo of Mary from the Incident board.

"Right, Jimmy," he said as he went into his newly-requisitioned office, "let's start with some photos. This is Mary O'Donovan, the lass who was killed. Does she bear any resemblance to the girl you saw in that car?"

Jimmy slowly removed his glasses from an inside pocket and perched them on his nose.

"Hate these things," he informed them, "they're too bloody small. Course they belong to the missus but I borrow them when she's not looking."

Morecamb stared in disbelief and watched all trace of a breakthrough crumbling before his eyes.

"Could be her," Jimmy said as he squinted at the photo.

"Were you wearing glasses on the day that you almost met your Maker?" probed Morecamb.

"Ah no, I can't wear them when I'm driving. They only distract me. I only use them for reading."

"So your long-distance vision is fine then?" asked Morecamb.

"Well, I wouldn't say that now," said Egleston as he leaned back in the chair. "Middling, I'd say. I'm grand when things are up close, like that driver. Course I didn't see him until the last minute. I thought it was a combine harvester at first. But harvesters don't travel at that speed, do they? And it wasn't until he nearly came through the window that I saw it was a kind of jeep thing."

A silence descended on the room.

Egleston was obviously re-living the nightmare, Murphy was sizing up the exit and Morecamb was doing his best not to launch himself across the table at their star witness.

"And that was when you saw the young girl?" put in Murphy.

"Exactly. Long hair. Brown. Young, as I say. Certainly no more than thirty. Twenty maybe. Could even be younger. Hard to tell_____"

He was interrupted by a rap on the door and Rooney's head appeared.

"We'll just be on our way now, Inspector. It's nearly five and....."

Morecamb pushed his chair back, knocking it over in his haste. Rooney had the good sense to edge closer to the exit door as he caught sight of an enormous vein in Morecamb's neck. McGrath had positioned himself behind Rooney and McClean seemed engrossed in writing up notes.

"Sit down," roared Morecamb. "And don't dare move a foot, either of you, or I'll have you both arrested. I want a comprehensive report, when I'm finished in here, from whoever went to that chipper place. And for your sake, Rooney, I hope you were one of them."

Then he slammed back into the office again, righted his chair and started to pace the room. Egleston and Murphy exchanged glances but nobody spoke. After a few laps Morecamb resumed his seat, took a deep breath and told Jimmy to go through his account of events one more time. Murphy produced a notepad and pen and Morecamb averted his gaze as his sergeant began to doodle on the page and he knew that if he quizzed him later on that Murphy would inform him that he had transcribed Egleston's account word for word.

"And, apart from that Twomey man who else lives up that road? Any other 'mad-man' who might be in possession of a big jeep?" asked Morecamb.

"Well….let me think.….there's the vet of course. Peter Kelly. Lives a few miles up that road as well. Do you know where the monument to the Blessed Virgin is? The turn beyond that."

Twenty minutes later Harrington was detailed to escort Jimmy back to his residence and Morecamb stood in the middle of the day-room and barked, "Report, please."

McClean was over at the far side of the room staring vacantly into space.

McGrath spoke up and informed him that there wasn't much to report as there was a new assistant on duty and he didn't seem to know 'his arse from his elbow.' But some of the regular staff would be on duty the following day, especially someone called Louise, so he suggested that himself and Rooney might venture back there.….His voice petered out as he watched Morecamb button up his coat and beckon to McClean and Murphy. Silently he handed the car keys to McClean and headed out the door. He couldn't trust himself to speak.

Nobody else spoke either as they slowly navigated their way through the thronged town. Locals mingled with tourists in brightly-coloured, summer clothing. Children bounced excitedly to and fro, many guzzling ice-creams with most of it on their hands and faces, and all screaming. Mothers frantically raced around trying to prevent the little ones from toppling into the Marina. Fathers trudged along behind, arms laden with discarded shoes, coats, wellingtons and spades and studiously ignored the partying on the yachts. And probably wondered where it had all gone wrong. The pubs beckoned which only added to their misery.

Old men with heads covered in various apparel, from handkerchiefs to hats of uncertain vintage, lined the walls of the various hostelries, the more able-bodied with one leg raised behind them, and all with pints in hand. They surveyed the giddy melee with detached resignation. They had seen it all before and soon they would have their town back and get on with righting the wrongs of the world. Quietly.

When Morecamb looked to his right he gasped at the most spectacular sight of the fiery sun slowly easing into a downward trajectory and casting a diaphanous light over the entire town. It was surreal and suddenly he felt vulnerable and insignificant. Against this backdrop a large Ferris wheel sliced through the tentacles of riotous colours and the young and not so young screamed and clung to each other in a mad cacophony of cries and laughter.

As soon as they were on the open road Morecamb turned to Murphy. "Give me your thoughts on our star witness."

"Well, reminds me of the time that Alderton sent me off to the North Infirmary to get a statement from a witness to a car crash. A casualty actually. Mrs Bourke, I seem to remember. She was a back seat passenger. Hooked up to all these machines and gadgets. No response from her but I ploughed on, asking all these questions and writing everything down. Until a nurse came in, switched off the machines and told me she was dead."

"And your point is?"

"Well, the whole thing was pointless, wasn't it? As witnesses go I'd say Jimmy Egleston is right up there with Mrs Bourke".

CHAPTER 7

Tuesday May 6ᵗʰ

When Morecamb reached Union Quay the following morning Alderton was ensconced in his office, cleaning his golf clubs.

"New hobby, sir?" asked Morecamb as he steered a wide berth of what could be termed offensive weapons in the hands of Alderton.

"Not exactly new, no. I used to be a dab hand at it when I was younger. You should try it. Not sure what golf club would have you but you never know."

"Well, I could join the same club as yourself, sir. They can't be that fussy."

"Was there something you wanted or did you just come here to insult me?" Alderton glared as he poked the golf bag to one side with his foot and took up position behind his desk. "A breakthrough in the case perhaps, hmmm?"

"Not yet but we're working on it. Of course ideally we should have been brought in immediately_____"

"More excuses," Alderton interrupted.

"I was wondering if we could have Finin? Another one of the Kinsale tribe has decided to abscond and we're actually quite short-staffed. I could do with him_____ "

"No. He's starting in Rosssarbery tomorrow."

"You see_____ "

"No. You have more than enough officers to solve it and solve it fast. You *do* know that the Commissioner is due in Kinsale in another few days. Likes to do a bit of sailing and entertaining on the Bank Holiday so if all the bungling and mayhem is at an end by then that would be hugely helpful. And don't forget_____ "

He was still rabbiting on when Morecamb slammed the door behind him and stormed off down the corridor.

He was immediately accosted by Finin as soon as he left Egleston. Did Morecamb know that he had spent the previous day caddying for Egleston?

Morecamb stopped and informed him that his worries were over as he had now been seconded to Rosscarbery for the foreseeable.

"Where's Rosscarbery?" roared Finin as Morecamb continued walking and headed for the sanctuary of the toilets. Thankfully Finin didn't follow him inside. When Morecamb re-emerged there was no sign of his pursuer so he made his way to the canteen and joined Murphy and McClean.

"Murphy, as soon as you're finished there we'll head out to the pathology lab and serenade our good friend, Pettigrew."

Half an hour later they entered the swing-doors of the mortuary and were met by a look of astonishment from the pathologist which immediately morphed into a glare.

They were ushered unceremoniously into Pettigrew's fairly spartan office. There were no family photographs to soften the austerity. Perhaps he didn't have any family. Just suddenly sprouted out of the ground. Plenty of certificates though, lining an entire wall. Morecamb had his suspicions about the origins of some of them, well, most of them actually. He seemed to spend an inordinate amount of time in the States where, it was rumoured, a tidy sum could equip you with the most bizarre qualification. Might try it himself, maybe, and set up in opposition to Pettigrew. The idea brought a smile to his lips.

"Want to share the joke with us, Morecamb?" asked Pettigrew, "or are you having a stroke?" he asked with an unnerving note of optimism in his voice.

"Just marvelling at your ever-expanding collection of awards. Is it my imagination or does the haul increase after each visit to the States?"

"Please state, briefly, the purpose of this interruption."

"Mary O'Donovan. You did an autopsy on her a few days ago. The girl who was murdered in Kinsale."

"And what business of yours is that? Don't tell me you're muscling in on other jurisdictions now. Isn't there enough slaughtering in your own back yard? I seem to remember a massacre some time earlier in the year that you presided over. Your Superintendent descended into a black hole of despair_____"

"And he's still there, I'm happy to say. Now, can you take me through the autopsy report in layman's terms, like a good man. We haven't got all day."

"Move your feet," he snapped at Murphy as he went over to a filing cabinet and spent a few minutes rummaging through it.

"Here we are," he sighed as he slapped the buff folder down on the desk.

"Okay, two separate blows. Weapon was wielded with a degree of force. Pretty much crushed the skull. There would have been_____"

"Is that what killed her?" interrupted Murphy.

Pettigrew lifted his head and studied Murphy as if he were some kind of foreign species.

"_____ a lot of blood," he rattled on. "No doubt an amount on the perpetrator but the victim also bled out quite a bit where she fell. The photographs of the body in situ_____"

"What photographs?" asked Morecamb, feeling his blood pressure starting to rise. "I was told there was only one."

"_____in situ bear that out. I would gauge that the first blow was to the forehead and then the second to the back of the head."

"But_____" spluttered Morecamb, desperately trying to grasp the import of Pettigrew's report. "But why_____"

"The position of the body would indicate that sequence of events. The second blow caused the body to fall face down_____"

"The body was faced upwards_____"

"Incorrect. The initial photos show the body face downwards."

"I don't believe . . .show me," snapped Morecamb.

"Well, Inspector, you see she's buried now. So, unless you want to exhume the body, for some macabre personal reason_____"

"The photographs, you twat!" shouted Morecamb. "Show me the photos."

"I don't have them and if the pair of you are not out that door before I count to five I'm going to call the guards."

*****

Morecamb insisted on walking back to the station, nursing dark thoughts. It was five miles away but he didn't remember any of it. He had ordered Murphy to take the car back and wait for him there. An hour later he stormed through the door of the barracks and headed straight for Alderton's office. But, just as he was about to turn the handle, Moloney handed him a note before speeding off in the opposite direction. He had bolted through the back door before Morecamb digested the contents of the missive. In an almost indecipherable hand Moloney had written that as soon as Murphy had returned and regaled them with the morning's events Alderton had been called to an urgent meeting and wouldn't be back until the following morning.

When Morecamb entered the canteen his men were huddled around in a group. Murphy was obviously filling them in on the trip to the Pathologist. A hand nudged Murphy forward whereupon he suggested that they should skip Kinsale today as Morecamb was, 'never right in the head after a meeting with Pettigrew.'

Morecamb ignored him and went back out to the reception and ordered Moloney to ring Kinsale and tell the men to present themselves in a straight line in readiness for the arrival of himself.

The atmosphere in the car was stifling. Within minutes the windows were all steamed up but nobody suggested opening them. McClean blindly negotiated the car and to his credit maintained a steady sixty miles an hour in fourth gear. Murphy made himself as small as possible in the back seat but Morecamb was larger than life in the passenger seat. Every so often he let out a deep sigh accompanied by a rumble of curses.

When they arrived in Kinsale Murphy contemplated staying in the car until the worst had blown over but Morecamb stood and waited until he got out and went in ahead of him. Neither McClean nor Murphy made eye contact with the Kinsale officers lined up inside.

Wordlessly, Morecamb gestured to McGrath to get himself into Spillane's office immediately. Twenty minutes later McGrath re- emerged. Murphy had never seen a man so pale in all his life. Unless he was dead. There was a strangled whimper from Harrington as McGrath indicated that he was up next. And still nobody spoke.

McGrath felt that himself and Harrington were being treated harshly and unfairly. All the bastards who had taken themselves off on holidays were just as culpable for the mayhem that had unfolded on the night that Mary O' Donovan's body had been discovered. So it wasn't fair that only two of them were now being treated to the worst of Morecamb's excessive wrath in the confines of Spillane's den, with no hope of escape. But, to their credit they stood by one another and put the blame squarely at Spillane's door. He was the one in charge of the scene-of-crime photos, he was the one who considered all the photos, bar one, too grisly to have on display. He was the one who said one photo would tell them all they needed to know.

And whose idea was it to turn the body over?

Once again the verdict was unanimous. Spillane.

He was one of the first to arrive on the scene, after McGrath and Hancock, 'coming back from 'The Spaniard', sir' – according to Harrington 'and I should know because I'm his driver.' Spillane had ordered Hancock and McGrath to turn the body over, 'for identification purposes', then ordered them to put her back in the original position, then decided that she looked better 'face up'.

Then Foley and Hancock stayed with the body and Spillane and his 'chauffeur' went back to the barracks to call the photographer.

And who was the photographer?

"Lombard, sir."

Yes, apparently Foley *had* spoken briefly to Lombard but when Foley explained about the body rotations there was "a scene." A passing motorist intervened and guided Foley safely to the squad car whereupon he drove straight back to the station to complain to his boss but Spillane had gone home – 'to sleep it off, sir' – again according to Harrington. "And I should know because I'm his_____"

"Shut up, Harrington."

Then, in an unprecedented moment of initiative, Foley, Harrington, McGrath and Hancock had gathered up some scene-of-crime tape which had been 'lying around' and when they judged that Lombard might have left, they returned to the scene. Then they 'hurriedly' erected the tape 'to preserve the scene, sir and to minimise the risk of contamination.'

Rooney, the smarmy bastard, had escaped 'the fall-out' as he was on his 'holliers'. "Still, I'm sorry in a way that I missed all the excitement. Can't remember the last time I was_____"

"Get out, Rooney."

Interrogation over and Morecamb went out through the secluded back exit and straight up to the 'Hoor and Hounds'.

In his absence another photo of the crime scene had been located on one of the shelves in the day-room, under a stack of papers, and McGrath, with the sweat pouring down his back pinned it up on the notice board, terrified that he wouldn't have it in position before Morecamb emerged from the office, renamed 'the dungeon'.

It was another half an hour before they saw Morecamb but he didn't emerge from the office but came in through the front door. He went straight over to the board when he spotted the additional photo.

"Is this the sum total of the photographs that Lombard took?" asked Morecamb.

"Those are the only ones he would give us," Harrington piped up. "He said Spillane couldn't be trusted with the others. He was afraid he might sell them to the local newspaper. For the price of a whiskey, I believe he said."

Several pairs of eyes swivelled in Harrington's direction.

Abruptly Morecamb turned away from the photos and paced over and back across the day-room, with his hands behind his back, occasionally letting out a string of curses which impressed even Rooney.

Eventually he asked if anybody had a photo of Trevor Sugrue.

"Is he dead now?" laughed Harrington; in fairness it was a nervous type of laugh but his colleagues made a mental note to give him a good thrashing later on.

"McClean, I want you to go straight to Sugrue's and get a recent photo of Trevor Sugrue. Don't come back without it. And go straight up to the convent with it, show it to this Mrs McCarthy woman and ask her if she's prepared to identify him".

As he headed off McClean decided that if there was nobody home he was simply going to smash a downstairs window and retrieve the requested object. Failing that, he was going to return straight away to Cork and seek the protection of Alderton, if he could find him. He was not going back to Morecamb empty-handed.

Back at the station Morecamb was still on the warpath.

"Now, Rooney, where's your report from your travels yesterday?"

"Right there, Guv, just as you asked," said Rooney.

"Well, write it up in the log….." Suddenly he stopped as he spied the page, hastily ripped from a copy book, a sum's copy book, and consisting of about two lines. He reached down, ripped it in two and when McGrath saw the spittle he hastily volunteered to write it up 'proper-like' and have it ready for inspection in 'two shakes of a lamb's tail.' Meanwhile, Rooney inspected his nails.

Without another word Morecamb beckoned to Murphy and announced that they were heading towards 'Lorenzo's', on foot, to interview 'this Louise lassie'. For once Murphy didn't complain because he secretly harboured the hope that they might get something to eat there. But he decided that he wouldn't share those thoughts with Morecamb.

But, as usual nothing was straightforward where the Kinsale cowboys were concerned and 'Louise' turned out to be 'Louisa' and didn't seem to have a word of English.

"Mr Lorenzo?" asked Morecamb hopefully.

"Si."

"No. Is Mr Lorenzo here?"

"Si."

"Where is he?"

"Si."

There was a stand-off for a few minutes while Morecamb considered his options.

"Stop!" he screamed, in the direction of the kitchen.

A young lad appeared immediately and almost stood to attention when Morecamb flashed his warrant card at him. Louisa meanwhile disappeared through the same door.

"What's your name, son?" asked Morecamb.

"Gerard. Though I'm thinking of changing it to Geraldus. More in keeping with_____"

"If you do that I'll arrest you," said Morecamb. "Now, do you work here on a regular basis?"

"Yes, sir."

"Did you know Mary O'Donovan at all?"

"Only to see, sir."

"Did you ever see her waiting around outside the shop here?"

"A few times."

"Do you know who she was waiting for?"

"No, sir. She never actually came in."

"So, you never saw her with anybody? Any man in her company?"

"No, but I can ask Louisa if you like?"

"The Italian?" asked Morecamb frowning. "Do you speak Italian?"

"Good God, no," laughed Gerard. "Whatever gave you that idea?"

"But. . . she doesn't speak English."

"Oh, yes she does. Well, a little. See, in the beginning she could only say, 'no'. She's my girlfriend, see," he added proudly. "Anyway, as I said, she only had one word but I taught her to say 'yes'. And now she has several words. You should hear her curse…….."

"Shut up and get her back out here straight away, please."

"Can't, sir. She just left. Her old man picked her up there a few seconds ago. It's her half-day, see. And she said earlier that she was going to Cork to do some shopping."

"Is that so? Well, when you see her tell her to come into the barracks first thing tomorrow."

"Sure. I'll tell her tonight. We're off on a date tonight. Only the second one but I'm hopeful."

Morecamb turned on his heel and left Gerard contemplating the nocturnal wonders ahead of him.

"I wouldn't trust that fellah with *my* daughter, if I had one. Would you, Murphy?"

"Yes."

They headed back to the station, at a trot, Murphy several paces behind his boss.

Thankfully, when they got back McClean had returned, mission complete, and announced that Mrs McCarthy is almost one hundred per cent certain that the lad in the photo is the same 'pup' who was hanging around outside the school gates, 'up to no good.'

"Okay," said Morecamb, breathing a sigh of relief. "Well, that's something. Now I have a bit of ammunition when I interview him today."

Murphy, McClean and himself left straight after a pub lunch and headed out to Sugrue's place. They were a bit early and no doubt herself would whinge about that and no doubt she would be present during the questioning. Well, this would soften her cough.

And sure enough, the reception was frosty.

They could wait 'in there,' a room that was little better than a scullery, 'until Trevor has finished his dinner. But you *did* say the afternoon so you only have yourselves to blame.'

"We'll give him five minutes, Mrs Sugrue," said Morecamb.

They could hear her footsteps echoing down the flag-stoned hall as she took off in a cloud of peevishness.

There were no chairs in the room and, in spite of the sun shining outside, there was no heat either. The room smelt damp and was cluttered with wellingtons and overcoats, rain macs mostly, hence the pervading stench of mould.

A few minutes later a head appeared around the door – Marcus? – and told them to come down to the kitchen. They followed the young lad and entered a gleaming, spacious kitchen presided over by Mrs Sugrue, arms folded, mouth pressed tight in a straight line and standing protectively behind Trevor's chair. As *if* he needed protection.

He was slumped nonchalantly on his chair and never lifted his head when they entered, eyes focussed firmly on his full plate.

"Sit there," snapped Mrs Sugrue.

When they were seated opposite Morecamb decided to go for the jugular.

"So, Trevor, tell us about your relationship with Mary O'Donovan."

That caught his attention and his head snapped up, glaring at each officer in turn. Mama drew herself up a few more inches and placed her hands on Trevor's shoulders.

"I think I've explained the relationship, officers," she announced imperiously. "Tom is a cousin of mine, distant of course_____"

"We have a witness who says that you waited for Mary outside the convent gates after school and then the two of you went off together", Morecamb ploughed on, ignoring her.

The few inches Mrs Sugrue had manufactured had now all but disappeared but her voice was still in good working order.

"Don't be ridiculous, sergeant_____"

"He's a Detective Inspector, Ma'am," put in McClean. Murphy, who usually jumped to his boss's defence in such situations, seemed to be entirely focussed on Trevor's plate, which now lay untouched.

"You're mistaken, officers," said Trevor. "Your so-called witness is a liar."

"We also have it on good authority, from another source, that you were actually dating Mary O'Donovan for a while."

"Rubbish," he muttered but with far less conviction. Meanwhile Mrs Sugrue had eased herself into a chair beside her son.

"Our second source also said_____"

"Leila is a fucking liar!" he roared as he jumped out of his chair, sending it crashing to the ground.

"Sit down, lad," said Murphy firmly, "or we'll bring you straight back to the station and throw you in a cell."

"I'd like to see you try," he sneered but he sat back down.

"Officers," Mrs Sugrue put in, "I really feel this is harassment_____"

"Leave it, Mother. I can handle this."

"Then I suggest you begin by telling us the truth," snapped Morecamb.

"No problem," drawled Trevor. "Leila asked me to take Mary out on a few dates. Show her the ropes, so to speak." The swagger was back. "I've had a fair bit of experience, you see."

Morecamb noticed Mrs Sugrue's head swivel towards her son, open-mouthed.

"Leila knew all about my 'talents', shall we say, in that field, so it was she who suggested it. Didn't last though. She was hopeless. Frigid, I think, is the correct term. Leila said she'd look it up in the school library; see if there was a cure for it. But I couldn't be bothered waiting. Anyway, I wanted to cast my net further afield, fish in the bigger ponds_____"

"He's excellent at English," murmured Mrs Sugrue. "His teacher says he has a way with word____"

"So, if there's nothing else, Officers," interrupted Trevor, "I have a bit of old study to do."

"Law," said Mrs Sugrue, in a last ditch effort to salvage some of her dreams.

"Yes, Mother. Whatever."

"Get your stuff, Trevor," ordered Morecamb. "We're bringing you to the station to give a formal statement."

"Shouldn't I have some sort of legal representation, Mother?"

"I'll get your father," croaked his mother. " Wait a minute, Officers. He's out in the yard. I'll call him and he can go to the station with him."

Trevor's shoulders slumped and the arrogance had all but disappeared. Moments later they heard his parents coming through the back door. A tall, bewildered looking man advanced into the middle of the kitchen and looked around.

"Anyone care to explain?" he asked, in a no-nonsense tone of voice.

"Dennis, these men, officers of the law, wanted a word with Trevor_____"

"I see," he said, glaring at his wife. "And what's he done now then?"

Morecamb decided to step forward and introduced himself and his men.

"We're here to ask your son a few questions about his relationship with Mary O'Donovan."

Trevor's attention was now riveted on the pattern of the linoleum.

"His relationship with . . . I don't understand," he faltered.

"He was stepping out with poor Mary . . . for a wee while," his wife stammered. "An act of charity, really . . ." Her voice trailed off in the face of her husband's scowl.

"Trevor doesn't *do* 'acts of charity', Bridie. Do you, Trevor? Other acts, no doubt, but none that would be found in The Good Book. So, explain yourself, young man."

"We're taking him down to the station, Mr. Sugrue," said Morecamb, "and we'd appreciate it if you could accompany him."

"No bother. Trevor, get your shoes on."

Trevor didn't need to be told twice and made a hasty exit.

"Dennis, dear, what about his study?" his wife interjected. "You know he's_____"

"A shit! Yes, I'm well aware of that. And if I find he ill-treated that poor girl in any way or harmed a hair on her head, he'll live to regret it. Charity my arse. You know we're related to the O'Donovan's, Officers? Decent people and Mary was a grand girl. Tom and myself were in the same class in primary. I've known him all my life. My wife here is a cousin of theirs and . . . there you are," he broke off as Trevor came back. "Shall we, Officers?" he said as he marshalled Trevor out ahead of him towards the squad car.

The journey back to the station was a tense affair and Morecamb decided he wasn't going to say anything to relieve it. Let the young pup sweat. He was securely wedged in the back seat between Murphy and his father, a man who seemed to have the measure of him.

When they arrived Trevor and his father went in first and Morecamb ushered them into his temporary office.

"Sit down there, please. Can I get you a cup of tea?"

Father and son shook their head.

Morecamb decided that McClean would take the dictation today. All too often Murphy's notes were in complete contradiction to what was actually said. As soon as McClean was seated, notebook and pen to hand, Dennis Sugrue sat back, folded his muscular arms across his chest and glared at Trevor as he delivered his version of events. This account was far more sanitised and far more subdued than the previous delivery. There was very little mention of his amorous dexterity or Mary's shortcomings in that department. But the substance was more or less the same as the earlier rendition.

The first thing that earned him a clip across the ear from his father was his assertion that "girls throw themselves at me and they only want one thing."

The only new piece of information was his assertion that 'bloody Leila'......... another clip on the ear ....'knows far more about Mary

O'Donovan than she pretends.' She had hinted to himself recently that maybe he was too young and inexperienced for Mary after all. "But I think she was just trying to get a rise out of me because she knows I'm the original stud......."

This time a fine wallop was administered to the back of his head and thus ended the interview.

"Wait outside for me," Sugrue growled at his son. Morecamb gestured to McClean to accompany the boy outside. As the door closed behind them the father turned to Morecamb.

"He's a bit of an eejit, Officer, and his mother has him completely spoiled. God love her, she thinks he's going to be a barrister. Dispensing justice. As if the world isn't in enough trouble. But I don't think there's any malice in the boy. Just a bit of a clown, as I say. I'm hoping he'll grow out of it. As soon as he's done those blasted exams he's going to be working the farm with me. See if I can straighten him out. But I honestly don't think he harmed poor Mary in any way."

Morecamb was inclined to agree with him on that score. Actually he agreed with everything the man had said though he wasn't too sure about the prospect of a successful working relationship between father and son on the farm.

If Trevor was *his* son he'd pack a large suitcase for him and ship him off to the building sites in London.

"Look, Mr Sugrue, I don't believe that Trevor is our culprit either. But the fact remains that he lied to us. So, for the moment he's a person of interest. It seems to me a good fright might make a man of him."

"Oh, I'll make a man of him," said Sugrue, darkly. "Just as soon as he has broken his mother's heart with his exam results. Don't know how Bridie will cope. But, she's resilient and she can focus on the twins. Until reality kicks in there as well. Because they're complete clowns altogether. Well Inspector, if there's nothing else . . ."

"That's fine, Mr. Sugrue," replied Morecamb, as they headed into the day-room. "And thank you for coming in. Garda McClean will drop you and Trevor home."

As the door closed behind them Morecamb almost felt sorry for Trevor. And maybe Mrs Sugrue as well. But then he thought of Tom and Moll O'Donovan and his resolve hardened.

"Well, boss, what do you think?" asked Murphy coming back into the room.

"Well, I think his father summed it up succinctly. Trevor is a shit. But I'd like to go back to Flynn's and have another word with the lovely Leila. Apart from anything else she obviously contacted Trevor after our visit to her and put him on his guard. Plus, I think she knows more than she's saying."

"Could I be excused for that visit, boss?"

"No, Murphy, you're coming with me. Actually, I want you to lead the questioning. She won't be expecting that and it might throw her."

"Well, it'll bloody throw me. I just don't know what to say to women. Simply don't understand them." Murphy was pacing the room in his agitation.

"Don't be such a wuss. You're married, aren't you? And, you have a young daughter. What age is she now? Eleven?"

"She's twelve," said Murphy, reaching for a chair. "And I'm terrified of her. Announced the other day that she isn't going to be confirmed because she doesn't believe in God. I expected the roof to fall in on top of us. And she's not even a teenager yet," he added bleakly.

"The phone, sir. Will I answer it?" asked the excitable Harrington. Both men ignored him so he decided to take the initiative and trotted off into Spillane's office.

"Don't they get more sensible as they get older?" asked Morecamb, grateful that it wasn't a topic with which he had the slightest experience.

"Christ, no," Murphy almost shouted. "No, no, they turn feral when they're in their teens. And the wife just laughed and said it was just a phase."

"Well, maybe she's right," said Morecamb.

"But she's been like this since she was two."

"Right. I see what you mean. But you're still coming with me to interview Leila Flynn."

They were interrupted by Harrington informing them that Alderton wanted them back at the station by five. "Apparently he has another important meeting with the Commissioner tomorrow who's demanding an update on the case. I tried to reassure him, sir but he became quite abusive."

Harrington looked most put-out.

"Thanks, Harrington. You can go home now."

Fuck, thought Morecamb, of all the advocates to have on your side.

Leila would have to wait. As soon as McClean got back from Sugrue's they would have to head back to Cork.

In a way Morecamb was glad to leave Kinsale behind that day. They really hadn't made much progress and no doubt Alderton would press all the wrong buttons and then sail off into the sunset, completely unperturbed by the flotsam in his wake.

*****

"So, I've re-instated Detective Inspector Spillane and, to all intents and purposes, you will liaise with him for the duration of the enquiry. Or at least while our Commissioner is in the locality."

Alderton fixed a belligerent stare on Morecamb who retuned it with equal ferocity. And bunched his fists. Murphy asked to be excused but was denied escape.

Morecamb noticed that McClean had sidled around to Alderton's side of the desk and he resolved that he would never again be allowed to sit behind the wheel of the car. Mightn't even allow him *in* the car. Might insist that he take public transport from now on. Or a bike.......

"Do I make myself clear, Morecamb? It's called, chain of command."

"No problem, sir. I shall take great pleasure in introducing your brother-in-law to the Commissioner. Would you like Spillane to be drunk or comatose for the occasion? You *do* know he has difficulty identifying what day it is? The chances of him being up to speed on the case are somewhat slim. No, non-existent."

"Well, that's where you come in," roared Alderton. "Fill him in. It's hardly rocket science."

"Your brother-in-law might find it hard to distinguish between the two."

"How about I take Joe aside and fill him in?" asked Murphy, in an effort to diffuse the situation. "Then Inspector Morecamb can get on with_____"

"Get out, Murphy." Alderton was almost airborne with rage. "Don't you bloody dare . . . lock the door, McClean." This was added as soon as Murphy had made a hasty exit.

"See what I have to deal with?" fumed Alderton as he spread his hands expansively, encompassing the entire room. "And I blame you, Morecamb. You're supposed to ensure that your men toe the line but of course your own attitude is so cavalier it's little wonder_____"

"Sir," Morecamb interrupted, "you can do what you like about Spillane___"

"Why, thank you," spluttered Alderton.

"_____and take full responsibility for whatever nonsense spews from his lips but I *will not*, I repeat *will not* be filling him in on the minutiae of the case or indeed anything at all about the case. I intend pursuing the case without any reference whatsoever to your brother-in-law. And *you* can explain to the Commissioner how a man who is barely sentient got to be in charge of the barracks in Kinsale."

Morecamb turned on his heel, vaguely aware of Alderton's mouth opening and closing like a fish and a look of consternation on McClean's face.

CHAPTER 8

Morecamb contemplated resigning as he made his way home. There must be easier ways to make a living. Maybe an outdoor job where there was no danger of consorting with the likes of Alderton. Something where he could be his own boss. Suddenly a thought struck him. He had read in the paper recently where some eejit was making a fortune from breeding dogs. As far as he could remember they were pedigree dogs and he wondered if Willow would qualify. He could stipulate that the breeding act could only take place under cover of darkness and ply the owner with drink while Willow tried to figure out what it was all about.

As he pulled up outside his house he wondered if he should broach the subject with Dot. She'd know all about delivering pups and if the progeny emerged with two heads and only one tail between all of them she could be persuaded to keep quiet about it and they could have another go.

Dot didn't think it was a good idea at all and felt there was every possibility of a prosecution. She also felt that she might be tempted to complain him to the authorities as she didn't think Willow was right in the head and would just pass on the madness to another generation.

Half an hour later she was still going on about it and Morecamb regretted bringing it up in the first place. All he wanted now was a bit of peace and it was a relief when Dot started to put on her coat.

"Can you imagine the embarrassment? We'd be the talk of the place. And you know what people around here are like for the gossip."

Morecamb decided to get an early night and trooped up to bed with Willow in tow. She had her own bed at the foot of his and rolled into it.

As soon as Morecamb's head hit the pillow he was fast asleep.

Alderton experienced no such relief. The wife was waiting for him when he got home. She had spotted the taxi pulling away from the kerb and quickly assessed the situation. The row had started before he had even managed to close the front door. Yes, of course he was drunk and he thanked her for pointing out 'the bleeding obvious'! Had she any idea of the trials and tribulations which he was subjected to on a daily basis? Surrounded by a bunch of incompetents. Yes, he had re-instated her drunken brother, as ordered. Nope, he had no plans for any further promotion for the imbecile. And no, he wouldn't be making him an Inspector and installing him in Morecamb's position. Even in his wildest and most horrendous nightmares, which were increasing in frequency and ferocity at an alarming rate, could he even countenance such a move. Finally, he may have inadvertently called her brother a disgrace and an out-and-out tramp, necessitating a hurried scramble to the parlour. Hastily he locked the door and make a bee-line for the drinks' cabinet. Thankfully the rest of the night passed in a blur.

CHAPTER 9

Wednesday May 7ᵗʰ

The following morning Morecamb woke refreshed. When he drew back the curtains he marvelled at the dappled light which transformed the surrounding trees. Because it was still early, the dew on the grass looked like sprinklings of silver coins and he had a sudden urge to walk barefoot in his back yard. Without thinking he bounded down the stairs, threw open the back door and walked gingerly through the soft, yielding grass. Almost immediately Willow joined him and Morecamb smiled as he traced their footprints through the grass. Willow's were big and flat. And his own were big and flat. Maybe fallen arches.

As he raised his face to the rising sun and spread his arms wide, 'master of all he surveyed' as far as the boundary wall a few feet in front of him, he suddenly spotted the twitch of the nets on his neighbour's bedroom window. Mrs Lonergan, the old biddy. Then he became aware of his semi-nakedness; bare-chested and sporting just his underpants. The priest would be informed no doubt and Morecamb couldn't care less.

But the magic was gone and he shivered as he slowly made his way back in-doors.

After a rushed breakfast and securing Willow in the back yard, he made his way towards the station praying fervently that Alderton wouldn't be there. It was one of the few times he prayed really and he conceded that it was more in the nature of a demand rather than a supplication.

He left the serious stuff to Aunt Dot who chewed the altar rails on a regular basis. But he couldn't get his head around any of it himself. He could only sympathise with Murphy's daughter, which in turn reminded him of Leila Flynn. Should be interesting to see Murphy do battle with her today, he mused. An uneven contest of course but it would allow himself an opportunity to observe her as she batted the questions and watch for any give-away signs of lying.

When he entered the station it immediately became obvious that God was having a laugh. Alderton was waiting for him, in full regalia, and announced that he would be accompanying them to Kinsale.

"Not in the same car obviously," puffed Alderton. "McClean will drive my car. Clear off now, Morecamb, with that other wastrel and we'll follow ye down."

Murphy's reaction when told of the new turn of events matched that of the previous day when he was told that he would be the one to question Leila Flynn. As they left the station Morecamb was vaguely aware of Finin smirking.

Murphy completely ignored the speed limit, ditches, road-kill and cyclists. And of course there was that spectacular moment when they nearly upended a farmer on his horse and cart as he slowly made his way to the local creamery with his three churns tethered to the sides. Miraculously they arrived unscathed, though the paintwork on the car was a little the worse for wear in places.

The news of Alderton's imminent arrival caused consternation among the Kinsale contingent. Even Rooney was dumbstruck. There was a mad scramble for the toilets to freshen up, straighten ties and tunics and spit on shoes. Serves them right, thought Morecamb. No bloody harm to put the frighteners on them. Only Harrington seemed calm and even expressed delight to be meeting 'the great man' at last.

Half an hour later the man himself thundered in with a very chastened McClean.

"A monkey! Do you hear me, McClean? Thirty bloody miles an hour. A god-damned blind monkey would……….. who are you?" Alderton paused as Harrington advanced towards him with his hand outstretched.

Anybody else would have seen the warning signs; the bulging eyes and spittle flying but not Harrington. Alderton brushed past him and cast a disparaging look around the barracks.

"Line the men up, Morecamb. I'm just going to inspect my office and then I'll deliver a motivational talk to the men. Watch and learn."

As the men shuffled into a chaotic semblance of a line loud noises emanated from the office. Trays of paper seemed to be hitting the floor at speed, a chair was sent from one side of the room to the other and finally there was the distinct sound of breaking glass.

Alderton re-emerged with popping eyes and delivered an ear-splitting tirade. Cannibalism, monkeys (again), bastards, degenerates and pigs featured prominently. As motivational speeches go, Morecamb mused, it left a lot to be desired.

And he was now taking himself off to the nearest hotel from where he would direct operations. McClean would liaise 'between my good self and the pack of clowns in front of me' and he demanded a full up-date by lunchtime.

A collective sigh of relief greeted his departure. They could now get back to work without fear of interference or indeed interest from Alderton. As he studied the men Morecamb could see that the 'pep' talk seemed very wide of the mark. Harrington looked crest-fallen. On the plus side the men seemed to regard himself in a new light. Respect might be too strong a word but certainly he emerged as the lesser of two evils. And, of course, he had sanity on his side as well. For the moment.

"Right. So, where were we? Okay, Murphy and myself are going back to question Leila Flynn. Murphy, just phone the convent and arrange a time. You can use my office. Harrington…..no, Rooney, will you take a statement from this Louisa girl from the chipper? She's to come in this morning. Ask her if and when she saw Mary O' Donovan hanging around outside the restaurant. And Harrington…..no, McGrath, will you call on a man called Billy Twomey. He's a farmer who lives just up the_____"

"I know him, boss," interjected McGrath.

"Good. Harrington, you can go with Rooney to Lorenzo's. Ah, Murphy, what did the nuns say?"

Murphy had a slightly dazed look and for a moment Morecamb wondered if it was Leila who had answered the phone up in the convent.

"Leila Flynn isn't in school either today, boss. The father rang in to say that she was poorly and would be spending the day indoors. Apparently he sounded quite distressed, they said. And, boss, the office in there is____"

"Don't want to know, thank you. So____"

"But..... Jesus, boss, I ____"

"Never mind the bloody office. Let's just go and pay the lovely Leila a visit. We might catch her off-guard."

As they headed towards the car they spotted McClean and Alderton struggling to heave Spillane out of the passenger seat of, presumably, his wife's car. Well, McClean was doing the heavy work; Alderton was holding the passenger door open.

Murphy wanted to stay and watch but Morecamb told him that they didn't have time and threw him the car keys and told him to drive.

There was a brand new, top of the range Mercedes parked outside the Flynn residence when they arrived.

"'A bit of this and a bit of that' seems to be paying dividends," said Morecamb, recalling Mr. Flynn's job description when he had asked him what he did for a living.

Murphy's jaw dropped as he surveyed the splendour all around him and had to be prompted to walk to the front door. This time a very glamorous woman responded to their knock. She was probably in her mid-forties, kitted out in a black, trouser suit and embellished with a gold chain which caught the light in a spectacular fashion. She looked them up and down by way of greeting and when they introduced themselves she ordered them to wipe their feet before they crossed the threshold.

They were ushered into the same room as on the previous visit but there was nobody thrashing the piano on this occasion.

"I believe you were here the other day questioning my daughter," she said as she gestured them towards a sofa. The temperature in the room seemed to plummet several notches when she spoke.

"That's right, Ma'am," said Murphy in a subdued voice. Morecamb could understand his trepidation. It was like being summoned to the office of a headmistress and knowing it was only a matter of time before she turned savage and laid into them with a hockey stick.

"You do realise that there should have been an adult with her while she was being interrogated and please don't mention my husband's presence."

"Well, I'd hardly call it an interrogation," retorted Morecamb, his hackles beginning to rise.

"And why are you back here again today, may I ask?"

"There are a number of issues which we would like to clarify," Morecamb responded, "so if you wish to remain while Sergeant Murphy____"

"Oh, I shall. Stay there. I'll fetch my daughter."

Morecamb stole a glance at Murphy as she left the room. He looked ready to cry.

"Please don't do this to me, boss," he whispered. "There's two of them now."

Almost immediately the door opened again and a very subdued Leila preceded her mother into the room. Both of them sat next to one another on the sofa, facing both detectives.

"Proceed," said Mrs Flynn, "and before you try any of your tricks, Inspector, be advised that I'm a barrister and everything will be done by the book."

Murphy's right leg started to twitch and there was an audible wheeze. Morecamb relented.

"So, Leila, we paid a visit to Trevor Sugrue, just after you spoke to him, I believe____"

"No, I didn't."

"____and he intimated," continued Morecamb, ignoring her interruption, "that you knew that Mary O'Donovan was in a relationship at the time of her death."

" 'Intimated', Inspector?" asked her mother, arching an eyebrow.

"Then he's a liar," Leila snapped.

"Interestingly that's exactly what he said about you. Now, were you aware that Mary was in a relationship?"

"No."

"Would you have known if she was? Would she have told you? I mean you were good friends so I imagine____"

"Try not to 'imagine', Inspector. I think my daughter has been clear in her response. If poor Mary was seeing somebody then my daughter was not privy to the fact."

"I would find that hard to believe, Leila," Morecamb ploughed on ignoring the twitch in both of Murphy's legs now. "Girls your age tend to confide in one another. You had even planned together what you were going to do when you left school this year."

"Leila isn't leaving school this year, Inspector. She will sit her Leaving Cert and then go on to university," stated her mother calmly.

Morecamb waited for the predictable outburst from her daughter. Murphy was obviously of the same opinion as his entire body now seemed to have gone into some sort of spasm.

But none came. Two pairs of steely grey eyes regarded them and Morecamb had to cede defeat.

"So, if there's nothing else? Any other flights of fancy? No? Then I'll show you out, Officers and, in future, I'd be obliged if you'd make an appointment before you disturb us again."

They had barely cleared the threshold before the barrister slammed the door behind them.

Murphy was full of praise for Morecamb as they drove away. Brave, clever, cool and calm but mostly brave. Morecamb didn't share his enthusiasm but knew that Murphy's paean was entirely motivated by relief. He had escaped unscathed and didn't have to utter a word or even look at their two adversaries.

"Bullshit," snapped Morecamb. "That little minx knows more than she's letting on and I have every intention of going back, just not when the barrister is there. We'll give it a day or two. Slow down, for God's sake."

Back at the station Spillane had acquired a secretary, purloined apparently from the barracks in Bandon. McClean was bringing her up to speed and she wasn't to leave Spillane's side "except when he goes to the toilet." Alderton had spoken, before beating a hasty retreat back to the hotel.

"Rooney," Morecamb called, "did you get that statement from Louisa?"

"Well, there was a bit of a problem. See, she's Italian and doesn't speak any English."

"That's not true," said Morecamb, gripping the back of a chair for support and to provide a safety barrier in case he lunged at Rooney. "Her boyfriend told us that she *does* speak English."

"Well, he's wrong there, sir," volunteered Harrington. "I have a bit of Italian_____"

"Fluent," smirked Rooney. "Did it for a year and a half in secondary school."

"That's right," Harrington said. "Then the teacher upped and left and never went back to teaching. Works in London now on the building sites. But it was my favourite subject. Ciao, Bella Bella, Sanctus____"

"Shut up, Harrington. So, ye terrorised a prospective witness because we're practically falling over them at the moment of course. Right, the pair of you go back to Lorenzo's and bring Louisa or whatever she calls herself straight back down here. And, Harrington, you're not to speak a word of Italian ....or English, for that matter."

Rooney took off like a scalded cat, followed nonchalantly by the linguist.

"What a clown," muttered Morecamb as he strode towards the office and pushed open the door. It seemed a little off kilter since Alderton's explosive visit. Spillane was propped up in a chair, behind his splintered desk, with a cushion on either side of him and a belligerent scowl on his face. Beside him was God's answer to birth control....long, grey, woollen skirt, black sensible brogues, black cardigan and the thickest lenses that Morecamb had ever seen in a pair of glasses. Beside her McClean looked depressed as they both pored over reams of paper.

"Who are you?" asked Spillane. "A reporter?" A certain light flitted across his features. "I only give interviews at the Hoor and Hounds so if you give me a minute____"

"Detective Inspector Morecamb. We met___"

"Are you sure? I could have sworn............"

As Morecamb backed out of the room he could hear the tut-tutting of the personal secretary. There was no sign of McGrath yet so Morecamb suggested that Murphy and himself should adjourn to the Hoor and Hounds for an early lunch.

When they returned after lunch Louisa was ensconced, making eyes at Harrington and they were having a conversation in full-blown Italian, while Rooney looked on, mouth agape, in horrified fascination. Harrington's contribution seemed to be a robotic nodding of the head and occasional shouts of, 'Bela, Bela!'

"Right," said Morecamb addressing Louisa's spell-bound audience, "Harrington, you can go and get some lunch. Be back here in twenty minutes. Rooney, get a notebook and take transcription. Now Louisa, we're investigating the murder of Mary O' Donovan. Do you understand?"

There was an elaborate shrug of the shoulders and a doe-eyed glance at Rooney whose eyes were fastened firmly on Louisa's legs.

"We've already spoken with your boyfriend_____"

"Chi?"

"____who informed us that you *can* speak English so you can stop____"

Morecamb was interrupted by a barrage of Italian, most of it no doubt peppered with curses. It sounded awful.

"Right, Rooney, get the handcuffs."

While Rooney rummaged through a drawer Spillane emerged from the office with his secretary in tow.

"Ah, the lovely Louisa," he boomed. "And how are you today, my lovely?"

"Very well, mon ami! You naughty man!"

They both giggled like a pair of school children as Morecamb fumed and Rooney threw the handcuffs down on the table with a flourish.

"Make sure you put those back again where you found them. I can never find them when I want them. Myself and Teresa are off for our lunch. If my brother-in-law is looking for me tell him I'm patrolling the town."

And with a wink at Louisa he was gone. McClean sidled into the day-room as he heard the front door close, reached for a chair in the furthest corner and put his head in his hands.

"Right, Louisa," continued Morecamb "Mary O' Donovan. See that photo on the board behind me?"

"She very pretty."

" *Was*, she *was* very pretty," Morecamb said. "She's dead now. Get the Post Mortem photo, Rooney, and put it in front of our witness here."

Its arrival set off ten minutes of hysteria and sobs and more curses in Italian. Morecamb saw McClean sink lower in his chair and was now rocking back and forth covering his ears. Murphy emerged from the toilets, saw the mayhem and retreated.

"Louisa, when did you last see Mary O'Donovan and where?"

"Chi?"

"You should speak more slowly, boss," opined Rooney. "And maybe less shouting."

"I'm not shouting!" roared Morecamb.

"You're shouting," came the feeble voice from the corner.

Morecamb took deep breaths and counted to ten.

"Was she with a boy or was she with a girl?" he asked slowly, trying to keep his temper in check.

"A girl."

"Could you describe the girl she was with?"

"Brown, big hair, tall, slim. Very pretty."

"Not as pretty as you, I bet," said Rooney, winking. She giggled at him. McClean moaned in the corner.

"You are naughty," she cooed at Rooney.

"Yes, he is," said Morecamb, "and the naughty boy will have to be punished. Locked in a cell and given a good thrashing if he interrupts again. So, what were the girls doing outside the café, Louisa?"

"Talking. I think maybe they waiting for someone? And then it get dark and the pretty one, the living one go away and the other pretty girl, the dead one, she stay."

"And then?"

"Chi?"

"Well, did the dead girl stay there all night?"

"Sir, I think_____"

"Shut up, Rooney. Go on, Louisa."

"Well, she go in car, just a little up the road and poof!"

" 'Poof'?"

"Si. Fast, no?"

"And what kind of car was it? Any idea of the make? Or even the colour?"

"No, dark. I said!"

Maybe I'll put the two of them in the cell for the night, thought Morecamb.

"And was that the only time you saw her waiting and then getting into a fast car?"

"Si. No. One other time."

"And was it dark then too?"

"Si, car dark."

"One minute. So you *did* see the car that other time?"

"Si. It was light."

Morecamb could hear Rooney suppressing a laugh.

"So, the car was light in colour?"

"No!" She actually thumped the table. "Car dark, day light."

Christ!

"And what time was this?"

"Four? Maybe? After school? She wearing uniform, no?" she said, glancing at Rooney who now had his eyes trained on her bosom.

"Long skirt. My blouse. White, si? Purple and grey tie? No? Brown shoes, grey stockings and grey jumper. And long nails. And her hair____"

Morecamb and Rooney were staring at her with their mouths open. Even McClean had raised himself out of his stupor.

"____was up with two pretty slides."

"And the car?" asked Morecamb.

"Dark."

But, in spite of their probing – Rooney had now joined in - she couldn't describe the car. She thought the driver was a man with grey hair or blond….. 'maybe he dye it?' But Mary O' Donovan definitely had very long nails and two pretty hair slides.

Morecamb ordered Rooney to write up her statement, 'such as it is', and McClean was told to drive the witness back to her place of work. Murphy, who had sheepishly reappeared, was informed that they were going to visit Alderton, to update him and, hopefully, throw him into a spiral of deep depression.

The walk to the hotel was all downhill so there were no complaints from Murphy. He even remarked on the beauty of the bay – "not half fucking bad" – and the bobbing yachts – "big bastards of boats" – in the bay.

When they enquired at reception on Alderton's whereabouts they were directed towards the dining-room and they spotted their boss at a bay window overlooking the harbour and tucking into a lobster.

"I hope you haven't come to ruin my appetite," was his greeting. "No, you're not sitting down. Update, please."

Morecamb gave him the bare outline through gritted teeth while Alderton continued to chomp through his meal.

"So, no progress then," he said as he reached for his glass of wine. "Well, as soon as I've finished dining I shall be communicating with the Chief Commissioner. I shouldn't be surprised if he takes you off the case and puts a monkey in instead."

"Actually, the monkey is having lunch in the Hoor and Hounds with his personal secretary_____"

"I left orders that he wasn't to leave the office," bellowed Alderton.

Several heads swivelled in their direction.

"Get out." Alderton had the good grace to lower his voice. "And tell McClean he's to collect me here in two hours. We'll be heading back to Union Quay. And don't try to contact me for the rest of the afternoon. I've done all I can do here for today. And get Detective Spillane out of that pub and lock him in the office. Shoo. Go, go."

Murphy and Morecamb left, like two recalcitrant schoolboys, feeling the eyes of all the other diners on them. The walk back was, needless to say, all uphill and Murphy was told if he made one complaint he would be thrown into the Marina.

His sergeant had the good sense to keep his mouth shut as Morecamb grumbled and cursed. It was a pitiful state of affairs really and once again his mind turned to breeding from Willow. In a burst of enthusiasm and desperation he decided to bounce the idea off Murphy, avoiding all eye contact. About half a mile later he realised that his sergeant was no longer beside him and when he looked back Murphy hadn't moved a step since the 'unveiling of the new plan' and seemed rooted to the spot. Suddenly he had an even better idea, set in train by Alderton's lush surroundings and fine dining. An over-night stay in a luxurious hotel, away from the mayhem, suddenly seemed very enticing.

When they arrived back there was no sign of McClean and Rooney informed them that McGrath had arrived back, starving, and was now having lunch.

"So, Rooney," began Morecamb, "what did you make of Louisa's testimony? Do you think we should take her description of the driver seriously? Of course I'd have more confidence if she actually knew the gender of said driver."

"Well, I thought she was a very charming young lady," said Rooney, sailing perilously close to the edge. "In fact, in different circumstances____"

"Rooney, get yourself up the street and order the men and that poor woman back in here. Now."

With Rooney gone Morecamb read over Louisa's statement and then passed it over to Murphy.

"Mmmm ....not much here, boss, really," was Murphy's opinion, "though young Rooney seems to have sketched a fairly good likeness of Louisa there in the margin. With no clothes on."

"Put it in that folder over there, Murphy, before I lose the will to live."

Just then the front door banged back against the wall and the diners trooped in with Rooney bringing up the rear.

" Rooney, escort Detective Spillane to his office. Teresa, will you take the detective through the events of the case____"

"I already did," she snapped.

"Again then," said Morecamb matching her tone, "And it's *Sir* when you address me. And Rooney, fetch yourself a chair and sit outside that office door until five. Boss's orders. Now, McGrath, how did you get on with that Twomey man?"

"Wasn't there, sir. But I decided to call to the next house up. A fellah called Peter Kelly and his wife live there____"

"Oh, yes, the vet," interrupted Morecamb. "And?"

"Yes, well worth a visit, sir."

"Good. Fill me in."

"He owns a farm up a bit the road from O'Donovan's. He's also the local vet. They know the O'Donovan's quite well. Actually Mrs O'Donovan cleans for Mrs Kelly. Suffers from her nerves."

"Who does?"

"Mrs Kelly. But a nice woman. Gave me a great feed. Loads of sandwiches and cake. Fruit cake."

"Apart from her culinary delights and dodgy nerves did she impart anything useful?" Morecamb interrupted.

Not really. Apart from the fact that Mrs O' Donovan steals spoons, 'no, forks actually,' he corrected as he squinted at his notes. She has been working for her about fifteen years and she'd have sacked her long ago but herself is so frail that after the slightest bit of work she has to lie down in a dark room with the curtains closed and loosen all her clothes. Smashing up the parlour, was another of Mrs O' Donovan's failings and, of course the house was often dirtier after she left than it had been when she arrived. 'And get this, sir,' she had once caught her spitting onto a cloth before using it to dust the hall table, 'no, I tell a lie, it was the kitchen table' and she spent two days in bed after that, in a darkened room. 'Poor woman'.

Morecamb gripped the back of a chair for support, Murphy contemplated early retirement, very briefly, and Rooney sniggered over at his perch.

"McGrath, this had better be going somewhere, like a bloody great revelation, before very long more."

McGrath seemed to have skipped the lesson on the definition of 'revelation' in school because he continued his narrative in the same vein. Mrs Kelly, 'and I feel this is important, sir', was always dressed up but you could still see the marks of the wellington tops around her fat legs. And she always wore lipstick and was always giddy when Mr Kelly was around......

"Who's always giddy?"

Mrs O' Donovan......... because she fancies him but he wouldn't wipe his feet on her. He has a third cousin who's married into the aristocracy. And besides, she suspects he's having an affair with one of the nuns in the convent. Mrs Kelly says she understands all that as she is so fragile herself that when she sees him unzipping his trousers she has to go into a dark room_____

Morecamb's jaw dropped and he knew that another potential witness had serious credibility issues. McGrath was ordered off the premises, with Rooney, ' before I have ye shot.'

"Boss," interjected Murphy, "Did he interview Mr Kelly by any chance? Just wondering, like_____"

"No," said McGrath, keeping his eyes fixed on Murphy, "He was out with some farmer de-horning cattle. His missus thought it might be a good idea to phone ahead to make an appointment. Goodnight."

"Did she indeed?" spat Morecamb to his retreating back. It was only after the door had closed that he realised it was still only three o' clock in the afternoon but he couldn't stomach much more of either McGrath or Rooney so he left them off.

As soon as McClean returned from the chipper he would send him up to the 'guru' in the hotel and himself and Murphy would head back to Cork. Morecamb wanted to have a word with Lombard to try to get to the bottom of that photographic shoot.

Five minutes later a sheepish-looking McClean put in an appearance with a smear of garish lipstick decorating his left cheek. He looked mortified when Murphy obligingly pointed it out to him and hastily retreated to the bathroom.

When he re-emerged Morecamb gave him the good news about escorting Alderton back to his lair. He didn't bother to inform the 'inmates' in Sweeney's office that he was leaving but he told Harrington who was outside with his head stuck under the bonnet of a garda car. Morecamb didn't ask questions; just hurriedly got into their own car and told Murphy to "step on it."

When they got back to the station there was no sign of Alderton. Moloney whispered to Morecamb that the great man had gone straight to the golf course when he came back, with McClean caddying for him today.

Morecamb wondered how McClean was reacting to his new role. Hopefully apoplectic.

He immediately got on the phone to Lombard to ask him about the other photos of the crime scene. To say that the reception he got was frosty would be an understatement. It was positively arctic.

Yes, there were more photos. No, Morecamb could fuck off if he expected Lombard to traipse over to Union Quay with them. He could collect them in Summerhill station if he wanted them that badly. And, even *he* was shocked to see the contagion of Morecamb's ineptitude had spread to the upstanding gentlemen of the State's defenders of law and order in Kinsale. Morecamb didn't bother to interrupt the tirade but vowed to throw Lombard and his cameras into the Marina if he ever saw him in Kinsale.

"Murphy," instructed Morecamb, "go over to the barracks in Summerhill and get hold of the other photos that Lombard took at the scene. Take Kilroy with you, he's back from his course. I saw him sneaking into the canteen a few minutes ago. Ask for Detective Moran. I'll ring him now and give him the heads up."

Kilroy had no intention of darkening the doors of Summerhill station. And, what's more, he shouldn't be here at all. He was entitled to two days off after attending that useless course. And now the possibility of running into that mad-man, Moran, was the last straw. There was bad blood between himself and Moran. Spilt blood, actually. A quick fumble with the Detective's wife at the Christmas 'do' two years ago. God, she was a stunner! Kilroy had no doubt that things would have proceeded nicely if Moran hadn't stumbled upon them. Much of the events that followed were still a blur but Kilroy could distinctly remember crawling desperately towards the door, with his trousers around his ankles.

"You're very quiet, Kilroy," remarked Murphy. "Cheer up, it's nearly knocking off time and then we'll go for a few pints. Clear the head_____."

"I'm not going in," interrupted Kilroy as he pulled up outside the barracks. "I'll wait here."

"No problem," said Murphy, noticing the scowl on Kilroy's face. "No need for two of us to go in and carry a few snaps back to the car. That's just Morecamb being too cautious. Thinks everything is complicated. But you're still on for that pint?" Murphy checked.

"Yes, just a quick one though. I have football training at seven and I want to have a bite to eat first."

As Murphy disappeared inside the barracks Kilroy slouched low in his seat, trying to make himself as inconspicuous as possible.

Twenty minutes later Murphy re-emerged and got into the back seat.

"What are you.......where are the pics?" squealed Kilroy.

"Slight change of plan," beamed Murphy. "I asked Moran to join us for that pint____"

"You did *what*?" spluttered Kilroy.

"And he's just gone to get a folder for the photos and his baton," continued Murphy airily, "though God knows why he'd need to arm himself," mused Murphy, "unless he's expecting some sort of____"

He was interrupted by the slamming of the driver's door and the sight of Kilroy hopping onto the 12A bus, bound for the city centre, well out of sight before Moran put in an appearance.

What the fuck, muttered Murphy.

CHAPTER 10

Thursday May 8ᵗʰ

The following morning Alderton was pacing up and down the station's car park when Morecamb pulled in. He really didn't have the patience to deal with Alderton's histrionics at this hour of the morning. As he got out of the car Alderton charged.

"Who's Peter Kelly?" Alderton roared.

"Who?"

"Some poor bastard called Peter Kelly."

For a moment Morecamb struggled to get his thoughts in order. He had skipped breakfast, having overslept, and all he could think of was a strong cup of black tea and a slice of toast. "Why are you so interested in Peter Kelly?" he asked as he locked the car door and prepared to head towards the station door. And then he stopped and turned back towards Alderton who seemed rooted to the spot.

"Kelly? Let me see......well, he's the local vet in Kinsale. Why?"

"Oh, no reason really", spluttered Alderton. "Nothing that would interest your good self. But I have been reliably informed – go on, get inside – that he was hacked to death sometime last night...." Alderton was practically roaring at this stage and had the attention of the entire station...... "and was found in a pool of his own blood...."

"Shit!"

"....in his own farmyard, by the postman. Bits of him all over the place," continued Alderton, close to tears now, "and the Commissioner due to arrive in the next day or two....."

107

"Any witnesses, sir?" asked Murphy who had foolishly positioned himself behind Alderton.

"Who said that?" screamed Alderton. "Murphy! Oh yes, about forty witnesses, I believe, all queueing up outside the station in Kinsale, volunteering to show where the man's fingers and toes are located..... get out, Murphy."

"My God, the Press are going to have a field day," Murphy threw over his shoulder as he headed for the toilets.

"Did you hear that, Morecamb?" gasped Alderton. "And the fiasco your great, big lump of a sergeant made of the press conference last year. My God, Kelly's manhood was apparently hacked to pieces. Makes me queasy to even think about it. And the Commissioner.....all hands on deck.....every man, woman and child....."

He was almost incoherent by the time he reached his office and slammed the door behind him.

Morecamb decided that they would take two cars, to make it easier to get round. Himself and Murphy would travel in the first one and he informed McClean that he would take the other one.

"Actually, sir," interrupted McClean, "I've put in for an immediate transfer so if you don't mind I'll be staying here. Just waiting for a phone call____"

"Sure you are," said Morecamb. "Murphy, take McClean and lock him in a cell___"

"Are ye still here?" roared Alderton putting his puce face around the door. "Get out. The lot of ye."

McClean put his head down and headed out to the car, thinking very dark thoughts.

Alderton slumped into his executive chair. He did feel decidedly queasy. That poor man......what was his name........his bits and bobs on display for all to see. And maybe even sneered at.

Gingerly he lowered his hands onto his lap. The 'Crown Jewels' a previous girlfriend had dubbed them. And who was he to argue? Of course he had his suspicions that she might have been a prostitute. Still...... After thirty years of marriage his wife had never offered any compliment in that department. In fact she had been quite derogatory at times......several times.

McClean was equally distraught as he jerked the car into motion. His vehicular manoeuvres bordered on insane.

He hadn't spent four years in University only to end up caddying for the likes of Alderton. Sociology, Logic and something called Cultural Identity. Or was it Geography? The Sociology was a mistake but he'd had it on good authority, before enrolment, that it was a dawdle. Some other 'Freshers', way past coherence in The Western Star pub, had advised him and, it was only through cheating that he had graduated. He still didn't know what the logic had been all about. But it now became clear to him that latching himself onto the coat-tails of Alderton had been a monumental mistake. And the thought of ingratiating himself with Morecamb turned his stomach.

Christ, was that a dog?

Going from first gear to fourth he contemplated throwing himself at the mercy of the Commissioner. Maybe.......

Another bloody dog?

That was actually an idea. Sweeney wasn't fit to hold office. Yes. He rather fancied Detective Inspector McClean of Kinsale barracks. He would immediately fire the whole bloody lot of them and instal his own team. Yes, he liked the sound of 'team'.........

Was that Morecamb's car?

He indicated to overtake them, pushing the car to fourth gear, expertly avoiding other cars parked on either side of the narrow street, but, perhaps, clipping Morecamb's wing mirror in the process. And maybe his own because it certainly wasn't where it had been when he had set out.

Abruptly he pulled up outside the barracks, engaged the hand brake and, when he spotted the contorted features of Morecamb advancing, he hastily bounded into the barracks.

Morecamb took a moment to survey the damage to both cars and silently vowed to sort out McClean at the first opportunity. But, right now, he had more urgent matters to attend to.

When they got inside McGrath seemed to be in charge, that is to say had his sleeves rolled up and was staring vacantly out the window.

When Morecamb cleared his throat Rooney nudged McGrath and the trance was broken.

"Have you heard?" asked McGrath. "We have a serial killer running around the place__"

"There is no evidence of any such thing," snapped Morecamb, "so don't start that. Tell us what you know."

"Well, a man has been slaughtered in his own home____"

"Yard," said Murphy.

"How did you know that?" queried McGrath.

"Continue," said Morecamb.

"And his balls_____"

"We know that too," said Murphy.

"How did you know *that*?" McGrath again, beginning to look at Murphy with something akin to wonder. "Anyway," he continued after a pause, "the postman found him and we believe the dog ate one of Kelly's_____"

"Oh, for fuck's sake," said an exasperated Morecamb. "Rooney, who's at the crime scene now?"

"Well," drawled Rooney, "that would be our erstwhile captain, Detective Sweeney. And before he left he rang the station in Bandon and asked for re-enforcements. Oh, and his secretary and Harrington are with him as well."

"What the blazes is the secretary doing there?" Morecamb exploded.

"Taking notes, apparently."

"Rooney, ring the 'Scene of Crime' unit in Cork and tell them we need a few lads at the scene. Explain about the extensive area which needs to be covered. And, Murphy, will you ring the Pathologist and let him know that____"

"Already done," said Rooney. "He's not exactly your number one fan, is he, sir?"

"Shut up, Rooney and go in and ring Lombard then and____"

"Done and done," interrupted Rooney. "And *he* absolutely hates you."

"Thank you, Rooney. Well, when Lombard puts in an appearance I want you to escort him to the locus. Oh, just a thought….I presume a doctor was called to certify death?"

Rooney looked at him as if he'd sprouted horns and then held his sides as he rocked back and forth, laughing uproariously and spluttering expletives about male genatalia and torsos skittering around on their backsides. 'A very vulgar man', was Murphy's opinion and went over and kicked the chair out from under him.

"Well done, Sergeant", cheered Morecamb. "Right, McClean you're coming with Sergeant Murphy and myself. And you'll be occupying the back seat, giving directions. McGrath, you go on ahead in your own vehicle."

*****

CHAPTER 11

McClean's directions to Murphy were monosyllabic and, in spite of the fact that he had spent his childhood holidays 'all over the place', they went astray three times, extending the journey by at least twenty minutes. Murphy felt that he might have been doing it on purpose because he wasn't allowed to drive but he didn't share his suspicions with Morecamb. Things were tense enough.

Kelly's farm was accessed by a long avenue, fenced off on either side by a wooden railing and the wonderful sight of horses, chomping at the grass and completely oblivious to the machinations of their masters. Young foals gambolled through the meadow, tails in the air and spindly limbs going in all directions.

Such noble animals, murmured Morecamb. Over to the left, two other Garda cars had been slewed to a stop all over the front lawn and were obviously just abandoned. The rear doors of one of them were still hanging open.

The body was smack bang in the middle of the yard. Slowly Morecamb approached it. Someone had attempted to encircle it with crime-scene tape. Morecamb brushed it aside and hunched down.

The body was at a grotesque angle, the head several feet away from the body. Enormous purple bruising covered the torso. Some of the fingers had been hacked off and, yes, the genetalia had suffered the same fate.

It was the most frenzied attack Morecamb had ever seen.

With difficulty he levered himself to a standing position and, for a moment, his vision blurred. Slowly he looked around and took in his bearings.

McGrath was over in a corner, stripped to the waist, throwing up the contents of his stomach and seemed to be in danger of falling into the water trough. Meanwhile, Sweeney was sitting on an upturned bucket and seemed to have delegated responsibility to Harrington. And then there was the Secretary.....Teresa, wasn't it........taking copious notes in her jotter and completely ignoring their arrival.

"Ah, Morecamb," boomed Sweeney. "It *is* Morecamb....... isn't it?"

"Detective Sweeney, what's going on?"

"All under control," he replied with an expansive sweep of his arm.

"Harrington," roared Morecamb, "get over here. What's going on? The short version, please."

Harrington seemed to have grown several inches and stood boldly in front of Morecamb. Murphy and those capable of any movement at all headed towards the far corner of the yard.

"Well, Detective Spillane has honoured me with the position of Scene-of crime supervisor and in that capacity_____"

"You've twenty seconds, Harrington!"

Right, Harrington had taken it upon himself to order the men to erect the crime scene tape......so himself and Teresa had to put it up themselves. In fact Teresa was proving an invaluable member of the force and if he might be so bold as to suggest that she be co-opted on to the Garda force. And now, if Morecamb would care to step this way he would introduce him to the lads from Bandon who were a great bunch____

Was that a garda tunic, wondered Morecamb as he surveyed 'the exhibits', suddenly fearing that he might be on the verge of a nervous breakdown.

Teresa was now, on Harrington's instructions, making a note of all the exhibits and taking down the registration numbers of all the vehicles, especially the garda cars. Oh, and himself and Detective Sweeney had spoken to Mrs Kelly, very sensitively, but she really had nothing to say. Actually, nothing at all. But..........

Morecamb left him in mid-sentence, strode across to the secretary and told her if she hadn't vacated the area in ten seconds, with Sweeney in tow, he would make her eat her pencil and notebook. He then ordered Harrington to tell Sergeant McGrath to put his clothes back on, cop himself on and stop vomiting. The Bandon crew was to take up position at the yard gate and nobody was to be allowed in, no reporters or photographers…..except Lombard, of course. Harrington himself was to go around discreetly and check if all of Kelly's anatomical appendages could be accounted for.

"C'mon, Sergeant Murphy, you're with me," and he headed towards the front door of the dwelling house, which was ajar. Hopefully things might be a little clearer after he had spoken to the widow.

They found her in a darkened parlour and, when Morecamb identified himself and Murphy and offered her their condolences on the terrible shock, she calmly informed them that she had been in shock for all of her married life. She loved her husband, of course she did, and she knew that men couldn't control their animal instincts but, notwithstanding all that, she felt she had to call the priest after poor Peter had assaulted her on their wedding night. And it was only on the rare occasion afterwards that he got out of hand.

And did they think that the whole business out in the yard might be an act of God……….

"Still a bit of the penis missing," announced Harrington as he barged into the room. Murphy excused himself to the nervy widow and frog-marched Harrington out the door.

"And can you think of anybody who might have had a grudge against your husband, Mrs Kelly?" asked Morecamb. '*Other than yourself*', he added under his breath, all the while trying to ignore the shocking spectacle of Harrington's entrance and the decidedly dodgy-looking specimen which he had been waving about in the air.

"Absolutely not," she answered. "He was a dedicated vet, a loving husband, would have been a great father but the Good Lord hadn't been particularly favourable in that department……in any sense of the word," she added darkly.

*This is hopeless, Moreca*mb realised.

"Do you have somebody who will look after you, Mrs Kelly, you know, maybe stay with you?" asked Morecamb.

"Oh, yes, my sister, Rosie, is on her way from Cork. With the tablets. She'll look after me, she knows how sensitive I am. And she thought the world of poor Peter. I even think she'll be as sad as I am."

One could only hazard a guess at how that 'sadness' would manifest itself, Morecamb thought. A knees-up around the kitchen table perhaps.

He said goodbye to Mrs Kelly and told her that he would call back tomorrow; he needed to ask her some questions and would also like a chat with Rosie.

When he got back outside to the yard the police photographer, Lombard, was stalking around the place with his camera, snapping at everything in sight. The rest of the crew was keeping its distance, especially Murphy. There was history between the pair of them from a previous investigation.

"Good morning, Lombard____"

"Oh, is it?" he sneered. "This must be one of your finer dramas, Inspector. Disaster seems to follow you, doesn't it? Yes, I've noticed that. And then it's left to us professionals to salvage the situation and restore some sort of order........."

"Get on with your work, Lombard, and don't forget to take the shutters off the lenses this time. Right, men," he called, walking away from the photographer, "gather round." He promptly told the Bandon lads to go away. McClean was to stay behind and not to let anybody in or out except the guys from the Pathology lab. Any reporters who arrived were to be told that there would be a short Press briefing the following day in Cork. Superintendent Alderton would notify them on the time later on. And Harrington was to wash his hands before he got into a car.

*****

Truth be told the Bandon lads were mightily relieved to be going back to their own station and there was a bit of a tussle as they hastily retreated to their cars. Their own base mightn't be the most progressive but, my God! When compared with the debacle in that farmyard and Harrington's assertion that he himself might well be leading the investigation in a few days, well, all dreams of advancing to the Serious Crime department were irrevocably dashed.

CHAPTER 12

Back at the station Morecamb noticed that there was no sign of Sweeney or his secretary and they were no loss.

"Right, everybody, listen up. We have two very serious crimes on our hands.......Murphy, will you answer that?" as the phone in Sweeney's office started to ring. "Take a message and tell the caller I'll ring them back. Now, Mary O'Donovan and Peter_____"

"Is there a connection, sir?" This from Harrington. "You see, I believe, based on my experience from events this morning_____"

"Sit down, Harrington. Where was I? Yes, and Peter Kelly, both brutally murdered_____"

"There's the connection right there." Harrington was on his feet again.

"Harrington, if you interrupt again you'll find yourself out in the corridor. Now, there's no reason to say that there's a connection but I'm not ruling anything out. Two suspicious deaths_____"

Rooney giggled.

"Rooney, will you stand in the corner over there."

"I was going to say_____"

"With your face to the wall."

"'*Suspicious*', you said," he shouted. "I mean the dogs in the street_____"

"Shut up, Rooney," said McGrath, "and do as you're told."

"Thank you, Sergeant," said Morecamb, surprised by McGrath's intervention. But judging by the sheen of perspiration on McGrath's face and his waxen complexion he wasn't too sure if McGrath knew where he was , much less what he was saying.

"Now, we'll have two dedicated, and I use the term loosely, teams. One group will focus on Mary O' Donovan_____" Harrington's hand shot up.

"........and the other on Peter Kelly."

Now McGrath had his hand in the air and he announced that he wanted to work on the O' Donovan case as he couldn't stomach the idea of wading through the terrible events of Kelly's slaughter. But Morecamb told him that he's do as he was told and promptly assigned him to the vet's case, alongside Murphy while McClean, Harrington and Rooney would solve Mary O' Donovan's murder.

Murphy's panic-stricken arrival interrupted proceedings and he informed Morecamb that Alderton wanted him to ring him back straight away. Actually he was quite curt with himself and Murphy couldn't understand why he was the one who was always asked to answer the phone when he knew very well.......Morecamb cut short his almost incoherent ramblings and told him that he would be joining 'Operation what the fuck' with McClean and Harrington.

"I'll be effectively working on the two of them," Morecamb expanded. See if, God forbid, there might be a connection...."

"Told you," crowed Harrington.

" ......which I doubt."

Finally when they were seated in their groups Morecamb decided it was probably safe to leave them and phone the Super.

"What do you want now?" barked Alderton.

"Well, you asked me to ring. Had you forgotten? Dear, oh dear........ anyway, we're definitely dealing with two murders here_____"

"Yes, well, I suspected as much," drawled Alderton. "I mean, when a man is hacked to pieces you usually find that life is extinct ____"

Morecamb calmly put down the phone and went to investigate the racket which had suddenly erupted in the day room.

Sweeney had returned in an inebriated state. Apparently, his secretary, though equally inebriated, had the good sense to rebuff his amorous advances and he was now calling for the 'spare set of handcuffs'. Harrington was told to drive Sweeney home and Rooney was to escort the secretary to her place of residence.

It was all hands on deck to get the pair safely into their respective cars, cheered on by the locals who had gathered outside the 'Hoor and Hounds'. Oh, to have Alderton here!

Murphy came flying out of the office as they returned to the day room to inform his boss that Alderton was on the phone again and was there no end to the torment?

Morecamb brushed past him and this time he didn't spare Alderton's blushes. He gave him both barrels, starting with the debacle with Sweeney and his belief that the secretary was going to file a law suit against Alderton's brother-in-law for sexual assault.

"So, I was wondering, Superintendent, if I should direct her towards the Commissioner when he arrives and nip the whole thing in the bud, so to speak. What do you think? Oh, and by the way, we've informed the hordes of reporters down here that you will be giving a Press briefing tomorrow. So I'll leave that in your capable hands."

If it hadn't been for the strangled breathing at the other end of the line, Morecamb would have sworn that Alderton had hung up. Morecamb sat quietly at the desk, taking deep breaths and decided that he was going to spend the night in Kinsale, with Murphy, and try to find out as much as they could about this Peter Kelly fellah. It had the added advantage of not having to meet Alderton that evening.

He poked his head around the door and beckoned to Murphy.

"Shut the door. You and I are going to book into a hotel for the night. I'm going to ring Moloney now in Cork and tell him to notify your good wife. I'll also get him to call on my Aunt. She'll have to look after my dog. We can buy toiletries and that locally."

Murphy was delighted. "It would be like a mini-holiday, boss. Just imagine, no nagging or complaining..........from Alderton...... That place where the Superintendent was staying looked nice. Perhaps....?"

"Sure. Why not? I'll book us in and make that call to Moloney."

When Morecamb re-joined the others he gave the thumbs-up to Murphy who beamed from ear to ear. Then he noticed Harrington hopping from one leg to the other, in a high state of giddiness. He called it 'a moment of inspiration' and felt they should return to Kelly's place of death to ascertain if he had engaged in the sex act before someone had taken a hatchet to him. Apparently that was as good a way as any to find out if his last assignation had been with a man or a woman and it would narrow down the field considerably. They could be looking at fifty per cent if his maths were right.

Christ, was there no let up?

"Well, what if he was a homosexual?" asked Rooney, who had just returned from his rescue mission.

Harrington's brow furrowed in concentration.

"I hadn't thought of that," he said, slapping his hand against the side of his head in a dramatic fashion. Murphy got up and hit him a belt on the other side of his head and Harrington meekly resumed his seat.

As McGrath was still looking wan Morecamb told Murphy and Rooney to call on all the houses and farms near Kelly's place and try to get a sense of what kind of man he was and if there was a reason why he might have been targeted. As he saw Murphy glance at the clock on the wall, he assured him that they would go for lunch when they got back. After all it was only eleven thirty now!

McGrath and McClean were dispatched to Mary's parents to find out if Peter Kelly ever had occasion to call on them in his capacity as a vet. "But, be gentle. Explain to them that we don't think there's a connection but we have to explore all avenues. Harrington, you're coming with me. I want to introduce you to Leila Flynn."

CHAPTER 13

Harrington was his usual cavalier self as they tore up the narrow roads leading to the Flynn's residence. Fields and ditches were all a blur and that car which had scrambled to safety when they overtook it on the hair-pin bend was still in the ditch when they were returning later on to the town.

Mr Flynn was outside practising his golf swing as they drew up in front of the house. He seemed delighted to see them and tried to persuade them to come inside for a drink. Morecamb declined and asked if Leila was still feeling poorly and perhaps at home?

He had no idea but he would ask the housekeeper. Moments later he returned with the news that she had gone to school, after all. That surprised him. He went on to explain that there had been an almighty to-do 'between my good wife and poor Leila' that very morning.

"Any idea what it was about?" asked Morecamb.

"Not really. I was busy reading The Times.......do you read it yourself?"

"The row, Mr Flynn?"

"Oh yes, well, as I say, a great bloody shin-dig. Women's stuff, you understand. Poor Leila said she was giving up school and going to be a hairdresser. Poor Marjorie got very upset......she's delicate too, you see, and she threatened to send poor Leila to the Gaeltacht if she ever mentioned that nonsense again. What do you think, Officer..........it's a new driver and cost me a packet but apparently your golf improves by.......Oh, you're off. Are you sure....."

Morecamb felt that the authorities of the State had got it all wrong. Children up and down the country were suffering at the hands of parents and teachers, telling them that if they studied hard they would end up rich and successful. Look at the Sugrue woman, for example. But that man Flynn gave lie to that nonsense. Morecamb doubted if he could even read and yet, here he was, in the midst of a most magnificent pile and his only concern was his prowess as a golfer.

Meanwhile Morecamb's own immediate concern was his blood pressure. In an effort to distract himself from his racing pulse he decided to talk very calmly to the idiot driving the car. He knew Harrington wouldn't ask for any clarification or take the slightest bit of notice of what he was saying.

"See, Harrington, there are all sorts of weirdos around every corner," Morecamb pronounced as Harrington went from first gear to fourth in one chaotic manoeuvre. "Mind the dog.......actually, slow down..... slower! Take Flynn, for example. Barking mad but I don't think he's any danger to his fellow human beings..........."

"I think I'll take up golf, sir____"

"Then there's Detective Sweeney.......slower, please......he's not the full shilling either........bad bend up here.......but again, no great danger......unless he starts driving....."

"I'm his driver, sir____"

"......or, God forbid, takes an active part in an investigation. That could be fatal. Of course, his secretary, Teresa whatshername, she might regard him as a bit of a menace_____"

"Oh, I wouldn't worry about Teresa, sir. She has a bit of a drink problem herself. All her life. I believe she was the only person in the entire county who refused to take the Pledge at her Confirmation. She was on half a bottle of whiskey at the time_____"

Right. This wasn't helping at all, thought Morecamb, as he loosened his tie and opened the top two buttons in his shirt.

They had pulled up outside the station before Morecamb realised where they were.

"What are you doing here, Harrington? Straight up to the convent, I said."

He hadn't but young Harrington wouldn't know the difference anyway.

"Right, sir. Bit of a hill up to the convent but it's great fun coming down. Boom!"

Morecamb resolved that he would walk back as he stumbled from the car and fought to regain his sense of equilibrium. He refrained from glancing at the vertiginous view of the harbour on this occasion.

They could hear a bell ringing somewhere inside the convent and, when the door opened, a horde of girls almost knocked them to the ground.

"Girls! Girls!" screeched a habit. "Remember you are young ladies."

This admonishment only served to exacerbate the squeals and pushing and Morecamb and Harrington flattened themselves against the wall until the worst of the stampede was over.

"You'll have to excuse my students, Officers." This from a young man, obviously a teacher, who was trying to keep up with them. "They all want to sit in the front seats," he added with a smug look.

"I'm sorry about that," apologised the nun who had tried to restore order. "I'd like to say that the rush was motivated by their love of Science but, who are we kidding," she added with a shrug. "Now, how can I help you?"

"We're investigating the murder of Mary O'Don____"

"Oh, yes, Sister Josephina mentioned that. If you follow me I'll see what I can do."

They were led into the same parlour, which seemed a million miles away from the mayhem they had just witnessed.

"Exciting, isn't it, sir?" exclaimed Harrington. "I've never been in a convent before. The nuns sleep in cells, you know. That's what their rooms are called."

"Are you sure that it isn't where the girls are billeted? I would have thought that_____"

He was interrupted by the appearance of Sister Josephina. She was full of apologies but she was under strict instructions from Leila's mother that her daughter was not to be interrogated again without herself being present.

*****

Morecamb was so incensed that he forgot his intention to walk back to the station and was exposed to the full horrors of Harrington's definition of 'Boom', a most terrifying experience.

"Just pray that we don't meet anything coming against us, sir. It's impossible for two cars to pass side by side. Roads are too narrow, you see."

And young Harrington had the solution apparently. The trick was to plant the boot and travel the miniscule roads as fast as possible and when any 'imposter' spotted you hurtling towards them they inevitably had a change of heart and reversed as fast as they could until the advancing menace was well out of the way. Morecamb wasn't sure if taking the corner at the Trident hotel on two wheels was part of the plan or their near submersion in the Bandon river. But he was definitely going to issue him with a fine for reckless driving.

CHAPTER 14

Thankfully McGrath and McClean had returned so Morecamb felt there might be a bit of sanity as he mopped his brow.

"Well, how did it go?" he asked.

"Well, considering the circumstances, I feel we maximised the occasion," began McClean.

Oh God, here we go, thought Morecamb as he reached for another handkerchief.

"Mr and Mrs O'Donovan were very generous really. Two whiskeys, was it, Sergeant McGrath? I myself declined naturally, as I'm on duty."

Morecamb was in no doubt that a beating would be administered. He might join in himself. Even Harrington looked appalled.

"Get on with it, McClean."

The upshot of their visit could best be described as a disaster. McClean had told Mr and Mrs O'Donovan that most of their resources would now be concentrated on finding Kelly's killer as that was the most recent and, as they knew themselves, it was easier to find witnesses and evidence in a fresh case than in a cold case. The O'Donovan's torture was further exacerbated by McClean's suggestion that it was possible that Mary was having a relationship with the dead man.

Two handkerchiefs soaked now.

"And what happened then?" asked Harrington excitedly.

"We got thrown out, didn't we?" roared McGrath. "Whipped the glass from under my nose. Mrs O'Donovan took hold of the sweeping brush. Poor woman was hysterical and poor Tom was crying….."

Morecamb felt ill. "I'm going for a walk," he muttered.

*****

It was a short walk. He went straight into the 'Hoor and Hounds' and ordered a double whiskey.

What now, he pondered. *He had thought that McClean had some savvy. Why, he didn't know. Maybe, like Alderton, he was impressed by the university education and the posh accent and the superior attitude and the supercilious bastardness of the God-awful twerp ......*

"Bartender! Same again, please."

....with a brain the size of an ant and the social nous of a gnat. He was going to kill him.

Decision made, he sat back and sipped at his whiskey. This benevolent hiatus lasted until his team trooped in, eyed Morecamb in the corner with his whiskey and meekly sat down at the table furthest away from him. Only Murphy ventured over, offered to get him a top up and tried to persuade him to eat something.

Morecamb reluctantly relented but he only picked at the food when it arrived and ordered another double whiskey.

He was nicely plastered when they went back into the station. Harrington wanted to chair the meeting but Murphy, with one eye on Morecamb, ordered him out to pick up the papers blowing around outside on the footpath.

"Right," said Murphy, from the head of the table, "let's hear some feedback from our actions this morning. Who's first?"

"Me!" said Morecamb with his hand in the air. "Do you know," he said, leaning across the table towards Rooney, "you can come down that hill from the convent at seventy miles an hour? What do you think of that? Mmmmm?"

"Inspector Morecamb," interrupted Murphy, "perhaps we should concentrate____"

"Seventy miles an hour.... in second gear........ It's called, 'Boom!' Ever heard of that?"

"That's fine, Inspector Morecamb." There was a hint of desperation in Murphy's voice now. "Any luck with Leila Flynn?" he asked in an effort to get his boss back on track.

"She's delicate, Sergeant Murphy, like her mother before her," he slurred. "But the really tricky part is stopping the car at that velocity."

"Yes," McClean chipped in. "Velocity is the time rate of change. And of course the speed is the time rate of change____"

That earned him three thumps.

"So, the thing is," continued Morecamb, oblivious to McClean's contribution, "the thing is…….. In order to stop you have to head for the quays at speed, right up to the edge and when you see your life flash before you, then you ram the car into reverse and…..boom over!" he finished on a hiccup.

Rooney thought the whole thing hilarious.

"McClean, hold the fort for a minute. I just want a word with Sergeant Moloney in Cork." He wanted to check that Moloney had carried out Morecamb's earlier instructions, check if he had notified Alderton, his own wife and Morecamb's aunt about the fact that they were staying in Kinsale tonight.

"Yes, Morecamb's aunt had been none too pleased."

"Alderton hadn't been informed at all because he had been feeling poorly and had already gone home with a rumbling ulcer."

"And Murphy's own wife had immediately called a taxi, arrived into reception in Union Quay………two hours ago…….. and was now sitting across from him and wouldn't be leaving until her husband put in an appearance. And if Murphy wasn't back at the station in one hour Moloney was going straight over to Alderton's house to lodge a complaint."

Murphy saw his 'mini-holiday' go up in smoke and staggered back out to the day room. In a fit of pique he decided that his Inspector could forget about *his* little jaunt as well.

"Right, lads, give us a hand here and let's get Inspector Morecamb into a car. Rooney, go out and check if there is a reception committee outside the pub first.

"All clear," announced Rooney, returning.

Morecamb was almost comatose at this stage and it took four of them to get him into the car.

"Is he dead?" asked Harrington as he hurried to open the car door.

"Not that car, Harrington," growled Murphy. "Open the other one...... the back door, you oaf."

After they had wedged Morecamb inside and shut the door Murphy got into the driving seat. Through the open window he told McClean to follow him and meet up with him outside Morecamb's house.

"And, Sergeant McGrath," he called , "will your lads update the notice board and write up the log for today. We'll see you all in the morning."

Murphy knew that, as soon as their cars had disappeared around the first bend that they would go straight into the pub.

*****

Morecamb's house was on the other side of Cork but Murphy, with huge misgivings, had decided to call there first. He fervently hoped that his wife hadn't cut loose in the station and made a holy show of him in the meantime.

Thankfully, McClean was right on his heels and with a superhuman effort they heaved Morecamb out of the car and wobbled up to the front door.

Dot opened the door to them and scowled when she clapped eyes on her nephew.

"Mother of God, look at the state of him. I knew it was only a matter of time before the drink got him. He needs a woman, you know." This was directed at Murphy.

"No, Ma'am, no, he doesn't."

"I'm telling you____"

"Where's his room?" panted McClean.

"Up the stairs and first door on the right. He listens to Classical music, you know......"

Murphy nodded towards the parlour.

"And that's not healthy......where are you going with him?" she cried. "Up the stairs........."

"It's too much," croaked McClean, "not the bloody stairs."

They deposited him on the sofa, turned him on his side and hastily left the house.

When Murphy reached Union Quay he exited the car almost before it had come to a full stop and dashed headlong into the station. And stopped. His wife was cocked up behind reception, manning the phone while 'that nice sergeant was having a well-earned cup of tea.' They would wait until they got home before they had their 'little chat' and would he 'fuck off now and inform the lovely sergeant that Mrs Murphy would have to be excused.'

CHAPTER 15

Friday May 9th

Morecamb had it on good authority, from his neighbour, that today was Friday so there was no chance of a lie-in to recuperate. Added to his misery was the fact that he had to walk to work as he felt there was still too much alcohol sloshing around inside him. As soon as he limped into the station the following morning he was summoned to Alderton's office.

"I'm going to have a pot of black coffee first, Moloney, so you can tell his lordship that I'll be with him in due course."

Moloney had no intention of passing on that message. It was way above his pay grade. Morecamb thumped himself down on the nearest chair and was quite proud that he hadn't spilled a drop from the pot.

Shit! He'd forgotten to get a cup. Up again but as he returned to the table the cup seemed to jump out of his hand and crashed to the floor in smithereens.

"Here, let me get you another cup, boss." Murphy to the rescue.

Morecamb gingerly lowered himself onto a chair and was horrified to see that his hands were shaking.

"There you go, boss. I'll pour."

Morecamb had drunk three cups before he felt revived enough to lift his head.

"Sorry about yesterday, Murphy," he mumbled. "Don't know what came over me."

But Murphy assured him that he shouldn't worry and went on to diagnose a nervous breakdown. It was nothing to be ashamed about. The same thing had happened to an uncle of his a few years ago and he was still up in the asylum. But there was great celebration recently enough when he was released from the padded room and the restraints removed.

"Think I'll go into Alderton," snapped Morecamb, glaring at Murphy before stomping out of the canteen.

Alderton was ensconced behind his desk with an array of pills spread out before him.

"Don't sit down, Morec_____" but Morecamb had already sat and managed to stay upright. Another minor achievement though his hands were still shaking. Hurriedly he put them into his pockets and almost careered onto the floor.

"Well?" asked Alderton.

"Well, what?" squinted Morecamb, getting up to close the blinds behind Alderton. Bloody sun. But when he turned around he realised that he wouldn't be able to find his way back to his chair so he opened them again.

"What the hell?" spluttered Alderton. "See, now you've made me swear. You look shite by the way. I hope you aren't going to tell me that you're sick.........."

"I'm sick," said Morecamb.

"..............because I'm not interested. The Commissioner has been on already this morning......" Alderton stopped to swallow two pills........."and he's not a happy man. The news has reached him about events in his beloved Kinsale.......don't know who squealed but I suspect young McClean. All that education. Anyway, he started to blame *me*. Me. I soon put him right....." Two more pills......... "so I'm happy to say that he's gunning for you now. And, you still haven't asked me," he glared.

"Asked you what?" sighed Morecamb.

"How I'm feeling," roared Alderton. "I specifically left a message with Moloney to inform you that my ulcer is on the point of exploding. I explained all this to you before........." Two more pills........... "how the doctor told me I'm on the edge of the precipice_____"

Something triggered in Morecamb's brain and he suddenly had flashbacks of the quays in Kinsale yesterday.

"Sick," he mumbled and headed to the toilets as fast as he could.

When he felt sufficiently revived he went back to the canteen and ordered Murphy to go into Alderton and inform him that they were leaving for Kinsale and they would update him this evening. He then told McClean that one car was sufficient for today, considering the damage he had managed to inflict on two vehicles yesterday. And of course McClean would be forking out for the repairs, fill in a report sheet on the incident and present it to Alderton for his perusal along with a large glass of whiskey. And, quite possibly, a letter of resignation. What did he think of that now?

Morecamb wobbled off out to the car, eased himself into the back seat and lay down. He put his cap over his eyes and was snoring by the time Murphy arrived.

"You don't look too well either, Sergeant," said McClean, ever anxious to point out the misfortunes of others, as a pasty-looking Murphy eased himself into the passenger seat.

"Just been in to see Alderton, haven't I?" retorted Murphy. "You drive, McClean and if you value your life you'd better behave today behind the wheel. There's a very unwell man in the back seat, who's liable to wake up at any moment. Of course it isn't strictly true that I've been 'in' to see Alderton as he didn't allow me beyond the door. Never does. I don't know if he's very well either. Has a sort of glazed look, I thought. And he roared laughing when I told him we'd update him on progress this evening. And then he clutched his stomach and groaned and I left."

"Maybe you should have told Moloney to take a look in on him," suggested McClean.

"Maybe," said Murphy, "but I didn't."

*****

As they began to pile out of the car in Kinsale, Morecamb almost collapsed when McClean slammed the car doors shut. He thought his head was going to fall off and resolved to give McClean the mother and father of all beatings when he felt well enough.

"How are you feeling today, sir?" sneered Rooney.

Morecamb immediately ordered him into the office to ring Alderton and remind him about the Press conference later on. Rooney sloped off, muttering, and slammed the door shut behind him.

And he would give *him* a good thrashing as well.

"Now, yesterday Murphy, you and Rooney went to question Kelly's neighbours. How did that go?"

"Well_____"

Another slam of the door signalled Rooney's return.

"Bit of a pig, isn't he?" he announced.

"Well, Superintendent Alderton isn't a well man_____" began Murphy.

"No. Your Sergeant Moloney," Rooney clarified. "Told me to get off the phone straight away. Said he needed to call an ambulance for the Super."

"Is he dead?" asked Harrington.

"Will you go in there, Murphy, and tell Sergeant Moloney to cancel the Press briefing and reschedule it for tomorrow. I'll take it myself if I have to. Otherwise they're going to start circling the station here and drive us mad. Now, Rooney, how did yourself and Sergeant Murphy get on yesterday?"

Well, Peter Kelly certainly wasn't a homosexual and, though his own amazing record of womanising was legendary, Kelly's escapades would leave him in the shade. He broke off when he saw Morecamb advancing.

"Okay, okay," said Rooney with his hands in the air. "Well, first off we called on a Mr Egleston......"

Several chairs in Morecamb's path crashed to the floor and Rooney sought refuge in the toilets.

"Moloney refused point blank," said Murphy coming back into the room. "Said it was up to Superintendent Alderton to call and cancel Press briefings. There had been a previous incident when Moloney had made a suggestion about something trivial and Alderton had threatened to blow his head off."

"Well, I don't care if it goes ahead or not," said Morecamb. "Now, Murphy, I've been reliably informed that you called on a Mr Egleston yesterday. Of course I'm sure I must be mistaken because I know for a fact that you and I already experienced that man's peculiar brand of eye-witness account and his rather dubious credibility. So, where else did ye go?"

"Well......where's young Rooney? He has the notebook."

"Get him, McGrath."

A sheepish looking Rooney emerged.

"Fetch the notebook, Rooney," Murphy pleaded. Suddenly Morecamb turned to Murphy. "Sergeant, I almost forgot. I sent you and Sergeant Kilroy to collect those photos which Lombard had dropped off with Moran. Where are they?"

"Um....they're actually still in Moran's car, boss."

"Well, have them on my desk tomorrow morning."

Murphy had to sit down. He had no idea where the photos were. The last place he recalled seeing them was on the counter of the Western Ho bar. Christ, that was two nights ago!

"Right, Rooney," said Morecamb, "Let's hear it."

"Well, after Jimmy Egles......we called at Billy Twomey's. His land is bounding Peter Kelly's.

He was dehorning cattle. There was blood everywhere. And the noise from the cattle crush......it was like World War......... right, yes, then we called to____"

"Go back," shouted Morecamb. "What did the Twomey man say?"

"Well, normally he gets Peter Kelly to help him to dehorn the....... right, well, he knew nothing. Didn't know of anybody____"

"His wife, Rooney," snapped Murphy, sensing a rise in temperature. "Tell him about the missus."

"Oh, yes, well we were invited in for the tea____"

Good God, fumed Murphy. Was the bastard doing it on purpose?

Her name is Mary, Rooney rattled on, and she absolutely hated Kelly. Said he was a ram. She didn't like the way he used to look at her daughter. Or herself. But, good God, the state of *her*. Even Murphy said he'd be hard-pressed to.......right; anyway, apparently Kelly was a wicked womaniser though that hardly seems a justifiable reason_____

"Did she know of anybody who Kelly might have been intimate with?" asked Morecamb, trying to control his temper. "You know, any *useful* information?"

Well, there were rumours that he was even friendly with one of the nuns in the convent. "Imagine that? Like letting a fox loose in a henhouse_____"

"Desperate vulgarity," muttered Murphy.

"He has an aunt in the convent," Harrington volunteered. "I believe they're very close but I hardly think_____"

"Thank you, Harrington," said Morecamb. "That's useful to know. 'Thinking', however, is over for the day now. You can give it a rest."

Harrington sat down, beaming from ear to ear.

"So, did this Twomey woman give any names?"

Oh, yes there were plenty. Some woman who owns a café in the town ..

"Mrs Fitzgerald," Murphy put in.

"Then she mentioned a Mrs Harrington.............Ha-ha! Gotcha!" screeched Rooney as he noticed the appalled stares and the stunned silence.

Morecamb reached over, snatched the notebook out of Rooney's hand and ordered him out the door.

"Murphy, you continue," said Morecamb, handing him the notebook.

Well, she also had her suspicions about Bridie Sugrue. And also Mrs O' Donovan. Then a Mrs Lysaght. But then her husband, Billy, had lost his temper and told her to shut up. He said it wasn't right to be blackening the poor man's name.

"So," said Morecamb, "it appears the only woman that he wasn't intimate with was his own wife. Could you believe anything out of that Twomey woman's mouth?"

"Well, he *was* a ladies' man," McGrath said. "But a fierce nice fellah for all that."

"Did you know him well, Sergeant McGrath?" asked Morecamb.

"Not very well but I sometimes met him in the local and we'd have a few drinks. Generous too. He wasn't afraid to put his hand in his pocket_____"

"And did you ever hear any rumours about his very public private life?"

"Well, I think there might have been something with the Fitzgerald woman_____"

"Is there a husband on the scene?"

"Oh yes, but I think they lead separate lives."

"But would he be the jealous type if he thought his wife_____"

"Ah no. He lives near the café"

"Well that wouldn't stop him____"

"...............with a man."

After a pause Morecamb said they would still need to interview her. And the husband.

"So, where next, Murphy?"

Well, the next place was the Lysaght place. Murphy didn't like the husband at all. Grumpy sod but the wife was nice, sounded English and he couldn't for the life of him understand why she had married him.

"Well, he's a very, very rich man," McGrath supplied. "Owns the finest herd of cattle in the entire county and he owns all that land on the other side of the Marina. Goes right down to the harbour."

"Next?"

"Well, that was it, boss. That took up the full morning."

"Of course if you hadn't wasted your time calling to Egles…….. " began Morecamb. And then gave up. McClean and 'that useless article, Rooney' were to go back to the Lysagh woman and question her about her relationship, if any, with Peter Kelly. She obviously wouldn't admit to anything if the husband was there. And they were not to start by accusing her outright of having an affair with him. Harrington and McGrath were to go back to the Louisa creature in Lorenzo's and ask her if she could remember anything else about that big car that she thinks the 'live' Mary O' Donovan got into. Himself and Murphy would pay a visit to Mrs Fitzgerald at the cafe before it got too busy.

"Boss. There *is* something," said Murphy as he struggled to keep up with Morecamb. "That Twomey woman *did* mention Mrs Harrington. But I told Rooney not to_____ "

"You're joking!"

"No. Her name was mentioned."

"Christ, do people do anything else around here? Apart from killing. We'll have to have a discreet chat with her. Don't want poor Harrington to get wind of it. Anyway, let's see what this Fitzgerald woman has to say for herself."

CHAPTER 16

The café was within walking distance and Murphy had high expectations of a substantial snack.

"We won't be having anything to eat here, Murphy. This isn't a social call," said Morecamb, as if reading his mind.

Murphy couldn't see how one precluded the other and did his best not to sulk. The missing photos served to keep his irritation at bay.

The door pinged as they entered and a middle-aged woman smiled at their approach.

"Table for two, gentlemen?" she asked, gesturing towards a vacant behind the door.

The café was quite full and several pairs of eyes swivelled in their direction.

"We won't be sitting down, Mrs Fitzgerald," said Morecamb as he made the introductions. "That's right," Murphy chipped in. "We just want to ask you a few questions about Peter Kelly."

The other diners didn't even bother to feign interest in their food and several removed their napkins and sat back in their chairs.

"Well, if you bastards would like to come through to the back........" she hissed with flared nostrils and teeth bared. She reminded Morecamb of a picture he had once seen of the Bull-run.....in Pamplona, if memory served him, just as the bull clapped eyes on its next victim before goring him to death.

She stomped off ahead of them into a pokey room at the back of the kitchen and slammed the door once they were inside.

"Your reputation precedes you, I must say", she snapped.

"Speaking of reputations.........can you describe your relationship with Peter Kelly?" asked Morecamb.

"Ah! Moral guardians now, I see. Well......the sex was great. Quite the adventurous type really." She noticed Murphy starting to squirm. "I think I've dressed up in every uniform going.........Nurse, Doctor, school uniform, police uniform, handcuffs of course, pilot............."

"Fascinating, Mrs Fitzgerald. And I trust they were all stolen," More-camb interjected. " Now, back to the real world. Were you still seeing each other?"

"Certainly not. I had moved on. Plenty of fish and all that. And some a lot more eligible than Peter Kelly."

So he had dumped her then.

"Any idea where his recent amorous acrobatics might have been directed?"

"I don't keep tabs on my ex-lovers. Now, anything else? Some of us have work to do."

"What about your husband? If he was aware of your little dalliance with Kelly....."

"You mean, if he decided that he preferred women after all and gutted Peter in a fit of passionate rage?"

"Nevertheless.....perhaps he would hold a grudge........"

"I don't see why he should. After all I didn't kick up a stink when *he* came home one night, informed me that he had completely gone off me and was going to give the 'old homosexuality' a go. And, from now on, he wanted to be called 'Cecilia', not 'Cecil'.

"Right. I guess you have a point there. Anyway, I'll need to talk to him too. Where_____"

"Four doors up, number twelve. And, when you see him, tell him I want my green cocktail dress back." She led them back out through the café, brazen as ever, and announced to all and sundry that the Officers weren't arresting her after all as they were 'on a promise'.

Murphy was distraught. What if word got back to his wife? The fall-out would make Peter Kelly's death look like an accident. Morecamb ignored his twitterings and had just raised his hand to knock on Fitzgerald's door when it was suddenly opened by............

"Mr. Fitzgerald?" enquired Morecamb.

"Cecilia, please."

"Detective Inspector Morecamb and Sergeant Murphy."

"Okay. Well, do come in but remove your shoes first, please. You can leave them out there on the doorstep. Germs, you understand." Cecilia shuddered dramatically and nervously twirled the three strands of green baubles around his neck. As Morecamb followed the 'apparition' in the floral skirt – Murphy had insisted on staying outside to look after the shoes - the Inspector wondered why Cecil hadn't gone the whole hog and shaved off the beard.

It was a short visit.

Yes, of course he knew that his ex-wife was engaged in unnatural acts with the vet. Odious man. They had flaunted it, for goodness sake. Perhaps she wanted to make himself jealous but he was *very* happy with Mark, thank you very much. Yes, he had heard that Mr Kelly had 'grown tired of my silly wife' and moved on to pastures new. Those types always did. And what about Kelly's poor wife? Simply abandoned. Marriage vows meant nothing to people now. What was the world coming to?

"Well?" asked Murphy as Morecamb escaped.

"He's very worried about the state of the world," said Morecamb. "Thinks there are no morals anymore_____"

"Who?" queried Murphy.

"Fitzgerald. The man in the floral skirt and green necklace, with the beard."

"But......" spluttered Murphy.

"Precisely. Let's go back and join the others. I think we'll have lunch before we listen to the various reports. Can't do that on an empty stomach."

CHAPTER 17

Morecamb decided to lift the alcohol ban and they were all allowed a pint with their lunch. Morecamb had a whiskey. Murphy eyed the amber liquid but said nothing. At least it was a single.

"Any sign of Detective Sweeney today?" asked Morecamb between mouthfuls. "Or that secretary?"

"His wife rang earlier," Harrington volunteered. "Seemed nice. He's a little under the weather, she said, but would do his best to make it after lunch. She also said there was a strange woman lying on her good sofa in the parlour and wanted to know if anybody had reported her missing. So I told her she could be a stray and she should notify the Gardaí."

Morecamb ordered another whiskey and everyone else took advantage and ordered a second pint. But when Sweeney and 'the stray' put in an appearance shortly afterwards Morecamb threw back the rest of his whiskey and ordered the others to leave their pints and get back inside.

Harrington and McGrath were first up to deliver their report.

"Any further information?"

"Si," said Harrington. "Do you want it in English or Italian, sir?"

"McGrath, a quick summary, please," sighed Morecamb.

"Well, we didn't get much further really," McGrath answered. " She was more interested to hear about the poor man who had been slaughtered."

"Uomo....Italian for 'man'.............."

"Please, Harrington," begged Murphy. He was sure that Morecamb's last whiskey might have been a double.

"Will someone take the 'sage' outside, please? Continue, McGrath."

"Yes, well, she still insisted that it was a big car and the driver was alive. And the dead girl was alive as well. So, no progress really."

"Okay, well I want yourself and that waste of space outside go back to Mrs Kelly and get a photo of Peter Kelly. She wasn't in any fit state yesterday to get one. But she said her sister was coming to stay with her. And tell the sister......can't remember her name, tell her I'll call in the morning to have a chat with her." Morecamb tried to ignore the ringing phone in Sweeney's office.

"Right, McClean, you and Rooney. Did you speak to Mrs Lysaght?"

"Oh, yes, sir. She was most charming _____"

"Murphy, will you answer that damned phone? So what did she have to say?"

Well, coincidentally enough, herself and her husband have a holiday home in Antibes, where his own folks had a summer pad as well. Imagine that! And she told himself and Garda Rooney not to hesitate to call____

"The 'lovely garda Rooney' I believe were her exact words", grinned Rooney. " What can I say? My magnetic charm. Young, old, middle-aged _____"

But she had stated categorically that she most certainly didn't have any illicit liaison with the deceased, McClean continued and her very good friend, Superintendent Alderton, would vouch for her impeccable character. And McClean was inclined to believe her as he thought she spoke very well.

"It's Superintendent Alderton," roared Murphy, coming back into the day room, shaking all over. "Why does it always happen to me?"

"And?" asked Morecamb, starting to lose patience with Murphy's sense of victimhood.

"You're to ring him. It's urgent. Said he wouldn't waste his breath on me."

"Of course it's urgent," said Morecamb going off into the office. But before he reached the phone it started to ring. The bartender up the road would appreciate if someone could come and collect Detective Spillane and his girlfriend as they were starting to get rowdy.

Typical. Now, for Alderton.

Morecamb began by explaining the embarrassing scenario in the Hoor and Hounds and then asked Alderton to define 'urgent'.

"The Press briefing," snapped Alderton completely unapologetic about his brother-in-law's conduct. "You'd obviously forgotten. Even in my hour of pain I remembered. Dereliction of duty, Morecamb. Get yourself up here straight away. I want the rest of them with you. We need a full show of strength especially as you've made absolutely no progress to date."

And you want to deflect the blame, of course.

Morecamb went back to the day-room, ordered McGrath and Rooney to fetch the two drunks and drop them straight home. "The rest of us are needed back at base. Press briefing. Complete waste of time. But, there you go. Eight o' clock here in the morning, everybody."

*****

They arrived back in Union Quay at ten minutes to three to find Alderton, in full regalia, in a high state of agitation.

Hadn't he specifically told Morecamb that the briefing would be at three? Luckily, he had put it back half an hour, knowing the extraordinary level of disobedience and insubordination which was widespread in Morecamb and his so-called team. He wanted them all in his office in ten minutes, tidy, and not looking like a bunch of hippies.

Morecamb went over to Sergeant Moloney and asked why Alderton wasn't in hospital.

Oh, the ambulance had called alright but didn't consider the situation critical. There was a lot of shouting from Alderton behind the closed door. Could hear him threatening the crew with a law suit if they didn't lift him onto the stretcher straight away. But they held firm and said there wasn't a thing wrong with him and he was the healthiest looking person they had seen in a long time. Alderton had perked up no end after that bit of news and had been throwing his weight around the place ever since.

With a heavy heart Morecamb marshalled his men into Alderton's office, where, as usual he was pacing. He knew there was no point in asking but was there any progress?

"Well, we're interviewing a number of people who we feel could point us in the right direction."

"That's a 'no' then. So, we need to dress this thing up a bit for the rabble. Would it be safe to tell them that an arrest is imminent?"

"Christ, no!"

"Mind your language. So, can I say, 'potential suspects'?"

"You can't say that either. We're interviewing people tomorrow and if they read in tomorrow morning's paper that they are potential suspects they'll clam up and tell us nothing."

"Why don't you say, 'people of interest', sir?"

"And why don't you shut up, Murphy," Alderton snarled. "Right. So, you're absolutely no help, Morecamb. I'll just have to improvise."

They were all lined up on the step of the station, each jostling to stand as far back from Alderton as possible. Morecamb had no choice but to stand beside his commander-in-chief, who was decked out in a suspicious array of medals. Every so often the glare from the sun seemed to give the illusion that Alderton's entire chest was on fire. Murphy had been wearing sunglasses when they came out into the sunshine but Alderton had ordered him to take them off in case the reporters and the entire population suspected they were all just on holidays. And, judging by their obvious lack of progress it would be a reasonable assumption after all.

And thus began the improvisation, spectacular in its own way.

They had narrowed the field of suspects down to two. He wasn't at liberty to be more specific but he could divulge that a man and a woman were in custody.

No, they were not related to one another. Yes, Inspector Morecamb was confident that there were two culprits, two separate perpetrators and he's very confident that he'd have the case wrapped up by the weekend.

"Did the female suspect kill the girl and the male suspect do for the man?"

"I'll hand you over to Inspector Morecamb to answer that. Inspector?"

"No, I have no reason to believe any such thing," said Morecamb.

"So, do you think that the woman killed the man, Inspector?"

"No."

"But you're still confident of having the case solved by Monday?"

"No."

"That's all for now, people," Alderton cut in as perspiration started to leak from every pore. "Great progress, as I say, and an imminent arrest. Arrests, I mean. Several, in fact."

Alderton, who had to be helped back inside, immediately ordered Moloney to call a taxi for him and told Morecamb that he'd see him in the morning, in order to demote him.

Morecamb realised that he needed to vent his anger somehow so he decided to ring the pathologist and rattle his cage.

"Ah, Mr Pettigrew, Inspector Morecamb here. Could I have an update on the Post Mortem on_____"

"No, you can't and for your information, one of your lot – possibly even yourself – has lost one of the body bags and we seem to be missing the head. Insignificant, I know but I was wondering how his poor widow would be able to make an identification without it. And please, no vulgarity."

"Well, I wasn't going to because in this particular case we certainly need the head. Without it there would be a long procession of women whose recollections we would have to rely on and as you know yourself_____"

"There you go, Morecamb. Couldn't resist, could you? Post Mortem at ten sharp on Monday. Try to be on time."

Well, all things considered, Morecamb didn't feel any great release of his pent-up rage.

"Right, men," he called coming back into the Incident room, "anyone fancy a pint?"

CHAPTER 18

Saturday May 10th

There was no sign of Alderton the following morning so it was with a relative sense of calm that they reached Kinsale.

The sight of Sweeney was a little unsettling but when he informed them that he would be in his office should they need him, 'only for an emergency of course', there was a collective sigh of relief.

"Bit unusual to see the Detective at this hour of the morning," said Murphy.

"His wife dropped him off," Rooney explained. "Don't think the car was even fully stopped when he got out."

"Okay, gather round, everyone. A small bit of housekeeping first, so to speak. It has come to my attention that a significant part of Peter Kelly has gone missing, namely the head. Anyone got any ideas?"

Harrington's hand shot up but Morecamb ignored him.

"How could it go missing?" asked McGrath. "Everything was bagged up and put into the Mortuary van........could somebody have stolen it?"

"Why, in God's name?" asked Murphy.

"Actually," McClean interrupted, "I seem to recall Detective Sweeney's secretary putting a black bag in the boot of her car before she drove herself and Sweeney away from the crime scene."

"Good man, I'll just pop in and ask the detective if he knows anything about it."

But there was no sign of Sweeney when he popped his head into the office, just the side door swinging to and fro.

Morecamb spent the next hour going back over all the information on the two deaths that they had garnered so far, omitting Mrs Harrington's possible involvement with the deceased and finishing with Alderton's promise that the case would be solved by Monday.

"McClean, I want you and Rooney to call on Bridie Sugrue. See if she had any involvement with Kelly. Probably just a malicious rumour but we need to cover all bases. It also occurred to me last night that we haven't actually spoken to Egleston's wife at all and it's possible that he may have mentioned something to her during one of his more lucid moments. So, McGrath, take Harrington with you and pay a visit to Mrs Egleston. And, for God's sake try not to antagonise her. Murphy, you and I are going to visit Mrs Kelly."

Murphy had discovered a new fear overnight. What if his wife ever got to hear about all the strange women that they were meeting and interviewing and got the wrong impression? His hand shook as he switched on the ignition.

"Your wife has ears and eyes everywhere, Murphy, doesn't she? For a woman who doesn't venture outside unless chauffeured by you it would be something of a miracle if she heard any snippet of what's going on in the outside world. She makes Mrs Kelly look like a social butterfly."

Morecamb had no time for Mrs Murphy. A complete nuisance. She was always ringing the station, ordering her husband home. She was constantly unwell and always needed 'urgent medical intervention'.

*****

As they drew up outside the house Morecamb turned to Murphy. "I still can't remember the sister's name. Can you?"

"Not a clue, boss."

As they got out of the car the front door opened and a woman stood there looking at them quizzically. Thank God the yard seemed to be cleaned up, thought Morecamb, as they approached her.

"Inspector Morecamb, isn't it? Poor Daphne said you'd be calling. I'm Rosie, her sister. Come in."

Morecamb expected to be led into the parlour but instead they were shown into a bright, airy kitchen with a fantastic view across the fields to a range of mountains in the distance. Mrs Kelly was sitting at the table tucking into a big fry and seemed to be in great form. Her hair was neatly groomed, bright red lipstick covered her thin lips and most of her teeth, an expensive looking black dress and a sparkling necklace adorned a rather plunging neckline. The glazed eyes struck the only bum note.

"So good of you to join us," she giggled. "Would you like a sausage? Rosie, perhaps these gentlemen ____"

"No, no, Mrs Kelly, we're fine," said Morecamb.

"A cup of tea, perhaps?" offered Rosie. She was younger than her sister and more worldly, Morecamb imagined.

"Yes, that would be lovely, thank you. May we?" the Inspector asked, gesturing towards the chairs.

"Of course," said Rosie as she went to fetch two more cups.

"Isn't this cosy?" said Mrs Kelly. "I can't remember the last time I entertained."

"Poor Daphne is still a little out of sorts," explained her sister.

Drugged to the eyeballs, you mean, thought Morecamb.

"Understandable," said Morecamb. "Actually, I wanted to speak to you as well. Perhaps in another room?"

"Oh, there's no need, Inspector. Daphne and I don't have any secrets. Isn't that right, Sis?"

"Or perhaps some black pudding?" asked Daphne.

"So, you can ask whatever you like. You're probably wondering about my relationship with Peter. Oh, don't worry," she said as she saw their startled look. "I know how tongues wag." Well, it started shortly after her own husband, Arthur, had been badly injured in a traffic accident, she recounted. The intimate part of their life had come to an abrupt end, sadly, so he told her she could get on with it. Which she translated as......

well......anyway, she knew how poor Daphne struggled with that side of things so they came to an arrangement. Daphne would sit and look after poor Arthur and Rosie looked after Peter.

It was all very civilised and she felt if there was more generosity of spirit and civility among people the world would be a far better place. Only good could come from such acts of kindness.

Morecamb decided not to mention the recent mess out in the yard.

As Rosie showed them out Morecamb asked if her sister's medication had been prescribed by a reputable doctor. He didn't like the fact that Daphne seemed to be having a full-blown conversation with her breakfast as they were leaving.

"Of course," came the spirited reply. "You hardly think I rifled through Peter's bag and simply snatched a few horse tranquillisers."

Morecamb hadn't even thought of that but now he wondered.

"Do you think it's all the fish they eat, boss?" asked Murphy as he turned the key in the ignition. "What other reason could there be for all the shenanigans?"

"Could be," responded Morecamb. "It's obvious that you and I are missing something from our diet. Let's go and call on Mary O'Donovan's parents. They'll feel we're ignoring their situation. And whatever about Peter Kelly, Mary O'Donovan was an entirely innocent victim. And Alderton barely mentioned her yesterday at the Press conference. Here we are. God, they live quite close to Kelly's. Didn't realise they were that near."

"Well, remember, Mary's mother cleans for Mrs Kelly, boss. Not too far to travel. And she doesn't drive."

Tom was in the yard mending a broken gate when they pulled in. He put down the hammer and walked slowly towards them. God, the man seemed to have aged ten years since they last spoke to him.

"Morning Tom," said Morecamb, extending his hand. "You're busy."

"Always busy on a farm," he answered. "Do you want to come inside?" he asked, heading towards the door.

"Thanks. We won't keep you long. How are you bearing up?"

"Ah, middling. Nights are the worst. Hard to sleep. At least during the day I stay busy. Herself will make some tea."

Moll was standing at the range, busy with a large pot, when she became aware of them.

"Oh, we weren't expecting you," she said. Morecamb thought he detected a note of anger in her voice.

"Will I make them a cup of tea, Moll?" asked her husband as he went over to the sink.

"No. I can make it."

There was an awkward silence and after a few moments Morecamb cleared his throat.

"I just want you to know that we're doing everything we can to find Mary's killer. We've interviewed several people and I'm hopeful of a breakthrough before long. Somebody will have noticed something. Sometimes they don't realise the significance of something they may have seen until....... well..... until they're questioned again."

God, he must sound like Alderton, clutching at straws and talking just for the sake of it.

"Of course there's Peter Kelly now too, isn't there?" said Tom. "Plenty of Garda cars and that going up and down the road yesterday. I thought maybe they might stop here, just.....you know....to update us and that." There was no obvious hint of accusation in his voice but Morecamb felt it all the same.

"Yes, there was a lot of activity," Morecamb agreed. "It's always like that when the initial discovery is made. But I want you to know_____"

Moll pushed three cups of tea into the middle of the table and resumed her stance at the stove.

"Thanks, Mrs O' Donovan, Yes, I want you both to know that all our resources will be spread evenly between the two cases."

"It's just I didn't see that many Gardaí or cars where our Mary was left," continued Tom. "Just a single strip of that red and white Garda tape. All torn now, too. I wanted to put some flowers there but Sergeant McGrath said I couldn't because it's a crime scene."

"Tom, of course you can put some flowers there," said Morecamb, reaching across and squeezing his arm.

"We have them on her grave, Tom," said Moll, fairly sharpish. "Why would we put them where she was killed?"

Tom said nothing, just stared into his cup.

"We'll see ourselves out, Tom and thanks for the tea, Moll."

Neither seemed to be aware of their departure, Tom hunched over and Moll clattering away at the pot on the stove.

They drove back to the station in silence.

CHAPTER 19

There was a slew of newspapers scattered across the table in the day-room to greet them when they got back.

"You're everywhere," said Harrington gleefully. "Look." And he thrust the 'Cork Examiner' in Morecamb's face.

'**GARDAI STILL STRUGGLING!**' screamed the headline.

"And look at this one," as he reached across for the 'News and Star'.

'**MANIAC AT LARGE!**' and underneath a very large photograph of Morecamb.

He might consider suing.

"And then there's this one." Harrington was almost giddy at this stage. There was a scantily-clad model on the left-hand column of 'The Mirror', right next to their banner headline, '**DOUBLE MURDER PARALYSES KINSALE.**' This time there was a picture of Alderton.

Good.

He noticed that 'The Irish Times' had shown a little restraint. '**PIC-TURESQUE TOWN TERRORISED**' and another picture of himself, scowling.

"Where did they get these bloody photos?" asked Morecamb.

"Oh, and sir, Superintendent Alderton has been on the phone several times," Harrington piped up. "You're to ring him immediately. Oh, that will be him now," he gushed as the phone started to ring again. "Will I get it_____"

"Leave it. I've better things to be doing."

Meanwhile, 'The Echo' had shown no restraint whatsoever with their headline; '**MYSTERY OF THE MISSING HEAD!**' and yet another photo of Morecamb.

"Where the hell did they get that information?"

"I think that's a little misleading, sir. See, when you read that headline and then see your photog__"

"You don't say, Harrington."

Morecamb noticed that none of the others was inclined to get involved in the discussion of the newspapers. In fact there was no sign at all of Rooney and when he enquired on his whereabouts he was informed that he had taken it upon himself to call on Teresa about the missing black bag.

"Oh, that'll be him again," said Harrington as the phone began to ring. "I really think we should answer_____"

"Let it ring out, Harrington, and then go in and take it off the hook. Now, folks, on to the more mundane things in life. Right, McClean, you and Rooney went to see Bridie Sugrue. How did that go?"

Well, that hadn't gone very well at all. She summoned her husband when she realised the direction in which the questioning was going. When he was, hysterically, brought up to speed he fetched his shotgun. McClean felt obliged to ask him for his gun licence whereupon he fired a volley of shots over their head and they left rather hurriedly. And, actually, Garda Rooney made a very good point on their departure. If the natives are armed shouldn't the Garda force have firepower as well. It was really only a matter of time....

"Right, get on that phone, McClean and tell Mr. Sugrue to make himself available here at the station on Monday. Say, twelve o' clock. This place is turning into the Wild West."

Harrington announced that it had never been like this before but his voice petered out when he saw Morecamb's face and he hurriedly sat down.

"Sergeant McGrath, how did you get_____"

"And me," said the incorrigible Harrington.

"....get on with Mrs Egleston?"

"Do you want to answer this, Garda Harrington?" asked McGrath.

Morecamb whirled around so fast that his neck almost snapped. "Sergeant McGrath, why would you even think that this crazed whelp here would have anything remotely relevant to say?"

"Anyway, I waited in the car, sir," said Harrington. "Sergeant McGrath said he wasn't going to bother going in because_____"

"I *did* go in," snarled McGrath, "but there was nobody there. I looked in all the downstairs rooms and called out but got no answer."

"How did you get into the house if there was nobody there? Did you break in? "asked Morecamb incredulously.

"Of course not," McGrath retorted. "The door was open."

"How do you mean, 'open'?"

"Well, unlocked."

"Nobody locks their doors around here, sir," Harrington explained. "Why would they? There's never any trouble_____"

"Found it," shouted Rooney, as he crashed through the door, waving a black bag in the air. There was a mad scramble to move back as he plonked it in the middle of the table. "One missing head!"

"A brief explanation, please," said Morecamb, "and get it off the table."

Well, he had called to Inspector Sweeney first, who's at home, not feeling great and he knew nothing about it. Actually he seemed surprised that Peter Kelly was dead. He thought he was in Intensive Care. So then he had called to his secretary's house. She remembered putting the black bag into her car but said that it only had Inspector Sweeney's wellingtons in it. He always carries a pair with him if he's going to a farm or anywhere mucky. Anyway, Rooney persuaded her, 'the old charm working again, sir', to show him and when she opened the bag and saw what was in it she fainted and hit her head a mighty crack off the boot of the car. So Rooney 'kindly' waited for the ambulance to come and, now, here he was.

"So, where are the wellingtons then?" asked Murphy while Morecamb struggled to steady his pulse.

"I believe the Pathologist would be in possession of those," laughed Rooney.

"Put that bag in the boot of our car, Rooney," ordered Morecamb, "and McGrath, go into the office and tell Superintendent Alderton that we're on our way back to Cork. C'mon lads, time to face the music."

CHAPTER 20

Alderton was sucking on an inhaler when Morecamb marched into his office, black bag in hand. He had decided on the way back from Kinsale that 'attack' was the best strategy and, with that in mind, he put the bag on Alderton's desk and waited for him to get his airways cleared. Looking down he spotted a pair of wellingtons on the floor by the desk.

When he judged the moment to be opportune he pointed to the bag and informed his boss that Kelly's head was now staring at him. Alderton snatched up the inhaler again, pointed to the bag and the door and was just turning an unusual colour as Morecamb took the exhibit and made his exit.

"We'll need some space in this fridge, lads," he said as he entered the canteen. "I won't be able to surprise Pettigrew with this until Monday."

"How did the Super re-act, boss?" asked Murphy.

"He didn't say much, Sergeant. Actually, he said nothing at all."

*****

"You're home early, Jim," said his aunt, as she wrestled with some lamb chops on the pan. "But it's nearly ready anyway."

"No worries," said Morecamb, "I'm not that hungry actually. And I'm not staying. I'm heading back down to Kinsale. I'll just have a quick bite to eat and then I'll grab some clothes and be off. And, will you do me a favour, Dot? Look after Willow and I'll collect her tomorrow evening."

Morecamb had decided on this course of action all of a sudden, as he pulled up outside his house. He tried to convince himself that it was work-related but, truthfully, he just wanted to get away for a few hours.

In spite of the horrors of the past few days there was still something magical about Kinsale and he suddenly wanted to see it through a tourist's eyes. He would also take a trip out to Garretstown. He had a sudden urge to walk barefoot on the beach. Maybe even pitch a tent and sleep under the stars. No, scratch that last bit. He was going to roll up at Acton's hotel, order lobster for his dinner and quaff their best wine. For the first time in ages he felt a flutter of excitement.

Hurriedly he packed, gave Dot a quick peck on the cheek and she was still complaining as he closed his front door behind him.

The journey to Kinsale was slow and leisurely. And bloody wonderful. Morecamb avoided the usual route and decided to stay as close as possible to the coastline. Passage West was his first pit-stop and he had a frothy pint in one of the many pubs. It was quite magical and Morecamb marvelled at the quality of light which seemed to be a feature of all coastline regions. He missed that in the city. All around gaily-coloured National flags fluttered in the whispering breeze and tired children and their exhausted parents emerged on the horizon, covered in sand and scowling.

American tourists seemed to disembark from buses every five minutes and Morecamb suddenly understood the plethora of flags of every nationality. The Star-spangled banner seemed to have prominence while the tri-colour would have benefited from a spell with the local seamstress. The noise levels inevitably increased in volume when one bus-load of Americans spotted their compatriots roll off one of the other buses. They hadn't seen one another since they had left Cork city, '*Imagine!*' and now it was marvellous to meet again and, '*Honey, you look so good and isn't this such a darling little town.*'

Morecamb finished his drink and left.

On through Monkstown and Ringaskiddy before a quick stop in Crosshaven and another pint. The light was beginning to fade as he sat on the wall by the quayside and listened to the local fishermen discuss their day's haul and the sagging fortunes of their local football team and who needed to be sacked. There were several options apparently and

Morecamb sat back and soaked in the atmosphere. He raised his glass to some of these men and they waved back, tipping an imaginary glass to their lips and calling, 'Slainte'. He was tempted to spend the night here but decided he would stick to his original plan and head for Kinsale.

When he entered the foyer of Acton's hotel with his battered suitcase he was glad that he had stuck to his original plan. He could feel his feet sinking into the plush pile carpet and had a sudden desire to lie down on it and stretch out.

"Good evening, sir. Can I help you?"

Oh, joy! Imagine someone asking *him* if he needed help. Morecamb suddenly remembered that he had never cancelled his previous booking so he signed the register as Sergeant Murphy and then took the lift to the second floor.

His room was palatial but it was the view across the harbour which took his breath away. Heretofore he had only seen it from ground level but from up here it was a whole new experience. Fingers of fire danced in the bay as the sun was packing up for the day and gracefully moving aside for the moon to take the stage. Some fishing boats puttered away from the quay and set sail for the open waters. All leisurely and unhurried.

Reluctantly Morecamb turned away from the window, had a quick shower and a change of clothes and went down to the dining room. Waiters hurried to his side and before long his lobster had arrived accompanied by the requisite bottle of wine.

He was on his second bottle of wine when his waiter finally managed to persuade him to *please* re-locate to the residents' lounge. But it was all terribly good-natured, Morecamb mused, though the stool at the bar where he was deposited seemed rather shaky. And a tad too high. Oops! Nearly fell there.

"Would sir like a drink?" asked the bar attendant.

"I rather think 'sir' has had enough, don't you?" said a voice to his left.

Morecamb almost sobered up at the audacity of this interloper and truculently told the barman he'd have a double brandy. Then he turned to

158

the 'voice' and almost sobered up for the second time in as many minutes. She was really quite beautiful apart from the scowl and Morecamb made a gallant effort to pronounce his own name without slurring.

"Jane Power," she replied as she hesitantly shook his proffered hand.

"Your brandy, sir," said the barman.

"Jane, would ....you know.... a drink? We could sit over there .... more comfortable."

"Why not? I'll have a mineral, please. Make that two, Stephen," she added, addressing the barman "and bring them over here. 'Sir' might cop himself on and realise that he's had a skinful and show some concern for his liver."

Morecamb snatched up his double brandy and tottered over behind Jane, steadied a little by Stephen who had suddenly appeared at his elbow.

Over the course of the evening Morecamb decided to lay bare his soul.

"*Did she know Alderton by any chance? Well............* "

"*What about Pettigrew?*"*............* "*Yes, She had heard of him.*"

"*Well, did she know this about the bastard................?*"

"*Now, Murphy isn't bad and aunt Dot is the best in the world but..........* "

By the time he had got to the saga of his ex-wife tears were streaming down his face so the janitor, the night porter and two bar staff, on Jane's instructions, hauled him up to his room and threw him onto his bed.

*****

Back in Cork sleep had completely eluded Alderton.

Earlier, as he had made his erratic journey home - fairly certain that he wasn't fit to drive - he wrestled to keep his car on the road, his thoughts from spiralling out of control.....or was that the car?....... and struggled to banish the image of a pair of wellingtons with a head sticking out of them. Some- where, in the midst of the fog, he knew that he had overdosed on the inhaler.

His wife had come to the same conclusion as she had watched him pace the floor and, rather hysterically, tell her about the wellingtons with a man's head. He was vaguely aware of her ringing the doctor and getting more strident with every utterance. 'I hope she isn't talking about me,' he muttered as he struggled to locate his pills. Ah, got them! He tilted his head and threw a few back, helped on their way with a glass of whiskey.

The bloody woman was making no sense at all now. She had definitely got worse since coming off the phone. But he was just too tired to figure it out. He decided to go to bed.

But, after an arduous journey up the stairs, he found his bedroom door locked. Well, the spare bedroom was around here somewhere. He didn't think he'd bother getting undressed. He needed to be up early in the morning and try to sort out this Mr Wellington business.

CHAPTER 21

Sunday 11ᵗʰ May

As Morecamb entered the dining room the following morning he immediately spotted Jane sitting at the far side of the room.

Perhaps he owed her an apology. He wasn't sure really as somewhere in the recesses of his memory he felt he had been quite entertaining the previous evening. Light-hearted even?

"Mind if I join you?" he asked as he reached for a chair.

She looked up, somewhat startled, and then arched an eyebrow.

"Well…..let me see," she pondered. "If you promise not to cry, demand a double brandy to help you to sober up, promise not to mention your dog or your ex-wife and generally promise not to bore me to distraction…….yes, you may sit."

"Ouch! That bad, was it?"

"And then some! And, by the way, there seems to be some confusion about your name. The staff seem to think you're a Sergeant Murphy but I could swear, in the midst of all the nonsense last night, you told me that your name is Morecamb."

"Yes, about that….." And he went on to explain his dilemma about checking in.

"So you're obviously involved in these local murder investigations. A working weekend, is it?" Both eyebrows were raised this time.

Right. This wasn't very conducive to digestion at all, especially on a delicate stomach.

"On-going investigation, Jane," he answered rather brusquely as he speared a sausage. "Can't discuss it."

"And Professor Pettigrew?" she asked, ignoring the clatter of the knife and fork hitting his plate.

"Who?"

"Professor Pettigrew. You mentioned him at length last night. He used to lecture me."

"He lectures everybody," said Morecamb dismissively. "But most people ignore him. What was your crime?"

"I studied under him in U.C.C."

Morecamb was lost for words.

"So, yes, before you ask, I'm a Pathologist as well."

Morecamb moved his half-eaten breakfast to one side and focussed on his coffee.

"Yes. Qualified a few years ago. And do you want to hear something funny?"

"Yes, please," croaked Morecamb.

"Well, your Mr Pettigrew is going on sabbatical." She paused, watching her companion's reaction as he reached to retrieve his breakfast.

"The States. So, there's going to be a vacancy and I've applied. I've an interview in the morning."

Morecamb could feel tears beginning to gather at the back of his eyes.

"Thank you, Jesus!" he roared, jumping up from his chair with his arms outstretched, much to the consternation of the other diners. The waiters quickly went into a huddle but relaxed a little when he resumed his seat. When he looked at Jane she was trying to sniffle her giggles.

"Please tell me you weren't joking," said Morecamb.

"Nope. Deadly serious."

Morecamb almost felt emotional. Imagine no longer having to confront the peevish and snarling countenance of Pettigrew. Now, if Jane was successful, it would almost be a pleasure to enter the pathology department. Hell, he might even go out looking for bodies. He had a sudden image of strutting into the lab with a dead Alderton slung over his shoulder. Very dead.

"So, if you could put in a good word for me with the great man?" laughed Jane, interrupting Morecamb's hastily configured vision of heaven.

*****

They spent the most amazing day together. Far from the sober and judgemental impression he had gleaned the night before, Jane was full of fun and teased him unmercifully and insisted that his ex-wife's name was Willow and, according to Morecamb, she still wasn't house-trained.

The morning was spent walking barefoot on the strand at Garretsown, paddling and skipping over the incoming ripples. All around the hills seemed to breathe in the tranquillity, holding the foliage in abeyance as they watched two child-like adults revisiting simpler times, where ghastly investigations and dead bodies had no place.

Lunch was a picnic on the Old Head of Kinsale under the shadow of the Old Lighthouse from the 17th century. The views were breath-taking and Jane, a native of Bandon, was a knowledgeable guide. She pointed across the Azure sea, approximating the area where the Lusitania had sunk.

Afterwards they shimmied down a shingle slope and once again found themselves on a beach. But as the place began to echo with the sounds of excited children and distraught parents they decided to move on.

The afternoon went past in an instant – Courtmacsherry, Butlerstown, Timoleague – and by the time they reached Clonakilty it was time to call it a day. It was dusk when they arrived back at the hotel in Kinsale but decided they would dine together before going their separate ways. Each was reluctant to return to the real world and each was eager to do this again. But neither seemed to know how to articulate that desire to commit.

Outside, before they went to their respective car Morecamb kissed her lightly on the cheek and wished her luck in her interview.

"Any advice you want to share in advance?" she laughed.

"Plenty, but nothing that would help," responded Morecamb. "Oh, let me know how it goes. You know where I am."

It was the closest he could come to telling her that he wanted to see her again. Was it enough, he wondered.

The euphoria stayed with him all the way back to Cork and, as he lay in bed later that night, he suddenly remembered that he hadn't collected Willow. Or was it Fiona! He chuckled at the memory before drifting off into a deep sleep.

CHAPTER 22

Monday May 12ᵗʰ

In spite of the rather hysterical note which Dot had left for him on the kitchen table Morecamb arrived at the station bright and early, and put aside Dot's dire warning that Willow was, in all probability, pregnant. Notwithstanding all that he was determined to make progress on the murders today. But first there was a summons to Alderton's office.

He looked dreadful.

"I'm not a well man," he began. "No, don't sit down. I spent yesterday in St. Finbarr's hospital, where they regard me as a medical phenomenon. The Consultant, a good friend of mine, was amazed that, not alone was I still standing but, also, that I could still perform in such a high-powered job with such distinction. Actually, I saw my friend, Mr Pettigrew being admitted as well. But, the long and the short of it," he added quickly as he saw Morecamb getting ready to bolt, "is that I'm to avoid any kind of stress. I explained about you and he was full of sympathy. Nevertheless, he took away all my medication and told me I need to be less hands-on. So, I want the case solved by this evening. No phone calls or any communication during the day and just leave a note with the desk sergeant saying, 'Yes, it's solved' or, 'No, I resign.' And he can pass it on to me."

Morecamb did a military salute and banged the door on his way out.

When he told his team they were full of sympathy. Why should Morecamb be the one to resign? Could it be a full-blown breakdown, boss? And had he asked Alderton about the mysterious appearance of the wellingtons?

But the only thing that Morecamb took away from the monologue was that Pettigrew, the Pathologist, was admitted to the hospital and they could now safely deposit Kelly's head without any hassle. It also meant that Jane wouldn't have to endure the monster as, presumably, they would simply wheel in a replacement for Pettigrew on the interview panel.

When they reached the pathology lab Morecamb ordered McClean to drop off the head at the reception desk and say that the Superintendent had sent it over, for Pettigrew.

But, of course, nothing was ever that simple. Didn't McClean know the receptionist and they had a friendly chat, recalling old times, until the smell from the bag started to permeate the entire reception area and McClean spotted Pettigrew advancing, his handkerchief clamped to his nose.

"That was close, Inspector," gasped McClean as he threw himself into the back seat. "In fact I think he may have followed me."

And, sure enough, when Morecamb glanced in the rear view mirror, he saw Pettigrew taking down the registration number of the car. Morecamb swore under his breath. Did that clown Alderton get anything right?

Down in Kinsale Morecamb was informed that there was a message from Alderton to ring him immediately.

So much for the communication black-out.

When Alderton eventually answered Morecamb could hear Country and Western music belting out in the background. Jim Reeves singing, 'He'll have to go', if he wasn't mistaken.

"In view of our earlier conversation this morning," began Morecamb, "I wasn't sure if I should ring you_____"

"No, you shouldn't. Mr Pettigrew said you're to attend the Post Mortem of that Kelly man this afternoon."

"Well, I'll hardly have time………." But his voice was drowned out by Jim Reeves as Alderton obviously increased the volume several octaves.

Back out in the day-room there was a new visitor.

"This is Mr Sugrue, sir," said McGrath before retreating into the toilets.

"Oh, yes," Morecamb suddenly remembered. "Come on through. McClean, will you join us?"

"I know I should apologise to you, Garda McClean, for my behaviour the other day," began Sugrue. " Rest assured I had no intention of shooting you."

"Yes, well, it was a rather drastic reaction, I must say," said Morecamb.

"Damned unorthodox," added McClean.

"See," continued Sugrue, "things are a bit tense on the home front. Trevor has decided to leave school. Has left, in fact."

"He's a bit young to take up farming, isn't he?" Morecamb said.

"A bit stupid, more like. I want him to go into the army. Straighten him out. But herself has her heart set now on him joining the priesthood. So, there's a bit of a stand-off at the moment."

A priest? Morecamb was glad that he wasn't religious.

"Right. Well, do you know why my officers called the other day?"

"Oh, yes. Can't see it myself, to be honest. Kelly involved with my wife? Naw. In fairness her whole life revolves around the children, trying to make something of them. Not easy. See, she was very poor herself growing up. Left school after Primary Cert so she is hell-bent on them getting an education and being a success. Not easy at all. I know she has airs and graces but she's a good wife. Can't see her having any truck with the likes of Kelly."

"Did you yourself have any dealings with him? Was he your vet?"

"No, I use a different vet. I don't mind saying that I didn't like Kelly. Smarmy git. And he seemed to pluck figures out of the air when he presented you with his bill."

"I have a vet like that too," said Morecamb morosely. "So you've no idea who might want to kill him?"

"Oh, take your pick. Could be a jealous husband. Bloody fellow used to boast about his conquests, I heard. Anything new on poor Tom's daughter, Inspector? Can't help feeling dreadfully sorry for him. And Moll, of course."

"No, nothing, but I'm using everything in my power to get a result as fast as I can. Tom and Moll deserve nothing less."

"He was mad about her, you know. From the day she was born. Proudest man in Kinsale."

There were unshed tears in Sugrue's eyes.

McClean escorted him out while Morecamb went to talk to the rest of the team. They were all there, even Spillane, who was all spruced up and even came go stand beside Morecamb as he addressed the troops.

"Allow me," he interrupted as Morecamb started to speak. "I want to apologise for my recent behaviour. Unforgiveable, especially as a young girl was killed on my patch. The only excuse I can offer is that Teresa was a very bad influence on me and you'll be relieved to hear that I have now sacked her. I went to see her yesterday in the hospital and told her. At least I think it was her............her head was covered in bandages. Anyway, her actions viz-a-viz Mr Kelly's remains and my good pair of wellingtons....well, as I say, very unprofessional. So that will not be happening again. Over you you, Inspector."

Morecamb wanted to slap him.

"All very commendable, Detective. Now, first off_____"

"Sorry. One other thing. By sheer coincidence the Commissioner is dropping by today so I'll take him up to the Trident Hotel for dinner and keep him out of your way. Now, carry on, Inspector."

"Actually, I need to speak to the Commissioner as well so let me know when he arrives. Sergeant McGrath, I'll leave that in your hands. So don't bring him anywhere, Detective Sweeney, until I've spoken to him first."

That shut him up and he went over and sat on a chair in the corner and sulked.

"Now, I've just talked with Mr Sugrue and I think I can safely say that he's off the suspect list. As is his wife."

Rooney never believed that a woman could have mutilated a man in such a fashion. From his own vast experience of women.....

"Shut up, Rooney. And, remember, we're also looking into the murder of Mary O'Donovan. In fact I believe we should prioritise that. It's just not good enough......Oh, my good God! It's that Flynn woman with the lovely Leila!" exclaimed Morecamb as he spotted them through the window, getting out of the car.

Murphy made a bee-line for the gents while Rooney straightened his tie and slicked back his hair.

"More trouble," muttered Morecamb, "and wasting my time."

"I need to speak to you, Inspector," Mrs Flynn began before she had even closed the door. "Is there somewhere more private?"

Morecamb ushered them into Sweeney's office, with Rooney hot on their heels.

Why not, thought Morecamb. Let's see him work his charm on this pair.

Leila sat down and brought her scowl to bear on the wall behind Rooney's head.

"Shouldn't you be taking notes or something, Garda, instead of leering at my daughter?"

"Oh, Mum, please, don't be disgusting," snapped Leila. "He's ancient."

"Well, in a way, that pertains to our visit, Inspector Morecamb. Tell him, Leila."

"There's nothing to tell really_____"

"Leila!"

"Okay, okay, it's just that Mary did tell me that she was seeing a mature man. She was in love with him."

"God's sake," muttered her mother.

"And he was in love with her," continued Leila, glaring at her mother. "And he was going to leave his wife to be with her. So there, Mother!"

"Leila, did she ever give any hint at all who the man was?" asked Morecamb, desperately trying to keep the interview on track.

"No."

"You sure? Anything at all?"

"I said, 'no'."

"And, how long ago was this?"

"Maybe a month ago."

"And where used she meet him? I mean, he hardly collected her at her home."

"Well, *hardly.*"

God, she's tough going, thought Morecamb.

"Leila, compose yourself, please," snapped 'Mother'. "Did she meet him after school, at weekends, when?"

"After school."

"There, Inspector. You just have to ask the right questions."

"And where did they arrange to meet?" pursued Morecamb. "Did he just pick her up along the road on her way home?"

"No. Sometimes she met him outside the chipper."

"The 'what', Leila?" asked Mrs Flynn.

"Lorenza's, Mother." A big sigh. "It's a fish and chip takeaway at the top of Mary Street."

"Never heard of it. I hope *you* don't frequent establishments like that?"

"No, Mother, I stay outside. Just looking in and wishing that I had normal parents who wouldn't swoon if I stepped inside. Look," turning to Morecamb and he wished she didn't, "I know he picked her up there. Once or twice I waited with her but she made me leave before he actually got there. I think she was afraid that if he saw me he might fancy me instead and dump Mary. I mean, I look quite mature for my age and I'm much better endowed, shall we say, than poor Mary."

"I'll say," exclaimed Rooney. "In fact_____"

"Shut up, Rooney. Leila, did you ever even catch a glimpse_____"

"Excuse me, Inspector," snapped Mrs Flynn, as she bestowed her daughter with a murderous glare. "Are you seriously telling me that you would consort with a married man? And, very possibly, a murderer?"

"Who says he's a murderer?" Leila snapped back.

"Well, Mary is dead, isn't she?" screeched Mrs Flynn.

"Yes, but he loved her," shouted Leila. "So why would he kill her?"

"Because......maybe he got tired of her and wanted to try someone new?"

"Well, Dad is tired of you and he doesn't kill you."

Jesus, this is awful.

Outside in the day room Murphy blessed himself. He reckoned the whole thing could be heard in the pub next door.

Meanwhile, inside, Rooney asked to be excused but was denied.

"Will the pair of you just shut up," said Morecamb, bringing his fist down on the table. "We've more important things to discuss than your little disagreements."

"They're *not* 'little,'" sobbed Leila. "She hates me. All mothers are the same. Trevor's mom hates him, Mary's mother hated her, Tanya's mother___ "

"Stop it, Leila," chided Mother. "You're hysterical. That's very unlady-like. What in God's name are those nuns ____?"

"And they hate me as well," gulped Leila. "And ye are all just jealous of us because we're younger and better looking and____ "

"Is there anything else, Inspector?" interrupted Mrs Flynn, as she calmly gathered up her handbag.

"No," said Morecamb, "I think that's everything for now though I may need to_____ "

"Come along, Leila, let's go and see what this chipper is like. Lorenzo's, isn't it?"

Morecamb felt he had done ten rounds with Cassius Clay. Groaning, he rested his head in his hands as he heard the door close behind him. Rooney also seemed a bit traumatised, speechless for once and wondering, if he moved, would he make it to the gents on time.

"Everything okay there, boss?" asked Murphy as he tiptoed into the room.

"Are they gone?" asked Morecamb, slowly lifting his head.

"Yes, boss. Was it awful?"

"Pretty much," he answered, levering himself out of the chair and heading towards the day room. "Let's just go and have some lunch and then I want everyone together in order to go over what I just heard."

"Oh, we heard everything, boss. But, if you want to get things off your chest____"

"What *are* you talking about, Murphy?" Morecamb snapped. "Let's just go and get a bite to eat."

Was it only yesterday that he had been feeling like a teenager, looking at the world through a new lens, completely oblivious to the outside world and the horrors waiting around every corner. God, he could cry.

*****

Everybody silently accepted what was put in front of them. Rabbit stew wasn't high on their list of favourites but who was going to object? And a big jug of diluted orange juice between all of them was the pits altogether. And each man paying for his own plate of mess was the final straw. But, who was going to complain?

Following lunch and back in the barracks once more Morecamb re-layed the meeting with the Flynn's. They already knew the details but nobody pointed that out. Morecamb was on a rant but everybody felt it was better to let him off. Therapy. It was only when the talk segued into Willow's possible predicament and the spittle started flying that Murphy decided it was time to intervene.

"Boss? Boss, please. What has Willow got to do with anything?"

"Sorry. You're right. That's another story. Let me count to twenty. That always helps. Done. So, where was I?" All said without breaking breath. "Now, in spite of all the extraneous stuff that we heard there were one or two snippets which are worthy of consideration. Actually, just the one. Mary O'Donovan was seeing a married man_____"

"Did he kill her, sir?" Harrington was on the edge of his seat.

"That's what we have to figure out, Garda," answered Morecamb.

172

"So, who killed *him*, then?" Harrington was on his feet now. "I reckon it was Trevor Sugrue. He was going out with Mary, got jealous when she dumped him and then, grabbed the billhook in the middle of the night and_____"

"Make him sit down, Murphy. Right, let's start with Mary's murder. Is it possible that her married boyfriend killed her? And, if so, why?"

"Well, obviously so that his wife wouldn't find out about the affair," said Rooney who, had regained the power of speech. "I mean, it doesn't take a genius to work that_____"

"And you're no genius, Rooney," snapped Morecamb. "So, let's go with this theory, then. The boyfriend killed Mary in order to silence her. Is there any possibility that Peter Kelly was the boyfriend?"

"Not at all," interjected Harrington. "My God, he's as old as my mother."

"You don't say!" said Rooney. "Now, there's a coincidence! And did your mother_____"

"Rooney!" barked Morecamb, "shut it. Of course, there's a problem with the Peter Kelly scenario_____"

"He's dead." Harrington supplied.

"And, that problem," continued Morecamb, glaring at Harrington, "is that Kelly didn't seem to care who knew that he was carrying on with other women. In fact, Trevor Sugrue's father said he used to boast about it."

"But, she was under age," said McGrath. "She was only fifteen."

"There is that," Morecamb acknowledged, "though I'm not sure he would have cared. You know, we really have to question that Egleston man again. He seems to be the only one who actually saw them together. But, of course there's the small matter of his near blindness. Sergeant McGrath, I want you to go back to him and try to jog his memory. Ask him straight up if he thinks that it was Peter Kelly who ran him off the road. Push him on it. The rest of us are heading back to Cork. There's a post mortem to endure. Mr Pettigrew awaits."

CHAPTER 23

Morecamb and Pettigrew had never seen eye to eye.

Morecamb didn't accord sufficient respect to the Pathologist who, on numerous occasions, had been obliged to complain to Superintendent Alderton. If the subject had been aired publically, Morecamb would have agreed with the assessment. He considered the pathologist arrogant, dismissive and over-rated.

However, the nature of their work ensured that they were destined to meet far too frequently for either man's liking. But, they had to make the best of it, and hopefully, if Jane was successful and Pettigrew farted off to the States and stayed there it would be a double bonus. In the meantime Pettigrew continued to incense Morecamb while the latter took great pleasure in watching the sometimes alarming changes of hue in the Pathologist's face. He regarded it as one of the perks of the job.

"You're late as usual, Morecamb," said Pettigrew as soon as they were suited up. "Tell your sergeant to stand well back. I don't want any contaminants and I don't know where he's been."

Murphy moved back a pace, not because he had any great respect either for Pettigrew but, any man with the tools which the pathologist had at his disposal, was not to be trifled with.

"So, what gems of wisdom do you have for us today, Pettigrew? Or is our guess as good as yours?"

"It's all guess work with you, isn't it, Morecamb? And, correct me if I'm wrong, but didn't this man's slaughter more or less coincide with the arrival of your good self? Drafted in to solve the straightforward death,

I would have thought, of a young girl and here we are with the second murder in as many days."

"I think that's a slight exaggeration, Pettigrew....." but the whirr of the saw drowned out Morecamb's voice as Pettigrew set about the further desecration of Kelly's torso.

Murphy moved closer to the exit but Morecamb stood his ground. It wasn't that he had a particular penchant for witnessing the gruesome spectacle that was unfolding but, he always felt that he owed it to the victims not to shy away from the awfulness of their final moments.

An hour later Morrissey, the pathologist's assistant, helped his boss to disrobe and turned off the tape recorder. Then Pettigrew stomped off into his office, issued an abrupt, 'Come' to Morecamb and glared at Murphy. As he sat behind his desk he carefully arranged his cuffs, straightened his tie and then started tidying some papers on his desk.

"So, what do you want to know?" Pettigrew's nasal tones always grated on Morecamb's nerves. "Actually, I have a better idea. I'll do the talking and you sit there and pay attention. You have a particularly nasty perpetrator on your hands, I'm happy to say. Liable to turn on anybody," he added darkly, favouring the two men with a smirk. "Now, I won't mention the cock-up with the head.....ooops, I just did! Moving on, his genatalia were particularly mutilated."

"That leads me to believe that it was an act of revenge," interrupted Morecamb.

"You can believe what you like. You usually do. Now, fortunately for the victim, I would say he was rendered unconscious by a blow to the back of the head. I know it's a silly question," continued Pettigrew, "but do you have any suspect in the frame for the murder of the O'Donovan girl?"

"Not just yet. Is it possible that both murders were carried out by the same person?" asked Morecamb.

"Well", drawled Pettigrew, " I wouldn't rule it out. But, then again, I wouldn't rule it in."

"So, you don't know," said Morecamb.

"Well, that would be your area of.......what's the word? God, I almost said 'expertise'. Must be the lack of sleep. I mean it isn't every day that you open a body bag and find a pair of wellingtons in it, a bag which was clearly labelled, 'head'. And, by the time that I had delivered them to your boss and spent an hour trying to calm him down, to no avail I might add, well, I felt quite nauseous."

"Yes," said Morecamb, "he makes me sick as well. Now, back to the matter in hand. You're saying that the victim was unconscious before his bits and bobs were scattered to the four corners of the yard and then he was decapitated. Is that right?"

"A reasonable assumption. You might be improving, Morecamb."

"And was the blow to the head the cause of death or_____"

"Decapitation. That's usually sufficient."

"This might be a stupid question_____"

"Usually is," interrupted Pettigrew.

"_____ but could a woman inflict those wounds?"

"Unlikely. Next question?"

"You mentioned the blow to the head. Same M.O. as Mary O' Donovan, right? So, it's perfectly feasible that both murders were carried out by the one perpetrator, and, at a stretch, by a woman."

"Yes."

"Rubbish!" said Murphy.

"Who said that?" asked Pettigrew, poking his head around Morecamb's bulk. "Get out, the pair of you. I shall be writing a formal letter of complaint to the Superintendent about_____"

"Just one other thing," interrupted Morecamb as he got up, "you don't by any chance carry out abortions on dogs, do you?"

Morrissey looked up as he saw the two officers hurrying out of Pettigrew's office and the sound of an ashtray smashing against the door behind them.

"Right, back to the station, Murphy. Time to fill in the troops."

"I'm going to walk back, boss, if that's alright with you. Clear my head."

"No problem. See you back there."

*****

Murphy was appalled. On several fronts. Why did his boss always rattle Pettigrew's cage to the extent that they were thrown out of his office. Every time. It was a traumatic enough experience without that. All he had to do was sit quietly and pretend that it all made perfect sense. That's what *he* did.

But the most awful aspect of the whole thing was the notion that a woman could have done that to a man. What kind of instrument could she have used? What had young Harrington said? A billhook? Murphy did a mental inventory of the tools lying around his own place. Time for a clear out.

He was fairly sure that there was a billhook rusting away somewhere in the shed. A rusty billhook. He felt a sudden stab of pain in his groin.

He decided that he wouldn't bother going back to the station. He would go straight home and start a bonfire.

*****

There was no sign of Alderton when Morecamb got back to Union Quay. But there was an 'urgent' message from him. The boss was going to convene, 'a very important meeting at 6.30 am in the morning', in the Incident Room. All were to attend. Moloney had been instructed to get the room ready. And, anybody who wasn't there on time would be locked out and would spend the day on traffic duty, in Princes street.

Wouldn't mind a bit of that myself, thought Morecamb, as he headed out to his car.

No point in briefing his team now and doing it again in the morning. Maybe he'd take Willow for a walk. It might calm him down a bit.

*****

Dot was putting on her coat in readiness to head back to her own house when Morecamb arrived home.

"I'm just off, Jim. There's something in the oven. Just heat it up."

"Before you go, Dot, what's all this about Willow?"

"Well, Maisie said that the Alsatian two doors down from her had been making lustful eyes at Willow this past while. And then, the other day, the deed was done and Maisie is still traumatised. You'll have to get her neutered."

"Who? Maisie?"

Dot glared at him and slammed the door behind her.

Morecamb was just sitting down to his dinner when there was a timid knock on his front door. Maisie had retreated half way down the path by the time he answered so he was forced to join her in order to be able to converse with her.

"Oh, Jim, I've been meaning to have a word. You know my son, Joseph, don't you?" she added, gesturing behind her.

Sure enough, when Morecamb focussed his gaze he saw the strapping six foot five giant beside her.

"Of course I do. Didn't we go to school together? How're you doing, Loopy?"

"Good. Yourself? Mother wants a word," he scowled without waiting for an answer.

Morecamb turned his attention to 'Mother'.

"Well……yes, Jim…..it's just…."

"Go on, Mother, tell him."

"Oh, yes….well, you see….I won't be able….."

"She won't be taking your mutt for a walk anymore," supplied the giant. "So there."

"That's okay, Maisie," Morecamb replied. "Did you find it all a bit exerting? Mmmm? All that walking?"

No, that's not fair, Morecamb chided himself. Poor Maisie was the salt of the earth. She was only doing Morecamb a good turn so it wasn't right to be rude to her. And, besides, her son was a brute. The schoolyard bully. Several times Morecamb had been at the receiving end of his fists and he knew for a fact that the Headmaster had fallen victim as well. He had foolishly confiscated Loopy's cigarettes one day and was later discovered smoking them, behind the bicycle shed, much to Loopy's chagrin.

"Tell him!" roared Loopy.

"Well," said Mother, "see it's a bit delicate, really. But there's this Alsatian......"Her voice petered out.

So Loopy filled in the gaps, none too delicately. The sanitised version was that the mad bastard of an Alsatian had cleared a six foot wall, ambushed Mother and the mutt and, as Maisie struggled to her feet and ran for cover her last glimpse of the canines was the spectacle of fornication between the pair of them.

"In broad daylight," Maisie twittered, shaking her head.

"Hammer and tongs!" shouted Loopy. "That's a terrible thing for my mother to have to witness!"

His pugilistic features were now only inches from Morecamb's face.

"Back off, Loopy," said Morecamb. "I'm not in the mood to haul you down to the station and go through all that paper work. So, shut it. Maisie, I'm truly sorry. And please don't blame yourself. It's not your fault_____"

"Not her fault?" bellowed her son, advancing again. "Not her bloody fault?"

There was an audience starting to assemble now, including a man with an Alsatian on a leash. It took all of Morecamb's resolve and energy to keep Willow, who had appeared at his heel, from re-uniting with her new boyfriend and, no doubt, the father of her numerous progeny. After a struggle Morecamb grabbed Willow, uttered a hasty apology to Maisie and, with as much dignity as he could muster, dragged Willow inside.

When he was sure that the crowd outside had dispersed he grabbed his car keys and headed to Dot's.

"Jim, come on in. I've just made tea and there's some cake_____"

"No, Dot, I won't come in. But, I want to ask you a favour. Will you bring Willow to the vet tomorrow and find out if she's pregnant and, if she is, tell him she needs an abortion."

"I'll do no such thing!" said Dot. "That sort of thing is against the Catholic Church! What would the Parish Priest say_____"

But Morecamb was no longer listening and he jogged back to his car as Dot went off on one of her rants.

*****

CHAPTER 24

Tuesday May 13th

At the pre-appointed, ridiculous hour the team grumbled their way to the Incident Room the following morning, led by Morecamb.

Alderton was scowling at the top of the room and when everybody was seated he ordered Morecamb to take the floor, 'and be quick about it.'

"Right, lads, Sergeant Murphy.....where is Murphy?"

Everyone looked around and shrugged. Alderton suddenly sprang to life, hurried to the door and turned the key.

"Anyway," continued Morecamb, "we called to the pathologist yesterday evening____"

"I know all about it,"snapped Alderton.

"____who was his usual charming self, apart from a few violent outbursts. In a nutshell, it is possible that both killings were carried out by the same person____"

"Possible," muttered Alderton.

" I've been thinking about what he said____"

"Good." Alderton again.

"____and in a rare moment of lucidity, Pettigrew agreed that the killing of Kelly could be interpreted as act of revenge. I think we're looking at a jealous husband. As for Mary's murder, we'll have to seriously examine Peter Kelly's role____"

"Who is dead," supplied Alderton.

"Is it possible that____"

"Possible. Here we go again."

"_____ for some reason, Kelly killed her in case she told anybody about their relationship? But somehow I don't buy that. According to people we've interviewed, it doesn't seem likely that Kelly cared if people knew about his philanderings."

McClean's hand shot up.

"I still think it's our best bet, sir. Kelly, for whatever reason, killed Mary and then a jealous husband killed him."

"That may well be but I'm still inclined to think that the same person carried out both killings. The blow to the back of the head in both instances_____"

"Sit down, Morecamb," barked Alderton. "It seems to me that the case is solved. McClean is right. A perfectly simple, straightforward explanation. With you, Inspector, everything is 'possible' or feasible' or 'can be interpreted'. No 'probable' and, least of all, certainty. Mary O' Donovan's killer is dead and all you have to do is find the husband whose wife was behaving in a disgraceful manner with the dead vet. While he was still alive. Keep it bloody simple."

"The only problem there," said Morecamb, "is the sheer volume of women who seemed to find the live vet_____"

"Rubbish. Kinsale is a very respectable place, lovely sailing club, good restaurants, golf clubs_____"

"And two dead bodies."

"There you go again, Morecamb. Complicating everything. Speaking of complications.......the Commissioner rang me last night for an update, God help us. And, you'll be interested to know, that he is planning to spend this weekend on his boat which, as it happens, is moored in the marina in Kinsale. So I assured him that this whole sorry mess would be cleared up by Thursday. And I'm not going back on my word. Well done, McClean," he added as he headed for the door, "I always said you can't beat a good education."

*****

As McClean headed out to the car to join Morecamb he felt extremely vulnerable. He didn't appreciate the Superintendent praising him in front of everybody, setting him up like that. He would have to spend the rest of the day grovelling, a prospect which was completely alien to him.

"Sorry about that, sir," he said to Morecamb. "I didn't mean to give the Superintendent the impression that I was contradicting you."

"Not to worry, McClean. You weren't to know that he was paying attention. You drive. I don't see any sign of Murphy. Did he turn up at the station at all yesterday evening, after the pathology lab?"

"I don't think so, sir."

"That explains it, so," said Morecamb. "He didn't know about the early start. Drive on, we've a lot to do today. You heard the Super. I reckon we've 48 hours! Hahaha."

*****

Sergeant McGrath and Garda Rooney were waiting for them in a high state of excitement when they reached Kinsale.

"We've got him," said McGrath, thumping the air.

"Who?" asked Morecamb as he took off his hat.

"Peter Kelly." answered the two men in unison.

"But…..he's dead," said Harrington, who had reached the station the same time as Morecamb and his men.

"Yes, we're aware of that," said McGrath, "but, we have it on good authority that he was driving the car that drove Egleston off the road."

"Well," said Morecamb, "not wishing to put a dampener on things but I'd hardly describe Egleston as a 'good authority.'"

"No," said McGrath," but I think his wife is."

"His wife?" queried Morecamb. "How would she know?"

"Well, she was in the car with her husband when it happened but she blamed him for the near collision. Said he was drunk and out in the middle of the road. In fact she thought that's why you had called the other day, to arrest him. She thought that Kelly might have lodged a complaint."

"I don't believe it!" gasped Morecamb. "Went on and on about how blind he is and never mentioned that the battle-axe was sitting beside him. I'm going to lock the pair of them in the cells for a few nights for obstructing our enquiries."

"Well, in fairness," said McGrath, "he was drunk so I suppose it's understandable_____" McGrath stopped when he noticed the look on Morecamb's face.

"Rooney, what did Mrs Egleston see?"

"Well, as Sergeant McGrath said.............right, she said Kelly was driving the other car and he had to swerve violently to avoid a crash. He obviously had to brake hard as himself and his passenger were thrown forward. And yes, Kelly's passenger was young, wearing what looked like a school uniform and had long brown hair. But she didn't get a proper look at the face because by then her own life was flashing before her eyes and it wasn't a pretty sight."

"And, she's sure it was Kelly?"

"Yes. She said her husband started cursing Kelly and blaming him for ending up in the ditch. But, after a few thumps, he quietened down."

"I don't bloody believe it," muttered Morecamb again.

"They're both coming into the station today to give a statement," Rooney supplied.

"I want to meet them," said Morecamb, darkly. "Oh yes, I really do. Right, now we're getting somewhere. McGrath and Rooney, write out the details as you remember them so that when the two clowns arrive we can just get them to read them and then sign them. Save some time before I have a little chat with them. Now, I'm going back to Mrs Kelly and, hopefully, her less daft sister will be there. I want to ask some questions. Harrington, you drive."

Once again it was the sister who answered the door and invited them in. They trooped in behind her. Harrington had refused to stay in the car in case the yard was now haunted after the terrible slaughter that had taken place.

"Daphne, look who it is."

It took a few moments for Daphne to focus and, when she did, it was clear that she shouldn't really have bothered.

"Will you have a sherry?" she asked as they sat in at the table.

"No, thanks, Mrs Kelly. We're on duty."

"How exciting! Rosie, I'll have a sherry, help to drive down the tablets. I think a few of them are stuck in my throat. A large one, dear. I'm sure there are at least four of them struggling to find their way....."

" Mrs Kelly," said Morecamb interrupting the nonsense, "this is a delicate subject and I'm sorry for bringing it up at such a delicate time____"

"Is it money?" she asked. "Do you need a loan? Rosie, get my purse, will you dear, please?"

Morecamb glanced at Harrington and prayed that he wouldn't say anything outrageous.

"Daphne, dear, I think they want to talk about Peter. Is that right, Inspector?"

"Yes. Thank you, Rosie. Mrs Kelly, were you acquainted with, or have you any knowledge of, your husband's women?"

"Oh, no need to feel embarrassed, Inspector. What a silly idea! Now, let me see....... Well, there was the nun in the convent, then a cousin of his in Dunmanway.......actually two. They were twins, you see. Mrs Kelly, of course, and my sister, Rosie....have you met her, Inspector?"

"There you are now, Daphne," said Rosie coming back into the room and putting a large sherry in front of her sister. "So, Inspector, has my sister been able to help you?"

No", said Harrington, "she's drunk."

"Well, she is on medication, Garda," Rosie shot back. "So, she does get a little confused sometimes."

Morecamb glared at Harrington and then turned back to Mrs Kelly.

"Mrs Kelly, did Peter ever bring any of his women back to the house?"

"Oh, no, he had too much respect for me. He loved me, you see."

"Oh, Daphne, you've forgotten. Remember that time he came back with Mrs Kelly's daughter? But she stayed in the car. And you said he was surprised to see Mrs Kelly here as you had threatened to sack her. She had broken one of your china figurines. And then, as soon as he had driven off you said that Mrs Kelly had broken the rest of them."

"Oh, yes," laughed Daphne, clapping her hands. "And did I sack her after that, Rosie? Can you remember?"

"Well, I think you said she didn't come back after that. You were most upset about the breakages. And rightly so."

"And rightly so," echoed Daphne.

"Well," said Morecamb, getting up to take his leave, "you've been very helpful, ladies and, look after yourself, Mrs Kelly. Rosie, thank you too."

"I hope we've been some help, Inspector."

"Yes, indeed," answered Morecamb, "probably more than you realise. Good day to you both."

"What did you make of that, sir?" asked Harrington once they were in the car.

"Interesting. Now, start the car. Nice steady pace, please."

CHAPTER 25

Meanwhile, back at the station there was a row going on in Sweeney's office. The Eagleton's had arrived and the pair of them were having a row. Egleston was sober and uncooperative and there was no way that he was going to malign the good name of a dead man. He said he was sticking by his story and nobody had driven him off the road and if his wife believed that then she was drunk.

McGrath pleaded with them to calm down whereupon Mrs Egleston hit her husband a belt across the ribs. She took grave exception to the accusation that she had been drunk. There was then a lengthy set-to about Mrs Egleston's assertion that she hadn't had a drop of alcohol since she had taken the pledge at her confirmation. Her husband reminded her that she was a Protestant and her lot didn't have any truck with that sort of thing whereas he was a Catholic and they took such things very seriously.

McGrath was beginning to perspire. What would they do if the statements weren't signed before Morecamb got back? Maybe they could forge the signatures.

Thankfully, Rooney came to the rescue and went up to the pub for a bottle of whiskey. After her husband's first glass Mrs Egleston said she was going shopping and she would get the bus home. After another snifter Egleston put pen to paper and then had another one to ease his conscience. Then he suggested they should all go next door and continue the 'session'.

But, before he knew what was happening McGrath and Rooney had hustled him out of the office and helped him into his car. Rooney even turned the key in the ignition for him and then both officers stood on the footpath and waved him off.

*****

Sweeney had decided to walk to work this morning. He liked to watch the lines of boats swaying in the marina and took pleasure in knowing that their movement wasn't as a result of any lack of stability on his part.

He had made a momentous decision as he had left his house. He was giving up the drink. Of course the fact that he hadn't a clue where he had left his car the night before played no small part in the decision. His wife's howls were still ringing in his ears. They had searched everywhere for his car keys, to no avail. Then, his wife had reluctantly handed over the spare key that she had, warning him not to lose it.

But, there was another battle when he went outside and couldn't find the car. Some of the neighbours were outside enjoying the sun and, as always, took a keen interest in Sweeney's movements. Foolishly, he went back inside and accused his wife of hiding his car. All hell broke loose, and when he asked if he could borrow her car instead, the neighbours were treated to details of their horrendous marital union and his multiple failings as a husband.

So, Sweeney, feeling much put-upon skulked off to work and was in no mood to take any nonsense from Morecamb. As he turned a corner he narrowly escaped being mown down by that clown Egleston, who seemed to think he owned the footpath as well as the road. It wouldn't surprise Sweeney if he was drunk. But, perhaps every cloud and all that because, there and then, the Detective had an epiphany. He was going to ring Alderton and insist that Morecamb be taken off the case and Harrington and himself would take over from here. After all, Alderton was family and that must count for something. Of course, his own wife was family as well.......but that was only through marriage.

When he reached the station he immediately took charge, aka, threw his weight around. Naturally, his men were surprised by his sudden display of authority and the speed with which he took command.

And how he moved, without falling over.

"McGrath, I want you to arrest Mr Egleston."

"On what charge, detective?"

"Being in control of a vehicle, that he had no control over. He nearly killed me and then where would ye be? It wouldn't surprise me if he was drunk, at this hour of the morning." It had just gone mid-day. "And, I think we should impound his car."

Maybe he'd commandeer it for himself until he could remember where he had left his own.

"Harrington, you go with him and drive Egleston's car back here."

"Harrington isn't here, boss," said Rooney.

"Ok. You go with him so and bring the car back here. By the way, where *is* young Harrington?"

"He's gone with Inspector Morecamb," answered McGrath. "They're calling on Mrs Kelly to ask her a few more questions."

"Who?"

"You know, Peter Kelly's widow, the man who was savagely_____"

"Oh, yes, my wellingtons. And there's another thing. I seem to have lost them as well. Have they turned up anywhere?"

"Last we heard they were winging their way to the Pathology Lab in Cork," laughed Rooney.

"I don't think that's funny, Rooney. What's *your* name?" he asked pointing at McClean.

"Garda McClean, from the Serious Crime Squad in Cork," he said proudly.

"You'll do. I want you to drive to Cork to the Lab and retrieve my wellingtons."

McClean was about to tell him to fuck off but then he thought of the beach in Garrestown and decided that an afternoon on the sand was very inviting.

All the men practically skipped out the door and Sweeney marvelled at the level of control he could exert and the willingness of his men to obey. Buoyed up by this realisation he decided that not alone would he relay his complaints about Morecamb to his brother-in-law but he was going to have a word with the Commissioner as well. What was the point in being sober if you couldn't demand promotion.

CHAPTER 26

When Morecamb and Harrington arrived back at the station they found it eerily quiet.

"Maybe it's been solved, sir and they've all gone off to celebrate," Harrington offered.

"Yes, that's probably it," said Morecamb, looking at Harrington with renewed disrespect. "Check the table there and see if they left a note or anything to indicate where they've gone. You know, maybe some forward planning and all that."

Just then the phone in Sweeney's office rang so Morecamb went in to answer it.

"Boss, it's me, Murphy. I'm thinking of joining you in Kinsale. I could get the bus down."

Murphy sounded more distressed than usual.

"It's okay, Murphy, no need. In fact, Garda Harrington believes that the case is solved."

"What?" squawked Murphy. "Without *me*?"

As Morecamb put the phone down he noticed that the side door was open. Did that mean that Sweeney was in the vicinity?

When he went back into the day room McGrath seemed to have materialised out of nowhere.

"Where have you been?" he asked him.

"In the toilet, sir. I didn't hear ye come in."

But, he had heard them. He'd arrived back early with Egleston and handed him over to Sweeney. Meanwhile, Rooney was struggling to get the 'impounded car' to start so he left him to it. He'd spotted Morecamb and

Harrington as soon as they'd pulled up outside the station and had decided to take refuge in the toilets where he'd pondered how best to reveal the strange events that had unfolded during their absence. Obviously, the main thing was to put the blame on Detective Sweeney but, even allowing for all that, he would still have to dress things up a bit.

"So, where are the others?" Morecamb asked.

"I have no idea, sir."

"But.....you've been here all morning, haven't you?"

"No, sir."

Morecamb looked around him, contemplating the most non-violent course of action.

Unwittingly, Harrington came to the rescue.

"Maybe we should go in next door, sir. It's lunch-time and they might be in there. Celebrating."

Morecamb wrenched the door open and took off to The Hoor and Hounds, followed by a beaming Harrington and a nauseous McGrath.

The place was thronged. There had been a funeral apparently.

"Old Mrs Martin," the barmaid informed Morecamb. "One hundred and two years old. Imagine? And still driving. There wasn't a bother on her. Hale and hearty. Except for the eyesight but other than that....."

"Nothing wrong with that," said Morecamb. "We find the best witnesses are blind," and he whipped up the drinks and made his way back to the table,

"Can I have a _____", began Harrington.

"No, I ordered bacon and cabbage for us. They're going to drop it down."

Just then an almighty roar went up at the far side of the bar and a very raucous group burst into song. When Morecamb glanced over he spotted Sweeney, who seemed to be the lead tenor and, if he wasn't mistaken, that man Egleston was stuck in the middle of it. McGrath felt his stomach heave when he looked up and identified the members of the 'choir'.

They were halfway through their lunch when Morecamb felt a tap on his shoulder. The Fitzgerald woman.

"God, it's a great country, isn't it. Here you are, stuffing your faces, while a murderer is roaming free and I saw another one of your crew in Gorman's drapery earlier on buying a pair of swimming trunks."

Morecamb didn't allow them to finish their lunch.

*****

Rooney had arrived back when Morecamb and his fellow diners returned to base. Rooney scowled at McGrath when he clapped eyes on him.

"You could have bloody waited for me, you know. Took me ages to get that heap of shite started....."

"Well, I had to escort the prisoner back here. I couldn't take the risk of him escaping and....."

"Right," said Morecamb, "will somebody tell me exactly what's going on? Let's start with you, McGrath. Enlighten us."

"Well, we arrested Mr. Egleston, on Detective Spillane's instructions."

"Ah, that's great. Which cell is he in?"

Harrington's hand shot up. "Actually, sir, I saw him in the pub_____"

"No, no, that can't be true. He's been arrested, remember? So, which cell?"

"See," stammered McGrath, "that's the thing. As soon as I came back with him Detective Spillane took charge of him."

"Ah, that's good. Next?" screamed Morecamb.

"That would be me," said Rooney. "As Egleston was deemed unfit to be in charge of a vehicle......I think that's subsection something or other of the Road Traffic Act........we impounded it. And, here's the thing.......the bloody brakes don't work if you go over sixty miles an hour so the car is now mangled against Jim Lucey's wall." Another glare at McGrath. "Course the bloody thing should have been towed but a certain individual was in too much of a hurry__"

Morecamb had once heard that if you pummelled a man just below the rib cage it would inflict maximum pain and leave very little trace evidence.

"Next!"

Silence.

"So, who's missing? Oh, yes, McClean. Anyone care to enlighten me?"

"He was sent to the Pathology lab, sir," answered McGrath.

"In a body bag, I trust?"

"He has to bring back Detective Spillane's wellingtons."

"Of course. One must prioritise."

"The phone is ringing, sir," Harrington piped up. "Will I answer_____"

"No, Harrington, I wouldn't advise that."

"And I haven't had any lunch," announced Rooney.

"Dear, oh dear."

There followed a long diatribe about the general state of affairs and the various roles played by 'the bunch of bastards in front of me.' Detective Spillane got special mention. He then went on to excoriate the entire denizens of Kinsale and their propensity to engage in acts of procreation, but only with somebody else's spouse.

He was interrupted by the, partial, appearance of Sweeney who put his head around his office door and then immediately withdrew.

"So, no more food while you're on duty. Or drink. And, from now on.............." He was distracted momentarily by the sight of Sweeney getting into a car, with Egleston in the passenger seat, and driving off. From now on, continued Morecamb, they would only take instructions from himself. McGrath was ordered to ring the lab in Cork and see if McClean had managed to collect the wellingtons; Rooney was to retrieve Egleston's car and bring it to the nearest garage or dump. And the bill was to be sent to Rooney. Finally, Harrington was detailed to go to Gorman's drapery and get a description of the man who had bought the pair of swimming trunks earlier on.

"So, that's the wellingtons, swimming trunks and smashed car sorted. And some people accuse us of doing nothing. Some even call us names. Want to hear some of them?"

They didn't but they heard them anyway. Even Rooney, no slouch in the profanity department, was impressed.

Once again the trill of the phone interrupted proceedings and McGrath was dispatched to answer it.

"That was Superintendent Alderton, sir," said McGrath on his return. "He said it's very important that you return to Cork immediately. There's been an urgent development."

"Right. Wonder what that could be? We'll just have to postpone those other important tasks. But, on the way back, I want to call on the O' Donovan's. I need to talk to both of them."

But, when he called there didn't appear to be anybody at home so he pushed a note under the door, telling them that he would call in the morning, at ten.

CHAPTER 27

Back at the 'ranch' Alderton was primed for attack. Morecamb was ordered into the Incident Room and Kilroy and Finin were told to come as well.

"Now, I've had the most appalling day and, as a man who has had more than his fair share of aggravation, I don't say that lightly. I've had several phone calls from the Commissioner, one worse than the other. Detective Spillane, in a moment of lunacy, rang the Commissioner, demanding a promotion to the rank of Inspector 'and beyond'. So, obviously he was given early retirement, effective as of this morning and now I have to go home and tell my wife that her brother is jobless_____"

"You said there had been an 'urgent development', sir" interrupted Morecamb. "See, we had to interrupt our work in Kinsale____"

"I'm coming to that. The second part concerns the Commissioner as well. For the first time in living memory he's afraid to go near Kinsale. He had planned to go sailing this weekend but will have to cancel. That's not a decision he took lightly but the news coming out of Kinsale is making the hair stand on his head. I told him that we are going to have a confession by Thursday, just a few tweaks here and there_____"

"Could you explain, 'tweaks', sir? asked Morecamb.

"No. So, I think I reassured him and eventually, I'm happy to announce, he said he'll reconsider. So, there's the time-line, Morecamb, and now let's hear your progress report."

Morecamb was acutely aware of Alderton pacing back and forth and, as his tale unfolded, there was a rapid escalation in Alderton's already puce complexion. Morecamb wondered idly if he had taken his medication. Or taken too much, perhaps?

"Much as it pains me to say it_____"

"Here we go."

"Peter Kelly could possibly be a realistic suspect for the killing of Mary O'Donovan_____"

"Isn't that what McClean said yesterday?" shouted Alderton. "McClean said......where *is* McClean?"

"We have reason to believe that he went for a swim_____"

The pacing stopped.

"Went for a .....what? Have you been drinking, Morecamb?"

"Not yet. But, Wonder boy was ordered by your brother-in-law to retrieve his wellingtons from the lab in Cork_____"

"But they're here," interrupted Alderton.

"Of course they are but that's not the point because McClean had no intention obviously of traipsing all the way to Cork for them. So he went for a swim instead. And I can't say I blame him."

"And, what? Did he drown?"

"Not as far as I'm aware. For all we know he could be half-way to France by now. But, time will tell. So, to continue, Kelly was definitely in a relationship with Mary. His widow confirmed that. It's also possible that Mary's mother was aware of the fact. Certainly suspected it. So, did she tell her husband, and, after Mary had been killed, did her father kill Kelly?"

"There you go. Arrest him tomorrow, I'll call a Press thingy for tomorrow afternoon and the Commissioner can set sail_____"

"It isn't that simple," snapped Morecamb.

"Of course it isn't," said Alderton. "With you, nothing ever is."

"Yes, Kelly was a philanderer but he didn't try to hide the fact. So why would he feel the need to 'silence' Mary? And then there's Mary's father. I just don't believe that he's a killer."

"But, if he felt that Kelly was responsible for killing his daughter then I think he would," suggested Kilroy.

Morecamb conceded to the possibility. "But having met the man I would find it hard to believe. However, I do think the killer is local. Or killers. These killings were opportunistic. I don't think they were planned. Kelly's killing was a frenzied attack, a spur-of-the-moment one and, in Mary's case, I don't believe her attacker was lying in wait. Remember, she had a puncture and was later than usual, so wouldn't normally be in that spot at that exact time. So, tomorrow I'm calling on the O'Donovan's____"

"And arresting the pair of them," finished Alderton. " Kelly is dead, Donovan is the killer and the wife is obviously covering for him. Case closed. And as I said, Press thingy tomorrow. I'll get the paper work sorted and give the good news to the Commissioner. See, that wasn't so difficult, was it, Morecamb? Just a case of admitting that you got it wrong. You'll have an early start in the morning so go on home now.

*****

Murphy was sitting in his car outside Morecamb's front gate when he arrived home. As soon as he stopped his car Murphy shot out of his own.

"If you're here to have a moan, Murphy, might I remind you that I've just come from a meeting with Our Leader so I'm not in the mood."

"Oh....okay, well I just wanted to check what time we're heading off to Kinsale in the morning."

"So have you been relieved of traffic duty in Princes Street? Were there incidents of mayhem?"

"I never got as far as Princes Street, did I?" said Murphy indignantly. "I was caddying for the Super."

"Well, congratulations. Only the chosen few get that honour. Fun, was it?" asked Morecamb as he locked his car.

"I was ordered home after the second hole. He cheats, you know, even when he's not playing against anybody."

"Sounds awfully like a moan to me, Murphy."

"He told me to keep the score and when I put down a quadruple bogey for the second hole he insisted that I change it to a hole-in-one. I refused. Then he turned savage so I left."

"Right. All very fascinating. We leave at eight in the morning. Don't be late."

"No fear. I'll never be late again."

CHAPTER 28

Wednesday May 14th

There was an air of despondency the following morning when they reached Kinsale, triggered by the news of Sweeney's removal.

The 'best detective' ever had been given his 'marching orders' and what hope was there for the rest of them?

"Well, he'll have a nice fat pension to console him," said Morecamb.

"No, he won't," said McGrath, " he's only been in the force about ten years."

"And what was he doing before that?" asked an incredulous Morecamb.

"He was a bouncer at the dance-hall in Dunmanway. Very good too, apparently. As soon as he left people started getting arrested for smoking marijuana. There was none of that while Joe Sweeney was on the door."

"The place closed down shortly afterwards," Rooney added. "Rumour has it that there's a fair share of it here in Kinsale now. You know that new place in_____"

"Shut up, the lot of you," barked Morecamb. "And get a bit of sense, for God's sake. Now, I want to fill you all in on the meeting which we had in Union Quay yesterday evening."

Briefly he went through the pitiful details and the Superintendent's equally pitiful assessment of those details.

"So, are we making an arrest today, sir?" asked Harrington.

"I can't see Tom O'Donovan as a murderer," said McGrath. "Doesn't make sense."

"But, if your daughter is murdered then any man would be capable, "Rooney countered.

"Look, we're not arresting anybody. I just want to ask them a few questions this morning".

*****

When Morecamb and Murphy reached the O'Donovan house they could hear Moll calling to the hens at the back of the house. Her voice sounded more impatient with each 'clucking' call. When they approached her the bucket clanged to the ground and, with her hands on her hips, she glared at them belligerently.

"I suppose you're here to tell us that you've arrested the man who killed our daughter? Otherwise why would you be harassing decent people and making our lives even more miserable. Well, which is it, Mr. Morecamb?"

She was spitting fire and for a minute Morecamb thought that she was going to lash out at them. In an effort to diffuse the situation he enquired on the whereabouts of Tom.

"He's inside in the kitchen," she snapped. "And he hasn't done a stroke of work for the last few days. Hasn't left the house since the last time your lot was here."

"I'm sorry to hear that, Mrs O'Donovan," Morecamb replied. "But, I'm afraid, I need to ask both of you a few more questions. Hopefully it won't be too long before we have it all cleared up. Maybe we could go inside?"

She marched off into the house without a backward glance. Meanwhile the hens fell upon the discarded bucket of meal but were immediately dispatched by a malevolent rooster.

Morecamb would never have claimed to be particularly sensitive to aura but the atmosphere when they went into the kitchen was leaden and seemed to descend on him and grip him in a claustrophobic stranglehold.

The hunched figure of Tom O'Donovan was barely discernible in the corner and he didn't even raise his head when the two men entered. Morecamb doubted he would be able to even if he tried. All semblance of the man they had first encountered had vanished and all that remained was an empty, deformed husk.

Morecamb wanted to turn around and leave. How could he question this man about the murder of Peter Kelly?

"Tea?" barked Mrs O'Donovan.

"Please," said Morecamb, not from any desire or need but simply to buy some time. He sat on the chair at the other side of the Aga, facing Tom. Murphy remained standing, cap in hand and stared at the floor.

When Moll had slapped the tea down on the Aga she went and sat at the table and cradled her own cup in her hands.

"I need to clarify something," began Morecamb, "and I'm afraid it's a bit delicate." He stopped and the only sound in the kitchen was the crackling of logs in the stove. "Look, there's no easy way to say this but, we have reason to believe that Mary was in some sort of relationship with Peter Kelly. Was either of you aware of that?"

No response.

"Did *you* know, Mrs O'Donovan?? I believe you used to help Mrs Kelly in the house and one day Peter Kelly_____"

The noise as she banged her cup down on the table was like a gunshot.

"Are you mad?" she screamed. "Mary was fifteen years old! What would the likes of Peter Kelly see in our daughter?"

"Nevertheless_____"

"Nevertheless nothing," she shot back, rising from her chair. "What exactly are you saying?"

"It *is* possible that Kelly killed Mary and then......perhaps in a moment of extreme provocation, and understandably so, one of you_____"

"What? Killed Kelly? Is that what you're saying? Is that the best you can come up with?"

She was beside herself with rage. Morecamb looked across at Tom, who had lifted his head a little, and he saw the silent tears coursing a furrow down his face.

Morecamb silently got up, squeezed Tom's shoulder gently and beckoned Murphy outside.

Neither of them spoke as Murphy guided the car down the rutted boreen and each was oblivious of any part of the journey back to the barracks.

As soon as they got inside Morecamb closeted himself in Sweeney's office and pondered the awful dilemma.

He was still sitting, staring off into the distance when Murphy interrupted him and suggested lunch.

Morecamb had no appetite and, looking around at his men, it seemed they had little either. A few of the locals cast a wary glance in their direction every now and then before returning their focus on their pints. It was a far cry from yesterday's exuberance at the post-funeral celebrations for the blind driver. Even the bar-maid refrained from her usual stream of chatter and scuttled back to her perch as soon as she had deposited their plates on the table.

They ate in silence.

*****

"I want to fill you in on our visit to the O'Donovan's this morning," said Morecamb as they all settled themselves back inside the day-room. "It gives me no pleasure to say that Tom O'Donovan seems to have emerged as the prime suspect. He made no attempt to deny that he was involved in the killing of Peter Kelly. Mind you, he didn't admit it either."

"Well, he hardly would," said Rooney.

"Still doesn't mean he's guilty," retorted McGrath.

"I agree," said Morecamb, "but, by a process of elimination, he seems the most likely candidate. He had the motive and the opportunity."

"Does that mean that Kelly killed Mary?" asked Harrington.

"It looks that way though Mrs O'Donovan strenuously denied that Kelly was in a relationship with Mary."

"Well, she would, wouldn't she?" Rooney again.

"But, Mrs Kelly and her sister said they saw them together," said Murphy.

"Well.......Mrs Kelly did," answered Morecamb. "And, if the Egleston woman is to be believed, she saw them too. Her husband's testimony isn't quite so credible. Actually, we can just discount his altogether."

"So, what now, sir?" asked McGrath.

"Well, we're heading back to Cork. The Superintendent is meeting the Press this afternoon so I want to tell him what he can and can't say. But, tomorrow morning I'll be going back to O'Donovan's and bringing Tom on to Cork, where he'll be officially charged. Sergeant McGrath, I want you and your men to write up the reports. I want all the testimonies and interviews carefully logged, sequentially. Every action has to be accurately recorded. Remember, that will form the basis for a conviction or, perhaps, an acquittal. Anyway, make sure everything is done by the book."

"And who'll sign off on it now that Joe Sweeney isn't here?" asked McGrath.

"You'll have to do it," said Morecamb, "and I'll counter-sign it in the morning."

*****

When they left McGrath went for a long walk. He felt depressed. There was no sense of achievement or elation now that the case was almost wrapped up. He had left instructions with the men to get started on the paperwork and now wondered how long he dared to stay away.

He felt envious of the fishermen as they loudly brought their catch ashore. He could hear the laughter and the banter and knew they would be heading for the pub after their day's work was done. No lives ruined. All pretty straightforward really. Surrounded by the vast blueness of the Atlantic, checking their nets, their weather-beaten faces wreathed in smiles as their nets closed in around their prey.

Tomorrow.

He was glad that he wouldn't be the one to put the shackles on Tom. He wouldn't be able to do it. Innocent or guilty, Tom O'Donovan was a gentle soul and if he had whacked *Kelly, well, more power to him. And McGrath knew that the events of the past week or so would leave a bitter taste. Tom was well-liked, always willing to help a neighbour, never had a bad word to say about anybody. That was a very rare quality around here. What was it they said about country people? Oh yes, we're grand people until you get to know us.*

Well, it had been an honour to know Tom O'Donovan. He was the exception. His bloody wife on the other hand............

*****

Alderton was outside in the car park when they arrived, soaking up the sun's rays. He scowled when he saw Morecamb and his men getting out of the car and beckoned them over.

"I'm almost afraid to ask but can the decent people of Kinsale sleep easy in their beds tonight?" Alderton liked to make a distinction between what he called the respectable, rich people and the 'riff-raff'. "And can our Commissioner venture into the town without fear of being slaughtered?"

"More or less," began Morecamb, "we went to_____"

"Good," interrupted Alderton. "Because I was going to announce to the Press that it was solved, whether or which. You're blocking the light there, Murphy. Move aside, please. Well, I always knew we could solve it. As I said yesterday, Morecamb, it's just a question of admitting that you were wrong. Still, we won't dwell on that, just yet. C'mon inside and fill me in on the details. What a splendid day."

Alderton didn't need anybody but Morecamb to join him on the steps for 'the thingy', and he was ordered to stand well back. The others were told to make themselves useful. They needn't think they were on holiday now that they had stumbled on a successful conclusion to the carnage they had left in their wake in Kinsale.

Even though Morecamb had primed his boss on what he could and couldn't say to the Press, it fell on deaf ears. He had distinctly warned him not to name the suspect. He did. Furthermore, Morecamb had begged

205

him not to announce that Peter Kelly had murdered Mary O'Donovan. He did. And, finally, he had asked him not to make a 'dog's dinner' of the whole thing and accuse the locals of questionable moral standards. He did.

*****

CHAPTER 29

Thursday May 15th

Alderton was in situ the following morning to wave them off. He informed them that everything would be in readiness for 'the mad bastard' when they brought him back to Cork. He was going to notify 'The Cork Examiner' to spread the good news followed by a phone call to the Commissioner.

He hadn't been able to sleep the night before with the excitement of it all. Images of promotion and sailing the high seas had kept him tossing and turning all night, so much so that his wife had suddenly appeared at the foot of his bed, complete with bandaged varicose veins, and threatened to throw him down the stairs if he didn't stop.

Eventually, in the small hours, he got up and contemplated going for a walk. But then he remembered the criminal elements who were probably at this very minute roaming the streets and decided to stay put. It was beyond his comprehension why somebody hadn't done something about them a long time ago. As soon as this debacle in Kinsale was over Morecamb and his bandits would be out patrolling the streets until every last offender was behind bars.

Of course that was little consolation to him now and he briefly contemplated ringing Violet. But the last time he had done that a man had answered the phone. It was hard to find loyalty in these immoral times.

*****

As soon as they reached the station in Kinsale Morecamb had a premonition of an unfolding disaster. From the outside the place looked deserted and when they went inside it may as well have been because there was only Harrington in attendance, playing with a pair of handcuffs, tossing them from one hand to the other.

"Good morning, sir," he beamed. "I decided to get the handcuffs ready. It's just the one set we'll be needing, isn't it? I mean Kelly is dead and you said_____"

"Where are the others?" Morecamb asked quietly. "Shouldn't they be here by now?"

"I think they might have been here already, sir. I've only just got here but I noticed the half empty cups on the table so that would indicate_____"

"Yes, I can see that, Harrington. And put those handcuffs away. We won't need them. I don't think that Tom O'Donovan will resist arrest. Have you any idea at all_____"

"They're outside, boss," said Murphy as he spotted the car pulling up outside the station. "That Rooney fellah needs to take a few driving lessons. Never seen anybody park a car like that in my life......"

Before he had finished passing judgement on Rooney's driving capabilities the door burst open and the breathless driver appeared.

Morecamb was on the point of ordering him to go back out again and come in properly like a civilised human being when he saw the look on Rooney's face. The words died on his lips.

"He's dead, sir. Tom O' Donovan shot himself at some stage during the night. The wife found him when she went out to feed the hens."

"I don't believe it," Morecamb mumbled.

"God's truth," said Rooney. "I was first here this morning and when I arrived Dennis Sugrue was already here, shaking. He said Moll had cycled up to their place and they tried to phone here. But of course there was nobody here_____"

"Well, we don't open until eight thirty," Harrington said, pre-empting any criticism.

"I know that," said Rooney. "Anyway, Sergeant McGrath arrived at almost the same time as I did so we followed Sugrue up to O'Donovan's. Jesus!"

"Where's Sergeant McGrath now then?" asked Morecamb, looking around.

"He's gone for a walk down to the Marina, sir," said Rooney. "I think he's in shock."

"Well, hopefully he won't fall into the water," said Harrington.

"Right, you go after him, Harrington. Just stay a few feet behind and keep an eye on him."

"And what happens if he falls in?" wailed Harrington. "I can't swim, you know. An uncle of mine died in a slurry tank and my mother forbade_____"

"Good. Now do as you're told," said Morecamb, "and, if you can, after a little while, try to persuade him to come back. Okay, Rooney, carry on."

"Well, Moll pointed to one of the sheds when we arrived and when we went inside......God, it was like something from a horror film. If you thought the scene at Peter Kelly's place was bad..... this was a hundred times worse. Sergeant McGrath got sick so I'm afraid the old crime scene took a bit of a battering_____"

"Right, you can stop there. Where's Moll now? Is there somebody with her?"

"Yes. Bridie Sugrue is there. And Dennis is there too, standing guard outside the stable door. Though who'd want to go in there_____"

"Okay, Rooney, you can shut up now. I need to think. Have you contacted a doctor to certify death?"

"Dennis Sugrue said that he would do that."

"Okay, well go back again to Donovan's and put tape around the perimeter and make sure there are no gawkers. Murphy and myself will follow. I need to make a few phone calls first."

His call to Lombard, the Police Photographer, was less than edifying. He was getting ready to go on holidays, he informed Morecamb, 'before your lot presided over another slaughtering and sure enough, you didn't disappoint. How many cadavers are we looking at today, Morecamb?"

"Just the one, Lombard. We try to keep things to a minimum for you, knowing your limited capabilities. And don't forget to bring your camera."

Next on the list was Alderton and, surprisingly, he was in his office.

"What is it now, Morecamb?" was the greeting he got. "I'm a very busy man. Don't tell me that you're already on your way back? The Press won't be here for another hour and you can't be here before them. And I'm waiting for a phone call from The Commissioner at any minute so get off the phone."

"Well, I won't tell you that we're already on our way back. Bit of a new development here, sir," and Morecamb went on to tell him about Tom O'Donovan's death. He did all the talking and, as he put the phone back on the receiver, he could hear his boss struggling to breathe on the other end.

When he came back into the day room Harrington was back, minus McGrath.

"Well?"

"He begged me to leave him alone so I just came on back," said a chastened Harrington.

"Okay, well, I've just informed the Police Photographer and, when he arrives, will you show him to the farm? And if Superintendent Alderton phones tell him he has the wrong number. C'mon, Murphy, let's go to O'Donovan's."

*****

Alderton was in deep shock. See, this was more of it! Could Morecamb do anything right? It wouldn't surprise him if he did these things on purpose. All he had to do was go down to Kinsale and arrest what's-his-name, read him his rights and, when Alderton was standing on the steps of the Station, resplendent in his full regalia, with the Press waiting expectantly, Morecamb would roll up, manhandle the prisoner out of the car and hustle him into the station, saluting Alderton on his way in. Alderton had spent a long time going over the choreography and now this!

What the fuck was he going to do now? And what about the Commissioner's call? He would have to stall that. Get Moloney to ring him and tell him…..what? Could he pretend that the culprit tried to shoot his way out of a tricky situation and accidentally shot himself? He'd need to think about that. Meanwhile, there was the matter of the Press. Alderton picked up his phone, rang through to the reception desk and told Moloney to summon Mc-Clean, who was confined to barracks after his escapades at sea, to his office immediately.

*****

As Morecamb and Murphy turned off the road into O'Donovan's' yard they were surprised that it was so quiet. There was none of the usual horde of onlookers. Suicides seemed to have that effect on people, Morecamb mused. Death from natural causes they could handle. He sometimes felt that country people were more adept at coping with the natural rhythms of life than their urban brethren. Murphy would say that it was a result of their propensity to murder and maim all around them.

But Morecamb reasoned that life on the land must surely take away the mysteries and unnaturalness of death. 'A season for everything', isn't that what the Bible said? Everything had a beginning and an end. Animals were born and died. Crops grew and sometimes failed. Litters of pups seemed to appear overnight and were summarily dispatched in the nearest river the following day. Ditto for kittens.

But a suicide fell outside that natural life-rhythm.

"C'mon, boss," Murphy's voice broke through his reverie and, as they got out of the car, Dennis Sugrue came over to them.

"Terrible business," he muttered. "Poor, bloody man. It must have been hell for him. And I don't think any of us did enough for him. I certainly didn't. You expect people to just get on with it, don't you?"

They were interrupted by the approach of another man. "This is Dr. Cauldwell," continued Dennis. "Look, I'll leave ye to it. I'll go back inside to the missus. And Moll of course."

Dr. Cauldwell had the complexion of a sea-faring man, his pristine white shirt accentuating the deep tan. Flecks of grey were starting to appear on a well-groomed head of hair. His manner was matter-of-fact and almost brusque.

"Unfortunate business, I'm afraid," was his opening statement. "But, an obvious suicide. Trajectory of the shot suggests that he held the weapon under his chin and then fired. All yours now," he said as he headed to his car.

Morecamb and Murphy reluctantly headed towards the stable. Rooney was standing in front of the stable door and for once he was quiet. Silently he handed Morecamb a torch. "It's a bit dark in there, sir. The wife said there's a tilly lamp around somewhere but we didn't want to trample all over the scene. You'll see more than enough with the torch anyway."

When Morecamb shone the torch on the interior he heard a gasp from Murphy. Deliberately the Inspector focussed on the barn's interior dimensions. It was quite large but seemed smaller because of all the bits and pieces of machinery strewn about. There was an old tractor which had seen better days and was now supported by concrete blocks. Bicycle frames were suspended from hooks on a wall. Old rakes and pikes without handles nestled among rotting bales of straw. There was one small window, affording little or no light, primarily because it was caked in grime.

Eventually the light found the remains of Tom O'Donovan, the shotgun still clutched to an out-flung arm. Surprisingly the torso was still intact. Above his shoulders there was nothing recognisable and Morecamb's thoughts immediately went to Moll and how she must have felt when she discovered her husband's body.

As Morecamb turned away from the scene he realised that Murphy had already left and then he spotted him leaning against an old chestnut tree over by the gate. Morecamb returned the torch to Rooney and rubbed a weary hand over his face.

"Lombard will be here soon," he said. "I'll notify the guys in the Pathology lab to come and retrieve the remains and transport them to the mortuary. A post-mortem will have to____" He broke off as he heard footsteps approaching quickly behind him and, as he turned around, he received an almighty blow across the face from Moll O'Donovan's fist. He reeled backwards and as he tried to maintain his balance he heard her scream, 'You bastard!' There was a shocked silence as they watched Moll march back inside her house.

Rooney was the first to re-act. "Are you okay, sir? Christ, she can pack some punch!"

"Yes. I think so. A bit dazed, if I'm honest. I think I'll head back to the station. You drive, Murphy."

As they retraced their steps to the car Murphy held onto Morecamb's arm.

"I'm okay, Murphy, I can bloody manage on my own," and he snatched his arm away. "I think we'll have a quick whiskey before I make those phone calls."

They had two whiskeys and then Morecamb reluctantly went back to phone the laboratory.

It was almost lunch-time when they set out on their journey back to Union Quay, all thoughts of the Press conference long forgotten.

CHAPTER 30

McClean had been both surprised and delighted that Alderton had chosen him to brief the Press. He had been afraid that his maritime exploits the previous day might have soured Alderton's opinion of him. But it was obvious now that Alderton still held him in high esteem, as he should, and surely it was only a matter of time before the inevitable promotion.

The word that had been circulating the station that morning was the imminent arrest of the murderer and all that remained was to bring him back to Cork. McClean rushed to the gents to check his uniform and slick back his hair before knocking on Alderton's door.

"Come," called his boss. "Ah, McClean, take a seat. Something has come up so I won't be able to meet the Press, unfortunately. So, I think this would be a good opportunity for you to dip your toes into the water, so to speak. The Press are due to start circling....ahem, gathering in fifteen minutes so, what do you feel about that?"

"It would be an honour, sir."

McClean felt almost humbled. At least he thought that's probably what it was, never having experienced such a lowly sensation heretofore. So Alderton briefly ran through the salient points. A successful outcome in Kinsale, the culprit identified, the safety of the good citizens of Kinsale guaranteed – *he wouldn't mention the riff-raff because, no doubt, they would continue to murder and maim but, hopefully, within their own circle* – and they could all continue with their wonderful pursuits, fine dining, yachting, golfing – *he wouldn't mention the whoring.*

"The main thing, McClean, is to keep it vague."

As McClean left the office he realised that he had no alternative but to keep things vague because he was armed with very little detail. But, no matter, he was more than capable of spoofing when the occasion demanded. Hurriedly he scribbled a few notes on a piece of paper and, shoulders back, he went out to meet the boys from the Press.

*****

McClean had once seen a documentary about a young deer surrounded by a pack of lions and then, as if they had received some sort of signal, they all pounced at once. McClean had felt a sense of awe as he had watched. You couldn't help but admire the speed and ferocity of the kill.

The 'signal' on this occasion was McClean's announcement that the culprit of the murder of Peter Kelly had been apprehended and was right now on his way to Cork, under heavy guard.

"Why was he under heavy guard?"

"But, was he not dead? They had it on good authority that he would be arriving in a body bag."

"Would the mortuary not be a more suitable destination?"

"Was it the guards who had fired the fatal shot?"

"Was it true that the widow was going to sue?"

As McClean stumbled back inside the station he decided that he wouldn't be buying any newspaper the following morning. And he would apply for an immediate transfer.

*****

Thankfully there was no sign of the Press when Morecamb and Murphy arrived shortly afterwards. Dealing with Alderton would be more than enough. As soon as they went into the station Moloney informed them that there would be a 'debriefing session' – Alderton's words – in an hour's time and he expected 'every half-wit' to attend.

"Will we have some lunch, boss?" asked Murphy. "I think the canteen is still open. I can smell food."

"Sure. Why not."

They joined the others – Kilroy, Finin, Moloney and McClean - at one of the tables and filled them in on the awful finale to the investigation. McClean just sat there with his mouth open and realised he had been duped. Finin no longer felt aggrieved that he had been denied participation in the investigation while Kilroy began to view his course in a new light. Nobody had much of an appetite but it was somewhere to sit and gather their thoughts. Morecamb's jaw was still sore and he found chewing quite uncomfortable. But, at least it took his mind off the scene back in the stable. Whether it would distract him sufficiently from Alderton's vitriol was another matter.

At two o' clock they all trooped into the Incident Room to be greeted by the frantic pacing of Alderton. Morecamb walked to the top of the room and they exchanged glares.

"I'm going to keep this short," snarled Alderton, to all and sundry.

An hour later he had run out of steam. The accusations were lengthy, all-encompassing and some, no doubt, slanderous. Morecamb kept his attention focussed on a spider's web on the wall behind Alderton and watched as a poor bastard of a fly became trapped. He willed him to break free, then watched in horrified fascination, as the spider stealthily approached to claim his prize.

*****

They all adjourned to the pub in the afternoon, except Alderton who was going home to lie down in a darkened room. There was no sense of celebration, now that the case was effectively closed and Morecamb knew that the image of Tom O' Donovan's body would stay with him for a long time. And the dread in his gut that they had somehow got it all wrong.

Sometime during the evening the bar-man approached him and said there was a phone call for him. Morecamb immediately thought of Alderton and reluctantly lifted the receiver.

"Jim?"

It took him a moment to recognise Jane's voice and he gulped back the tide of emotion which threatened to overwhelm him.

"Are you there, Jim? This is Jane and I read about your case in Kinsale. I'm truly sorry. I wondered if you'd like some company."

In a strangled voice he said he would and they agreed to meet outside the pub. Jane was in Cork sorting out accommodation as she had been offered the job in the Pathology department. Morecamb felt a weight suddenly lift from his shoulders and he felt a little more able to face the dark days ahead.

He left the pub quietly and stood with his hands hanging limply by his side. After a few moments Jane pulled up in her car, got out and went over and hugged him. Slowly he wrapped his arms around her and they just stood there, silently, savouring the moment. Then she took his hand in hers and the warmth of her softness seemed to melt the icicles which had engulfed his very being since the start of the investigation in Kinsale. Together they walked slowly up Oliver Plunkett street, merging into the throng of other couples, content in the moment and daring to dream.

CHAPTER 31

Two days after Tom's funeral Moll locked the stable door. She would never again re-enter. But she could still feel his eyes on her, accusatory, just as they had been in the days leading up to his suicide. But, if he had suspected, he had never said anything.

Of course there were moments of regret, but they were fleeting. All her life she had endured, a shadow in the background. And then Peter Kelly had entered her life, albeit briefly, and for the first time it felt as if she mattered. She had been devastated when he had cast her aside. Relegated to the shadows again. She had felt dead inside. Until the day Kelly had pulled up outside his house and Moll had seen her own daughter sitting proudly in the passenger seat. And a rage burned inside her, almost suffocating her.

When she had confronted her daughter that Tuesday on her way home from school, Mary had taunted her. Peter was in love with her and he was going to leave his wife and marry her. A red mist descended and Moll picked up the nearest rock. She had seen her own father stun animals on their small farm. Calling a vet would have been considered wasteful. Moll now smiled at the irony.

At her funeral Kelly had stood in the shadows but, even from a distance, Moll could see the look of sadness.

And, she hadn't meant to kill him that night in the yard. She just wanted to confront him, to understand why. But he had dismissed her protests, swatted her aside as one would an irritable, buzzing fly. As he turned his back and walked away Moll picked up her weapon. All the pent-up fury and disappointments were unleashed and she didn't remember the first blow. Or the last.

Now, as she looked around her, she conceded that it wasn't a very big farm. But it was all hers. Not many women could boast of owning their own farm. A laying hen. And, in time, who knew..............

The End

ABOUT THE AUTHOR

Susan is a retired teacher of English and this is her second novel. Originally from Co. Cork she now lives in Limerick and is the mother of four grown-up children.

The success of her first novel was a great impetus to complete and publish 'Betrayal', the second in the series of Inspector Morecamb stories. Both books are of the Crime fiction genre and both are set in the late 60s in rural Ireland.She has had a number of topical articles published in 'Headstuff' and devotes most of her time to writing. She also enjoys gardening and walking.

PLEASE REVIEW

Dear Reader,

If you enjoyed this book, would you kindly post a short review on Amazon? Your feedback will make all the difference to getting the word out about this book.

To leave a review, go to Amazon and type in the book title. When you have found it and go to the book page, please scroll to the bottom of the page to where it says 'Write a Review' and then submit your review.

Thank you in advance.

Susan